About the Author

Georgia Chadburn-Jones was born and raised in Enfield, London, where she spent her time running ruckus and reading fantasy books. These days she lives in Stockport, England, with her wife, Abbie, and their excitable Yorkie, Charlie. Georgia writes around her nine to five job and treatment for Stage Four Breast cancer, telling the stories that she wanted to read growing up and into herself. The Forest of Kasia is her first novel. You can find Georgia cosied up with blankets at home with Charlie.

The Forest of Kasia

Georgia Chadburn-Jones

The Forest of Kasia

Olympia Publishers
London

www.olympiapublishers.com
OLYMPIA PAPERBACK EDITION

Copyright © Georgia Chadburn-Jones 2024

The right of Georgia Chadburn-Jones to be identified as author of this work has been asserted in accordance with sections 77 and 78 of the Copyright, Designs and Patents Act 1988.

All Rights Reserved

No reproduction, copy or transmission of this publication may be made without written permission.
No paragraph of this publication may be reproduced, copied or transmitted save with the written permission of the publisher, or in accordance with the provisions
of the Copyright Act 1956 (as amended).

Any person who commits any unauthorised act in relation to this publication may be liable to criminal prosecution and civil claims for damage.

A CIP catalogue record for this title is available from the British Library.

ISBN: 978-1-80439-509-7

This is a work of fiction.
Names, characters, places and incidents originate from the writer's imagination. Any resemblance to actual persons, living or dead, is purely coincidental.

First Published in 2024

Olympia Publishers
Tallis House
2 Tallis Street
London
EC4Y 0AB

Printed in Great Britain

Dedication

For my wife, my light, my love. All three wishes.

1

Faeryn

Alone. Surrounded. Busy bodies. Anxiety. Creeping. Numb.
Awake.

As was each morning, the same, in which Faeryn awoke in her white castle of her own quiet solitude.

A pretty young thing, Faeryn had always been blessed with the magical touch of the Fae, as was her name sake. With long auburn hair waving down to the dimples that grace her soft, alabaster skin right at the bottom of her back. Emerald green eyes flecked with gold, around pupils so deeply black that you would fear that a spell had been cast upon you if you looked too long into them, with a sense of deep calm washing over you, drowning almost in the abyss. One thing did mar this perception of beauty that was rumoured to be a magic touch, ten nails, adorning her long slender fingers that seemed to be bitten down to the wick. A sure sign that maybe not everything is as it seems in the Castle of Ekoni.

Faeryn's life had always been perceived with a rosy hue, but growing up in a castle wears off pretty quickly when you are essentially isolated. Not knowing of anything else and left every day to wander, yet never allowed to leave the castle walls. Every day, the same, go to lessons and do her duty, every day. Cleaned by others, touched with the rough cloth of the cleaning materials on hand, without being touched by the real warmth of human skin touching human skin. The servants refusing to talk to her in fear of offending the Queen, only murmuring to give instruction, a "Raise your hands, mistress" so quiet and meek you would wonder whether it came from a mouse.

Being sent to bed only to repeat the exact same pattern the next day, and the next and the next.

The castle was expansive, glistening white marble shone in the sun and the moonlight looking as if it had come straight out of a fairy-tale book. Fairy tales that her mother, the Queen, had once told her as a young child, fatherless with a bedroom in a tower. She now saw the similarities her mother was trying to ingrain in her mind from a young age, teaching duty through child's stories, always duty.

Faeryn was like every other princess that her mother had told her about in the way that she had a four poster, dark mahogany bed frame with bedding made out of the plushest royal red silk, clothes of the softest materials, jewels that would make a dragon weep with joy. Except Faeryn wasn't like the princesses from her mother's tales, not really. The bedding to her was the colour that would remind you of blood if you had ever seen enough of it. The glistening stone of the marble would feel cold against her skin and she would feel as if it was a chill running through her entire being with every footstep she took. It was like taking a step onto ice; the mornings getting out of bed seemed like such a hardship because coming out into the snowy disposition that was the castle was terrifying in and of itself. A prison of her mother's making, unintentionally built to foster ill will towards not only her mother but also the Kingdom, the Princess longed for something more, something different.

With this solitude there came the inevitable wish for friends, Faeryn would imagine the games that she would play with the friends that she would have if she were just allowed to play with the children that served in the castle. The games of tag, running through the winding corridors that scattered the castle. In winter she would dream up that the cold of the floor when getting out of her four-poster bed was the cool touch of another, the way she imagined it would feel when you are touched by someone after playing in the snow having had a sleep over with her many friends. A sore point of hers as she had never been able to do this like the village children she would see from her bedroom window.

Faeryn was stuck, that was probably the best way to put it, and she was well and truly stuck. This was of her mother's making; the Queen who used to be so young and free was now like a shrivelled flower, thirst unquenched in the Sarno Wastes. Her hair once long and lustrous was now limp and lifeless. The skin, thin like paper with a grey hue that would have even the most studious of painters unable to produce a masterpiece. But the worst were the eyes, once green like her daughter's, now misty with no sight of the golden flecks so famous in Faeryn's own eyes. The change that Faeryn only knew about because of the portraits that littered the walls of every great room of the castle that depicted not only her as a babe but also her father standing tall and strong next to her mother. It had all started with the first Pirate War.

For you see her father, King Koni, had died when Faeryn was not yet three turns, fighting the war against the Pirate King of Nonas to secure the kingdom and its surroundings from the wrath of a merciless man, hell bent on seeing the world go up in flames. They say it was a glorious death, clashes of steel until the last breath, whereas King Koni was struck down he managed with one last show of strength to bring his sword down on the

Head of the Pirate King, ending an era of fire and heartbreak for many across the realm. It is difficult to understand how one's death is glorious when surely the glory should be of life. Yes, he died saving everyone from a threat that we did not quite understand but surely it would have been more heroic to have lived and been there to see his daughter grow up? King Koni was an understated man flitting from one subject to the next quite rapidly from day to day, hyper focused and fixated almost to obsession on whatever task, goal or adventure he had set himself. His moods would follow this like a mountain range, climbing up before peaking and stumbling down into valleys of slight despair before finding the next new piece of knowledge to acquire, skill to perfect, or, in the case of the Pirate war, a battle to win or kingdom to save. However, Princess Faeryn would see none of this as yet she was not old enough to remember the quirks of her father the great king of Ekoni when he passed but that she soon would learn were the same as her own.

It was easy to see why Princess Faeryn did not want to stay cooped up in the castle constantly, despite all its grandeur. She yearned for adventure and the day-to-day lessons she was so accustomed to consisted of the Kingdom, family history and her duty, something she would get drilled into her for the next fifteen years of her life. Nothing of exploration or the world outside the city wall. As time went by, music had become boring with lifelessness, the waltz nothing more than a walk in the park, art became colourless rather than the figures she drew dancing off the page they became dredged down, stagnated in their own lack of creativity with no new stimuli to feed the imagination. Princess Faeryn's life had become nothing but sheltered with her mother, the Queen, becoming quite over protective in her fight to save Princess Faeryn from the same fate as her father, constantly saying they were "one and the same", completely and utterly unpredictable.

It was during one of her many lessons with Tutor Tobin, a great historian of the Royal line, with five generations of his family documenting the life and rule of the Royal family Koni of Ekoni, that Faeryn decided on change. A dangerous and difficult pursuit for one stuck in the same routine and watched so carefully as the princess. This brings us to the present day as Faeryn stared listlessly out of the Princess's study's window into the inner garden of the castle, buzzing with life, chewing absent-mindedly on her already nibbled fingernails, deciding just how she would go about breaking out of her current boredom and to do what.

"Princess Faeryn, are you paying attention, my dear? I swear, it's as if you've gone away with the fae these days. Head always somewhere else, no wonder your mother, her highness, is so exasperated with your progress," exclaimed Tutor Tobin.

Faeryn jumped out of her stupor and looked down to her hands, now nervously picking at her fingernails before a bolt of mischief ran through her as she lifted her head slightly to the side, chin up and locked her green eyes with Tutor Tobin's and said, "I'll have you know, Tobin, I have heard every single thing you have just droned on about for the last thirty minutes and I could repeat it all to you but as I am sure you know, with only lessons to sustain me, I am quite aware of my own family's history! What I really want to know is why there are no god damned books in the Royal library about anything to do with The Unknown or the Fabled Pirate King and Lords my father, the King, died protecting this kingdom from!"

Taken aback Tobin looked at the Princess, unable to quite understand what had just happened, as a child and throughout her years under his tutelage she had never been so disrespectful and rude, wistful yes, head to engage on occasion but never rude. And so blatantly.

Fixing her with one of his best, "you will do as I say" stares he proclaimed "You know perfectly well that your mother does not like to have reminders of the loss of your father around her every day and does not think it is healthy the obsession you have with him or the Pirates of the Unknown. Now you will read the end last chapter of the chronicles of Koni, the original Royal, by tomorrow's lesson or I will inform your mother of your uncharacteristic insolence."

Tobin proceeded to pick up his cloth satchel laden with books, slamming down the First Chronicle and marching straight out of the library with little more than a glance in the Princess's direction.

Faeryn felt guilty about the way that she had spoken to Tobin, he had always been her favourite tutor, giving her the benefit of the doubt when she would ask questions about her father and the pirate war: entertaining her fancies of adventure and not growing outwardly tired of her constant requests for the stories of old, describing the different battles and quests won by her ancestors. She had never challenged him as she had done today, but she could not help herself. Today was the day for change, she wanted to not only see the world and the life and people within it from a window while she worked, mused and lived trapped in her own castle but she wanted to feel the buzz of excitement running through people's veins, touch the heat of another's skin as they smiled at her, not influenced by who she is but simply from knowing her as a person. She wanted to smell the spices she saw being sold in the village market and taste the way each town, port, island and village made them differently. Faeryn wanted to follow the stream to the ocean and feel the spray of sea salt water on her skin, feeling the way it dried differently on her skin and through her hair. To laugh in the face of adventure and say, I will be.

The room had gone quiet now without the consistent murmur of Tutor Tobin reciting the chronicles of of the third generation of the Koni Family, Queen Erin and her bibliographic collection. Left to her thoughts Faeryn realised that she had approximately thirty minutes to search about the room she had never been unaccompanied in before. Perhaps in here she would be able to find something, a clue maybe, to the world outside the city walls. Surely the tutors must have something hidden in here.

Faeryn looked about the room, there was the tutors desk standing grand near the side of the room, blood red leather sitting on its top with the golden crest of the Koni family emblazoned in the middle. She looked to the door and back to the desk and tiptoed across the room to the desk to see if she could take a look inside the drawers.

Faeryn grabbed one of the ornate brass handles of the top right-hand drawer and pulled. Locked. Rattling the other drawers Faeryn soon realised that all of the drawers had been locked in case of this very situation. No matter, the walls in the study were lined with shelves upon shelves of ancient looking, leather bound books from marbled floor to ceiling, giving off a musty smell so unique to books. Faeryn's eyes scanned the titles, faded and barely legible, it seemed to her that yet again these books had been censored, only containing the topics her mother thought appropriate. She continued her search, pulling some of the more faded books off of the shelf.

"Nothing," she sighed and began to get agitated, forgetting that she would be in trouble if she was caught snooping the way that she was. Faeryn threw herself down into one of the forest green wingback chesterfield armchairs that surrounded the room's large open fireplace. Just as she was about to give up and put the room back into its original order ready for her next, oh so thrilling, lesson, she spotted one last tome on the edge of one of the large oak shelves, that she had somehow missed. Looking around once more, Faeryn snuck across the room, making sure to keep as quiet as possible realising that she may have been rather loud in her pursuit of change. She went to grab the tome off the shelf; larger than usual, it seemed to be quite stuck on the shelf. As she tried to snatch it, it lurched and gave way along with an outpouring of dust coming from a crack down the side of the bookcase. Faeryn's face scrunched up with confusion. Feeling rather flustered she realised she now might as well continue her journey as there was no way she would get away with what she had done now due to the mess. She gave the bookcase a shove with both hands, it creaked but there was no give.

Deciding a run up should do it, Faeryn ran from one side of the room to the other, shoulder first into the bookcase with the crack down one side. As her shoulder made contact there was an almighty crash and she stumbled straight through into a dark and dusty passage way.

"What the fuck?" Faeryn exclaimed as she brushed the dust from her dress. "God, mother is going to kill me now, I'll be confined to quarters for a week, at least." She looked up and tried to squint to see down the corridor that had clearly been abandoned for decades at least but could not make out a thing. The space around her and the smell of damp and cold felt familiar to her, she began to rattle her brain to remember where she knew this place from when out of the way through to the study she could hear the sound of footsteps and the guard outside the door moving. Faeryn scrambled to run back into the room and at least close the door to the passageway that she now realised might be her only chance for a bit of freedom.

Managing to get back through the door, slamming it quietly shut, she collapsed back into her desk chair just as Tutor Tobin re-entered the room.

"What on earth have you done?" Tobin stood gobsmacked in the door way with none other than the Queen stood at his back with a face that could turn the most courageous to stone.

Faeryn knew she was in for it now, but at least her secret was safe as she glanced across to the hardly-there crack in the bookcase. She didn't even think to find an excuse and simply looked down to her feet staring determinedly, jaw set and eyes still, waiting for the explosion that would be her mother.

2

Faeryn

The Queen took a breath and slowly walked into the room, practically gliding with her light of foot grace, her gown brushing along the floor. Faeryn noticed how the dust lingering from the passageway caught in the hemming of her deep purple dress, the red stitching turned dull the further into the room her mother got. She held her breath as the gown came to a stop a mere foot away from her downturned head.

"How is it with a familial line as dutiful as ours I have been given a daughter so insolent that I am called by a tutor, the best in the kingdom, to deal with her and worse, arrive to find that she has all but laid waste to that very same tutor's school room? Mark my words, Faeryn, this will be your last warning," the Queen said in a deadly whisper.

Raising her voice once more her mother looked to the personal guard. "Call the servants, have this room cleaned up immediately, my daughter is tired and will retire to her rooms now."

As the guard marched away to fulfil her mother's wishes, she turned back around to Faeryn with one last murmured warning, danger flashing low in her voice. "You will learn to become a productive member of this family or I swear to all that is holy that your father will be looking down in shame as I name the first non-Koni successor this realm has ever seen."

With those final words her mother left, the maids bustling in to usher Faeryn out and down the long hallways to her rooms in the West tower of the castle. She ambled along in shock at her mother's words, she never had had her mother speak to her with such disdain and lack of love before. It lit a fire in her belly stoking a rage that had laid dormant for so long, removing any form of acceptance of her current situation. Her resolve to plan a change to her life becoming clear as ever, and it would all start with the passageway that still seemed so familiar.

The usual cleaning of her body and changing into her bed clothes went by in a daze and as she slid in between the blood red sheets she fell to sleep with one thought in her mind... The passageways were going to be her freedom.

Sweat marked skin, red from the heat of her own body, tossed and turned that night as sleep came easily but marked with the hand of nightmares. Running down passageways, childish giggles echoing from the ways, the sense of anxiety and fear creeping through her chest and running, always running. Fire flickering off the walls reflecting shadows of monsters as she ran. A hand comes out to push against the wall as she turns down a new passageway, small, not yet big enough to be more than ten turns of the cycle. Silence. Stuttering breaths. The sound of heavy footsteps come closer and closer as she pushes her tiny body tightly against the wall praying to god that she isn't seen; praying to anyone that will listen that they don't hear her breathing. They stop, an indecipherable murmur breaches the silence and echoes off of the walls in a garbled mess of syllables that her young ears cannot make out. The footsteps and fire flicker begin to move away from her hiding place, the sound getting shallower and shallower as her breathing begins to return to normal. Backing backwards through the small turn her escape gave her she moves slowly trying to make no sound as to attract those who have just moved away. Her hands touch a wall, the smell here is damp, musty almost, a smell she can't quite put her finger on, and there is a certain coldness to the air that you feel in your nose and through your bones. She goes to push to the wall closer, the wall gives out as she falls further and further into darkness, her eyes firmly held shut, afraid of what she will find when she opens them. A growl permeates the silence and as she dares to open her eyes she is met with a face she cannot make up.

Faeryn bolts upright, cold washing over her, fear freezing her heart and paralysing her lungs. A million thoughts are running through her head, and the fear gripping her slowly dissipates as she comes back to reality, gasping for air. A dream, a memory unlocked by a smell. She remembered little only that she had seen, no, not only seen but been in and run the passageways before as a young child. That's why the smell felt so familiar to her, she had smelt it before in a moment of abject terror, ingrained covertly in her memory forever, waiting to be unlocked.

Looking out across her room past the small polished desk shoved next to her window and into the dark night's sky, Faeryn could see the moon in all its glory and she resolved that come morning light she would go about her day as to her mother's wishes and gather information, and remember as much as she could about the passageways in the castle. She would create a plan to explore, unfettered, and gain a new semblance of freedom that she had been wishing for so long. That night she went to sleep again with determination of steel, knowing that if only she were to gain access to that passageway again she would know what way to go.

The sun rose that morning throwing orange light across the

room, chasing the shadows of night away.

Faeryn went about her morning, eyes hard as stone, the servants paid little notice, hurrying along with their tasks, knowing not to linger for too long.

Breakfast as always a grand affair, as Faeryn entered the dining hall that morning, her mother was sat at the end of the long mahogany table, carved with intricate vines and roses. Papers to hand and apparently ignoring her daughter's entrance, the Queen's eyebrow raised slightly as her eyes looked up over the documents to her daughter before the slight shake of her head and going straight back to her royal duties. Faeryn took the reprieve from her mother's barely noticeable attention to inspect the security around her, around her mother and the people present in the room. For the first time she noticed how the guards, dressed in tunics the colour of the family, always held one hand to the hilt of their swords. Faces stoic in their expressionless gaze held straight ahead with eyes darting from side to side as a lizard moves his tongue. The servants, garbed in rough cloth, clean yet seemingly dirty, pottered about doing their tasks, menial labour, eyes lowered to the floor to ensure they did not catch the eye of the guard or one of the royals. It was clear to see that they shouldn't be a problem, perhaps she would need to find shoes that matched those of the servants so that if she did stumble into one of them in her pursuit of freedom of movement they would not recognise her shoes, clearly too expensive and fine to be those of a servant who regularly wore burlap sacks fashioned into shoes with some sort of bark material fashioned into shoe soles: twine for laces.

Yes, it would be the guards that would be a problem. Always alert, always watching, they lined the walls some days and walked the corridors in pairs, there was barely ever a time that she did not seem to have the presence of at least one in the room with her it seemed. This would be something she would need to think on. The smoked salmon in her mouth taste turned metallic as she realised with a start that her mother was now looking at her with her full attention. The silver fork came out of her mouth with a clink against her teeth as she cringed.

She did not like being observed so closely by her mother and kicked herself mentally for having been so careless as to not pay full attention to her mother's movements across the course of breakfast having been enraptured by her own observations of the room.

"Faeryn, close your mouth, it's impolite to stare open-mouthed like a guppy," her mother sniggered at her. "You should not be looking at the help this way, soon it will be a time for you to start looking at noble suitors from across the realm, lords and dukes that will bear worthy adversaries for your wilder ways. We do not need rumours of your fancy for the wrong sort being spread across the land rendering you tainted."

Faeryn flinched at this. "But, Mother I am only fourteen turns, why would I possibly entertain such absurd ideas?" she huffed out before pausing and whispering under her breath, "Plus, I do not wish to marry."

A loud yelp came of Faeryn in shock as her mother appeared next to her and with a pinch of the ear threw Faeryn out of her chair.

"You will do as I say, child, or you will face disownment." With one last swift turn the Queen stormed out the room leaving a shout behind her. "Get to lessons, Faeryn or you will be late."

She stood staring after her mother as she walked out, opening and closing her mouth, furiously she turned on her heel and skulked out of the room the opposite way her mother had just gone. Faeryn new that she must remain calm, if she was to access the passageways again she would need to be clear headed.

Weeks passed and with each spare moment Faeryn planned, examining the study room while her tutors droned on to their usual tune. It was only today that something was different; Faeryn felt a shimmer of hope stirring deep within her gut. Tutor Tobin was pacing caught mid rant when a breeze hit her right in the nose; the smell that haunted her dreams came pulling her closer. "Tutor Tobin, I feel quite strange. Would you possibly mind calling it a day?" The words came tumbling out and she was no wiser to stop them, she stood and teetered for a moment.

Tobin rushed a step towards her. "What has happened, Princess? I must admit being caught in my musings, do you need the physician?" Tobin flustered, moved once again away from the Princess and muttered under his breath, "I hope it isn't catching." Rubbing his hands that had barely whispered a breath near the princess against his silk britches, he rushed to the door almost dazed, "I will fetch the physician for you, Princess, lay on the arm chair if you must and rest"

"No, no, Tobin, I will just retire to m…" She trailed off as she realised she spoke to an empty room. Something filled her with energy, the instance of faintness forgotten in the rush of realising she was in the room alone once more. The first time she had been grateful to be truly alone.

Heart pounding, Faeryn approached the bookcase where the crack of a doorway was barely noticeable. Faeryn set aside her fear and reached out, running her fingers along the shelf and its seam. Gripping the shelf she pulled at the edges — and there, yes, it began to give way — now faced with the very passageway that had woken her night after night since her first discovery, she had the choice to follow the call or hide away back in comfort. With little more than a look over her shoulder and shuddered breath, Faeryn ran; she moved quickly like the Mountain leopards of legend that roamed the Mountains of Epicurus, grace in the way her heels never really seemed more than to skim the ground. She brushed her fingertips along the hallways, no mind the where she was going, feeling and absorbing the cool, marble feel of the walls enclosing the passageway and seeming to promise hope.

Further and further Faeryn ran into the winding passageways that were clear now to be throughout the entirety of the castle, she began to slow in her pace as she noticed small pockets of light coming from parts of the walls. Slowing enough to reclaim her breath and calmly approach the light that already felt unfamiliar, she pushed her eye up to the small hole in the wall.

Holding back a laugh Faeryn could not believe her eyes, there before her was the kitchen, a part of the castle she had not seen since she was small child. Cook was leant over a stove across the way and all Faeryn could make out was the back of a mane of lightly sweat slicked blonde curly hair, a heaving behind covered and swaying to an imaginary beat in the cook's head as she slaved away to cook the dinner for the inhabitants of the castle. To the right was a long oak table, covered in different types of vegetables and meats being prepared by the cook's assistants, two young girls who looked similar in that they both had blonde masses of hair but remarkably they looked exactly the same in features, the same eyes, and faces down to the freckles on their nose. She could hear them giggling to themselves and wished that she could make out what they were saying, accepting with reluctance that she would just have to make the conversations up in her head. She will name them Flora and Dora.

Before Faeryn could begin to imagine and play with the

dreamed-up lives of the sisters, a bell rang in the kitchen to announce that dinner was to be served soon. Reality came crashing into Faeryn like a ton of bricks, she must get back to the Study she had already been gone so long. She began feeling her way backwards. "Oh what turns did I take, do I go left or right or straight or back? How the fuck am I going to get back without getting caught? Mother warned me that this was the last straw."

As Faeryn began to run back through, turning which way and next, she began to hear the clashing of swords, her heart jumped into her throat, she began to think of all the possibilities. "We can't possibly have been raided while I have been gone, what has happened? If only I could just see."

Light was now entering the passageway blinding the Princess as she tried to adjust. Thinking the worst, she cowered down into a ball and leant against the cold marble of the wall that now seemed the polar opposite to how it had, cold and uninviting. As her eyes adjusted she began to be able to see, the light had been a window of sorts high in the wall up ahead. Crawling from her place she approached the window, fully prepared to peek through and see Guards in the midst of battle with the Pirates of the Unknown. Instead she was met with the sky of dusk and the guards, a scene practicing their swordsmanship. She watched fascinated and thrilled as they danced across the courtyard, swords swaying and catching the light, curling and curving through the air with a grace that screamed magic within Faeryn's heart. This was something she could watch forever. She wanted to try, she wanted to dance the way the guards did with their swords. Faeryn no longer cared about the repercussions; she would risk everything if only to come back here every night and watch the sword dance. Taking one last glance at the dancing swords, she began her journey back more reassured, following her gut to where she was certain she was meant to be.

Time moved quickly as she walked with her gut in the dark of the passageways, beginning to think she had gone crazy as her belief wobbled a slight lightening in the grey of the wall ahead caught her eye and yet again she felt the calling. Moving forward, as if pulled by ghosts of the past, her hands met the patch she had seen and rather than the cold marble stone she had been expecting to feel she was met with a rough material as if made from rug wool.

As her fingertips began to play with the material the sudden urge to push forward met her body and created a chain reaction that led to Faeryn falling.

"Oh fuck, fuck, fuck. Ahhhh," was all that could be heard as a dark tumble ended with the princess flat on her back, looking around the new light-flooded room she realised three things.

First, she had somehow stumbled into her own room in the castle.

Second, she needed to get better balance because falling from a hole apparently behind the tapestry above her head hurt. Bad.

Lastly, she was free. This was her magical moment, she would be able to sneak around the castle now to explore and listen and learn of the truths her mother would not allow her to learn during her tutorship.

As the emotion was getting too much to contain, clatter from outside the door alerted her to the guards and possibly another coming into her room. Knowing she was supposed to be sick and that everyone must have been looking for her after her teetering in the study room she scrambled into her bed and feigned sleep. Just as her eyes closed she caught a glimpse of the door to her room opening.

"Here she is, damned girl, I thought I had heard her say something as I left the room but I was in such a hurry to find the physician that I did not stop to listen. Apologies, my Queen, please forgive this humble servant!

Faeryn wished she could see the faces her mother was bound to be making, she had known Tobin since she herself was a child and presumably played with him as a child herself.

"No matter, Tobin, we have found her now, perhaps we should leave her be for the night, she looks like she is exhausted even as she sleeps." The touch of love to her voice could be heard even by Tutor Tobin whose clothes she could hear shift with a nod before the footsteps of him excusing himself could be heard.

Straining to hear if anyone followed, Faeryn remained as still as possible.

The love in her mother's voice was a rare yet wonderful thing and she hoped that she would continue while she thought her daughter was asleep and protected from the warmth of love that could lead to the pushing of boundaries. As the thought came to mind a hand brushed alongside her face, nearly making her jump, ruining her falsehood of sleep. No words were said but a quick kiss to the cheek and the quiet footsteps of her mother leaving the room was enough to leave a tear rolling from an eye as Faeryn slowly opened her eyes to the dark of her room and sank in the bed underneath her, relaxing to a degree barely known to her. Things were changing.

Faeryn began sneaking away every night through the small opening above her bed, presumably unknown to the other inhabitants of the castle as she had never seen another soul in the passageways, nightmare forgotten and dismissed as nothing more than a child's imagination. The same energised pull led her back to what she now thought of as the guards' viewing window, to watch them train and mimic their movements in her restrictive passageway.

The Royal Guard not only trained to always be ready for another Pirate war at any moment, fearing that the dreaded Pirates of The Unknown once again would rise up to challenge the Koni Family's right to the throne, but also because the highest-ranking Guard members aspired, like most in the military, to enter the prestigious world of the Personal Guard, the only way to gain entry to which was to become a master swordsman. Only the very best of swordsmen would be able to make it to this rank with a competition being held every two years for guards to prove their skill and determination, only the top five making it through to the Personal Guard. The head of which being the Head of the Personal Guard, shadowing the Head of the Monarchy every day, the highest honour the Military allowed.

These passages would become Faeryn's lifeline; she would use them to sneak away from her lessons claiming to feel faint and needing sleep. The passageways and viewing points were vastly different from day to night and the urge to listen in on the drama of the day-to-day servants' lives, was strong. No one knew that Faeryn was doing this; no one understood that maybe the Princess might have been lonely growing up without any friends, that she would become slightly mad in her pursuit of friendship and compassion. Obsessive, much like her father.

With the obsession she became sloppy in her need to be in the passages, forgetting to return to bed at the right times to continue her feigned illness. Missing lessons and raising the suspicion of her tutor and her mother.

On one such occasion it wasn't until the rumbling of her stomach brought her back to reality after having spent hours dancing through the passageway outside the guards' viewing point that she looked down and realised that she would need to go and find food. Sneaking through passages back to where she remembered the kitchen to be, she felt round for an entrance. There seemed to be a small hole you could crawl through if you scrunched up your body to get through into the kitchens. With one last look through the peephole to ensure the coast was clear, she crawled through making sure to tightly close the handleless door behind her. As she did this the bright orange peel of a tangerine across the table caught her eye and she went to cross the room to pick up the food, her stomach rumbling. Fingers wrapped around the fruit and shivers ran down her spine as the shouts of Flora and Dora could be heard coming down the steps to the kitchen. Wide eyed and looking around for somewhere to hide, Faeryn didn't know what to do. As she turned back to the door all she could hear was the "ommphh" as the Cook slammed into the backs of the two girls stood still as statues staring at the Princess.

The cook was not one to mince words and came straight out with it. "Princess, you are not supposed to be down here under any circumstances! I have half a mind to call your mother down here to reprimand you." Wagging her fingers and tutting her overly large lips together like a disappointed nurse maid.

A new pull crossed Faeryn in that moment, words she barely heard bubbling from her own mouth much like the day she first found the passages. "This is bullshit. I'm the Princess, I'll be where I want and there is nothing Mother dearest can do about it!" Her foot rose and came back down with an almighty thump, stamping her foot like an adolescent unable to control herself.

Cook's face swelled with tomato red anger and Faeryn could swear on it that she saw steam coming from behind the curls near her ears. "Right that's it! Girls, get Tutor Tobin; he can report this straight to Her Majesty and we will see about what is and what isn't bullshit!"

Faeryn couldn't believe that this was happening, twice now she hadn't been able to control the words coming out of her mouth, twice she had felt he pull and call that had led to involuntary actions on her behalf. She must be under some spell surely, a curse from an enemy of the crown. Before she knew quite what was happening she was in front of the Tutor, his lips moving but she was unable to hear a thing, only keep silent looking on in dismay. Eventually she was reprimanded back to her quarters where her mother was waiting looking beaten down and tired, gone was the mask pulled over her worn face, disappointment and disgust now marred those features that only a few weeks previously Faeryn was sure would be filled with love. Self-loathing washed over her like a warm bath, enveloping her the longer her mother sat there without her mask.

Slowly standing she looked at Faeryn and began to speak in a low dull tone. "I wish from the very heart of me that you would behave, you are so much like your father. In that respect, he was a courageous man, determined in his pursuits of knowledge and righteousness. But, Faeryn, he was kind, he followed his duty even when his interests lay elsewhere, and he looked to the good of the people, not just what was best for himself. That, my child, is where you seem to differ. I have tried too hard to mold you into the young ruler that he would have wanted but I feel as if I am failing my duty not only to him but to the people." A sigh escaped her lips as she looked around the room once bright with colour that seem to now be faded and dull. "Perhaps it is my fault that you have ended up this way."

"Mother, no, I am sorry. I let my heart get before my head. You raised me to look out for what is good for the kingdom but

I keep letting my own wants and fears get in the way of what should be the time for learning. I just wish for more freedom." The words poured out of her as if they had been trapped behind a dam fifteen years now in the making. Her mother's face switched almost immediately, it had been the wrong thing to say Faeryn now understood as she backed up with a puttered step towards her bed.

"Freedom?" roared out the Queen. "You are the Princess of a realm; do you not want to live to see past your teen years? We have enemies everywhere, what would happen if the Pirates of the Unknown reappeared tomorrow and you were out 'being bloody free'?" Heaving, the Queen came to her fullest height, gone was the dull and broken mother Faeryn had seen when she entered the room. "You want to make out as if you are a prisoner, I'll give you prisoner. Confinement, you will be confined to this room."

"Guard!" called the Queen. In response a burly middle-aged guard came in from the hall way.

"Yes, Your Majesty," came the brisk reply of the guard.

"Set up a watch on my daughter. She is not allowed to leave this room. Have her checked on once an hour." And with that she strolled out of the room, chin high in the air, slamming the door behind her, leaving the guard to awkwardly reopen it and take up his post on the other side.

"Shit, I really have done it now," Faeryn whispered in disbelief to herself as she ambled towards the bed.

There's no way I can get back into the passages now, not when I've left her like that. Well... at least not while the guards are checking in on me.

Faeryn huffed a sign and resigned to her fate chucked herself backwards onto her bed. It was fun while it lasted.

3

Faeryn

The sky passed by slowly for Faeryn locked in her room. From her place on her bed she could see the way the colours of the sky would change slowly with the falling of the sun and the rising of the moon. She could see the way slowly the stars in the sky would wake up and begin to twinkle. The way the colour would deepen as the hours passed, from the pinks and purples to the deepest of blues, she imagined that this is what the ocean looked like. As the night began to wane away the blue would lighten, the birds singing calling the sun to take its place once again, visible in the sky.

With a huff Faeryn turned away from her window, she had been unable to sleep all night worrying over what the future would hold and the way she had hurt her mother. It was easy to feel conflicted in this moment because why should she feel bad for wanting more freedom, to get out and see the world and learn about the kingdom she would one day rule? Travel to other places to understand the entirety of the realm and the place out of her mother's watchful eye. How was she supposed to rule diplomatically and for the good of the people living there if she had no idea of their culture or customs? Her points seemed valid enough for her even if she still did not have a single solitary person to bounce them off of. However the hurt so clear in those moments with her mother rather than just the Queen would catch

Faeryn and the anchor weighing down her chest would renew its pressure in the ever-present guilt that she was beginning to become accustomed to since being locked into her quarters.

It had been two days since her mother had walked out on her. Two days and all Faeryn had done was wallow in her self-pity. Her lessons would begin again in the morning and she needed to make a decision on how she was going to approach her new situation. With questions of whether she should submit and give up her dreams of adventure or whether she should push it further and try to make change swimming in her head, she walked across her quarters and sat on the window seal looking out across her city.

Lost in memories Faeryn remembered how she would look out this window upon an evening after the servants had washed her, lonely, often crying wondering why she was never able to leave the castle completely. She'd look out on the village and the people in the village around her all the way through to the wall which surrounded the city of Ekoni and she would think, is there a single person out there who would be my true friend and not just a friend because I am royalty but a friend who would be able to touch my very soul? She would look out in the villages and see the markets and hear the children giggling and crying because they did not want to go to sleep and then she would as she did many nights look out in further across the wall and the stream into the forest of Kasia. Now the forest of Kasia was a dark and mystical place just beyond the wall, forbidden not only to her but also to the castle staff and the villagers and anyone in the Kingdom who did not wish to "die a gruesome death". The forest was said to be the home to magical creatures: squirrels that can fly, dogs that had no bark, snakes that could talk, anything you could really think of, but the most important and the thing that always caught Princess Faeryn out was that the forest was said to be home to fairies and her namesake is that of fairies. Faeryn would look out to the forest nightly and think of what her life would be like if she were not a princess, she would imagine a life of adventure, exploring the entirety of the realm. The moon would glow and shine brightly on the leaves of the trees of the forest as if to almost twinkle in the moonlight, calling to her to come to them, to explore, then find the fairies and make home and peace with them.

As these memories washed through her, she realised her decision had already been made for her, as she had decided upon many times already across the last few months, it really was time for change. First she would need to become stronger. Perhaps she could copy the movements of the guards' muscle-strengthening training to build her strength instead of just mimicking their sword fighting steps. That night Faeryn went to sleep peacefully for what seemed like the first time in a very long time.

The next day Faeryn realised that confinement didn't have to mean the end of her tasks, she could begin training in her room. She would watch the people from her window and she would mimic until she felt confident enough that she could sneak out through her passageway to watch the guards again.

After this the days came easier to Faeryn and she would stick to her routine in order to fulfil her mother's wishes while confined to her room while sneakily taking purchase of the movements of the villagers and guards from her window. Taking time to understand which movements she could copy without anything other than her body that seemed to make her muscles tighten and shake with effort. These are the things she decided would help her get stronger. Whether that be leaning all her weight onto her hands against the desk or wall and bending her elbows down to bear the weight or duplicating the action of falling down to use her hands to push herself and jump back up. Faeryn would struggle with them alone, realising her childhood of luxury and staff had stopped her growing strong in body. At lights out Faeryn would fall into a sleep that was almost comatose. Waking up feeling weak and sore, getting out of her bed would feel like each limb of her body was weighted down with gold. Luckily for Faeryn this tiredness went unnoticed by the tutors that came each day and the servants even if they did notice did not say anything. She would practice with each spare moment of the day that her quarters emptied and wore herself out quickly. She had no idea how long she would be confined for, all she could do was go along with her punishment rebelling in secret until she could come up with a firm plan to enact change.

It was on one of these such occasions while Faeryn was jumping into the air after one of her exercises that she heard a key in the door, it was too early for her tutors to be here and with the slight distraction and the panic of "would she get caught?" she lost real focus and came down to her feet with a jolt twisting her ankle over and slightly to the side.

"Aagghhh, oh shit that hurts, ahh," Faeryn exclaimed as she jumped around clutching her ankle to her chest, the new presence entering her quarters completely forgotten.

"Ahhemm," a new voice in the room broke through Faeryn's pained jumping. She looked up and forced her eyes to focus on this person that stood before. He was a young boy of twelve or so, tray of food in his hand. Brunette hair swept to the side with a bit of a ruffle, clearly this was his first day on the job, no seasoned servant would be so obtuse as to not be neat and tidy within the castle with how strict the rules were on this. Or have the courage to make a sound when not spoken to. She could see herself making an ally out of this one if she could get a hold of him long enough before he was indoctrinated into the way the rest of the staff behaved.

Clearing his voice slightly with a thick swallow in his throat and eyes darting to the side he brought Faeryn out of her thoughts with the words, "Princess I have your lunch. Tutor Tobin is going to be early today and requested your food ar… arri… arrive early." He stumbled over the end of his sentence in surprise as Faeryn rolled her eyes quite harshly at him. Forgotten was the thought of having this boy as her ally and in came the rage, flooding her clarity.

"Oh really, and what else has Tutor Tobin requested for me? Hmmm? Bet he doesn't have his lunch time dictated to him," she snarked almost to herself, looking up quickly and sighing as the young boy shook in front of her, her rage ebbing away as the guilt of scaring him creeped in. He was so young, she noticed during her musings, that he kept looking to the door.

"Go on then." Sighing flinging her hand in the general direction of the door, watching as the boy scampered away.

She plopped herself down on the floor where she stood to inspect her ankle that was still pulsating under her dress. She went to pull her dress above her ankle to see what the damage was. She looked down to her ankle and saw that it was beginning to turn blue and purple in certain areas, slightly swollen in appearance but definitely not broken.

At least that was something.

This would stagnate her progress slightly, she would need a few days of rest from her usual exercises to let it heal.

The rest of her day went by as usual — if you don't include the rushed exercises in between lessons and almost passing out from exhaustion. It wasn't until Faeryn lay back in her bed wondering what she would do to pass the time that she realised that up until now she had been running on fumes, passing out each night rather than falling asleep, she could feel that she had gotten slightly stronger yet here she was unable to fall asleep, mind blank.

A calm washed over Faeryn in that moment that she had never before known, she felt her body move carrying her to the window seat she had fashioned out of her old desk and took residence there. Looking out across the usual landscape her eyes moved once again past the village and the city wall to the Forest. She could stay here for hours just staring into the trees; it would be here that she could find peace.

4

Wren

The market was hot and sticky and the smells of a hundred different spices would overwhelm your senses taking root in the space between your nose and brain. The stalls were so close together that the sellers could reach out and brush alongside each other's clothes with nothing but a finger's stretch. The noise a cacophony of voices, high pitched mixed with the low bellows of men.

"Come and get your chilli, mixed herb half a gallon, a bag." Jumbled in with, "Lilies for your beauty, Roses for your love, get some flowers for your paramour," came the squeaks and bellows of woman and men alike.

Right in the middle of all this a girl could be seen running in and out weaving her way like a skilled dancer through the stalls being chased by two street children. If your eyes could move fast enough you could see the way the girl's olive skin was tanned from the sun yet still glowing and smooth without a mark to her. It would seem to reflect the light's rays as she moved. Her hair flowing in a curling mane behind her, smooth in its ringlets and shining as if it were not the hottest day of the summer months. And her eyes could be seen as she skidded to a halt in front of a flower seller as blue as the ocean, pupils darker than the night with a glistening of what could only be described as akin to the North Star.

"Five minutes faster than last time, you're improving. Now tell me why the street children are chasing you?" the flower seller said with a smile as she looked down in to those ocean eyes looking innocently up at her.

"Well you see, Mother dearest, the boys here" — looking back at the boys the girl began to smirk — "bet me that I could not get back to the market stall from the tavern before them without causing disruption. I seem to have proven them wrong," the girl said as she turned her body slightly across to now face the two young street boys who were stood two paces away watching and waiting.

"Lads, I do believe you owe me a favour, no worries, I will collect at a later date. Now off you go and tell the others that I am still undefeated." With a wink the girl turned back to her mother as she caught the boys giggling and scampering off to the other street children of the city of Ekoni.

"You should not goad them as you do, my daughter, one day they may beat you or be fed up of games and you never know what will happen then. What do we always say?" The mother looked to the daughter with amusement written on her features.

Sighing but standing straighter and raising her chin slightly to her mother the girl said fiercely, "Maintain humility, retain dignity and always show kindness." The glint of pride was clear in the girl's eyes as she said these words. Strong words to live by in the market village in the shadow of the castle of Ekoni where the market sellers lived and the street children hid in every nook and cranny.

Seeing the change in emotion in her daughter, the mother knew that nothing else needed to be said on the matter. "Now report in."

"Father is still at the tavern, Mother, he has been there since the sun rose after you left for the market day. Half the money for the week seems to be spent and the guards are keeping an eye on him. What is my next mission?" The role play of mission and spy master was now a common occurrence for the two of them.

"Time to stand down my Wren. Time to stand down," the mother whispered, knowing they would need to make enough money today off the flower stall to make up for what her husband was spending on ale in the tavern across the village next to the guard keep.

Wren had been named for the bird, small and inconspicuous in appearance but bold and loud in nature. From the moment that she had been born, this description seemed to fit her like a glove, being born into the world with a cry that sounded like bird song loud and beautiful. It was not until she started grow that the inconspicuous nature of her footsteps and sneaking became clear, small though she was she had an unnatural beauty to her that caught even the most stoic off guard and gained her favour with the people of the village surrounding the market.

The market village where they lived was in the shadow of the North West side of the Castle that stood atop the hill that centred the city of Ekoni. One of five villages that made up the city, the market village was known to be for the merchants and the veterans of the Pirate war like Wren's father. The stipend that they received when he first came back from the war injured with a sword to the leg paid for their little house two kilometres away from the market stalls. Their home backed onto the hill face which made up the backing wall for the structure, housed both sides by limestone walls and a thatched roof. A single story with three rooms: a living room and kitchen, the main bedroom for her parents and then Wren's room. Wren's room was just about big enough for her single bed, a pile of wood stacks with a hay mattress and a single side table with two drawers that held her clothes.

Although small, the house was kept immaculately tidy and as clean as humanly possible in the conditions. Wren knew how important this was to both her father and mother and would make sure that the house was in order every morning alongside her other chores. Despite having no visitors to see this immaculate home, Wren was still unbelievably house proud and the act of cleaning and keeping the home in order filled her with a sense of motivated calm that she lacked during her day-to-day life.

Wren's father, who was now at the tavern spending their weekly veteran's allowance, had been a strong man when Wren's mother, Maggie, first met him. A sharp jaw line cut from the very marble the walls of the castle were made from, with eyes like icicles and a warm smile that would melt her heart. That man had left to fight for his King in the Pirate War when Wren was yet to be born, with Maggie's stomach swollen and the birds singing from across the wall he had marched away with the other soldiers from the market village they had found home in. It had been Wrens singing that day as she watched him leave and not two months later her baby Wren was born to the world with that beautiful cry. What they hadn't understood on that day that the birds sang him away was that he would not be returning for three full turns of the seasons.

The man that came back to them was not the man that had left. Gradually over the years that followed he became more and more cold. Silent in their company, he would stare off into space, eyes darting around as if watching a scene play out on the wall behind his family's heads.

One of Wren's earliest memories had been of climbing up the bookcase in their living room in front of her father trying desperately to get his attention when her hand slipped and she fell. Her father did not even lift an eyelid to look at her, not one flinch of movement to save her.

Falling she landed on the pot of quills that had been knocked off the shelves on her journey up. Three quill tips poked out of her shoulder in an odd triangular pattern as her mother had come rushing through from the kitchen alcove screaming at her father, why didn't he do something?

Wren just stared blankly up at her father from the floor as her mother picked her up and took her to the kitchen to clean her up and remove the quills from her skin.

She had been six years old by then and she still to this day at fourteen years of age had three brown circles tattooed into her shoulder's skin where the quills had been soaked in dark brown ink for correspondence. It had only taken three more years after this for her father to begin disappearing. At first they could not find him, thinking he had gone to market or out for walks to build strength. Eventually they began to understand the more he was gone, and from the smell of him when he returned, that he had begun visiting the taverns of the village. One in particular that sat near the guards' barracks slowly became his local haunt and from then more often than not Wren's father could be found on the same stool at the tavern's bar.

It was at this time that Wren's mother Maggie began working the markets, stealing money from the weekly allowance while her father was drunk to pay for the stock of flowers to begin her own small stall in the market to keep food on the table and Wren in clothes. It was the following years that Wren learnt to weave between the stools, quicken her pace, strengthen her arms and discovered a soul deep longing for exploration and adventure around the villages in the city of Ekoni.

The older Wren grew, the more she understood that her missions and spying games were not just games but also lessons: how to be honourable, how to be just, humble, determined, but also quiet and sneaky, able to move without being heard or seen. Her missions would bring her to taverns across all five villages within the city wall in search of her father, she knew not to be seen or heard; she was to observe, find out when he was going to arrive home, ensure her mother knew what was happening so that she could get home before him. The make was her and the villager's secret, unknown by him due to his almost constant drunken state.

Now at fourteen Wren knew the city like the back of her hand, she had run the streets across the villages, seen all of the taverns and knew the rooftops like her very own private stairway.

The only ones that could rival her knowledge were the Street Children. A group of about thirty children that had been orphaned by the Pirate War that had no home, no relatives and lived in the empty houses on the edges of the Villages, mainly the market village, edging closest to the wall that surrounded the city. This area of housing had previously been left empty when older single male soldiers had gone to fight in the Pirate War but had never returned. It was thought that the area was haunted by the spirits of the soldiers and a dangerous place to go due to its proximity to the part of the city wall that backed onto the Forest of Kasia. Yet the Street Children never seemed to be afraid of either the spirits or the Forest that the village mothers told tales of to their children warning them of the magic that hid within the trees.

Wren and the Street Children had a unique relationship because of her snooping and had developed a sort of unspoken rivalry that often led her to situations where she would prove her agility, strength and stealth through races across the villages often beset with obstacles to pass or guards to avoid. It was one such of these races that led her to her mother at their Flower stall that day, five minutes early, that threw the timing of the rest of their day off completely.

5

Wren

Maggie had always been Wren's biggest supporter, no questions asked, she would roll with the changes that Wren would go through with ease. So when one day Wren announced that she would no longer wear dresses it came as no surprise to Maggie who proceeded to trade some of her flowers for some red and navy cloth to make britches and shirts. Of course it helped that she knew that this particular step would make carrying the flowers and baskets to and from the market a lot easier for her daughter and the other sellers wouldn't bat an eyelash because of her age. Maggie thought perhaps that Wren may grow out of this and wish to wear dresses again when she got to a stage where marriage was a consideration, certainly before she began to bleed.

The day to day for Wren had moved as she grew to encompass not only her spying missions but also working on the stalls with her mother in the market.

Every morning she would have to go and set up the stall before going back home and waking her mother and father, cleaning the house then going back to the market to begin the day of flower selling. An hour before the heat of the sun would hit the highest peak of the sky it would be time for her mission of the day, find her father.

The process of elimination that Wren had gotten used to

across the years would come as second nature to her as she searched through taverns, quiet as a mouse and unseen. The mission would be to find her father, ascertain how much longer he would be by the state of drunkenness he was in, try and find out how much money was left and then get back to her mother before the hour was up.

Today the bet with the Street Children's two older boys put an extra pep in her step and she flew through the sky as she ran as her toe tips would just about touch the ground, before springing off again for another leap allowed her an extra five minutes shaved off her best time, this time finding her father in less than forty-five minutes and making it back in time for a good lunch break.

As she sat triumph still present in her chest despite her mother's reminder of humility she closed her eyes and breathed in the smells around her. The aromatic spices filled her lungs filling her body up and allowing her every muscle to relax a fraction of an inch. The market had always felt safe to her, it was where she and her mother could be themselves away from the judging eyes of her now alcoholic father. It is where she learnt to speak her first words, where numbers began to make sense in the counting of change and where the talent for negotiation began to take hold, bartering with the locals trying to buy flowers for cheaper to then sell for more to others. Buying in new cloth for clothes for her and her mother, learning about the spices in their deep colour and learning what would stain and dye cloth, what would add flavours that watered the taste buds to meats and rices and then bartering with the seller to get the price down low enough to justify the purchase. This was almost like tradition for Wren by this point in her life, she lived for it, the routine gave comfort and she knew who she was and where she could go, feeling as if she had the respect from those around her.

Opening her eyes she saw her mother unwrapping a fresh pork pie for their lunch, the paper wrapping crinkling as crumbs started falling away from the unwrapped pastry. Wren flipped a knife out of her right boot for them to use to cut the pie in half to share between them. This was special, usually their food consisted of whatever they had managed to save from the evening before supper, half stale and cold. This, however, seemed to be a special treat that Maggie had scrounged up for them, rare enough that Wren kept her mouth shut and didn't want to question the occasion. The first bite had her mouth watering and her insides going warm. Wren felt her mood lifting even more than she thought possible after her win this morning against the street boys. She just felt like today was going swimmingly and that nothing could ruin her mood.

The rest of the market day continued on in very much the same fashion. The cloth sellers sold her new ruby coloured cotton for mere pennies in comparison to what they were actually worth. The Spice merchant, after a very passionate conversation over the best flavouring cooking methods for rice, gave her a discount in return for a promise to try a new flavour combination and report back to him on the results. And the carpenter had a whole stack of new creations: beautiful wooden training swords, bows, arrows and shields that he had let her play with despite knowing that she did not have enough money to buy any single item from him. Yes all in all it had been a brilliant day.

As Wren made her way back to her stall and to her mother she could see the stall topper being carefully folded away and the small smile on her mother's face as she sang to herself. This was what peace was, it could be felt in every pore she had and every step that she took, and this was what happiness felt like, in this moment.

"Mother, let me carry those, it's been a long day. You must be tired," Wren said as she took the baskets of flowers from her mother and tucked the stall topper into an empty section of the highest basket.

"As the sun sets on this day I can only say that I am the luckiest mother in the city to have a daughter as helpful and as smart as you, my Wren." Maggie usually came out with sentiments like this when tired after a good day's work, especially when Wren had done well on the market.

"We do what we must, Mother." Smiling at the compliment her mother gave her, she knew her response was what her mother would want to hear from her at this time of day.

"Perhaps, Wren, one day we will not have to work on the market stalls any longer."

"Hmmm, it's odd, I quite like being here, and the market feels like home. We would still need to at least visit, I wouldn't want to leave altogether." The thought gnawed at Wren's insides, the prospect of leaving behind the market and her daily routine making her squirm.

"Wren, there will come a day where we are able to make choices, choices that will not be out of necessity, but out of love and want." Her mother stopped and lightly touched her arm as she lowly spoke "If you could do anything, be anything, what would you want to be Wren?" Her eyes intensely focused on Wren in this moment.

Wren could not take her eyes from her mother in this minute of time, she had thought, of course, about life beyond the city, but had never let herself hope, or dare to think, of that becoming a reality. She had imagined grand adventures with friends, sword at her side and then returning home to parades and the applause of the people. She looked down slightly so as to not lose her step, she could not tell her mother this surely.

Looking back up at her mother, Wren had meant to reassure her mother that she would never leave her but what came out was vastly different. "I want to travel the world, become a master swordsman, meet the people from across all of the realm and feel free." Wren's eyes widened in shock at what she had just admitted to her mother out loud. Cheeks colouring in embarrassment, a feat considering her skin tone rarely allowed for the tinges of pink that Wren tried desperately to hide.

A laugh bubbled up from her mother, not one of mockery but one of pure joy. "Then, my blessed Wren, that is what you shall have." This time as she looked to Wren she reached out and used her finger tips to gently raise her face to level her with her eyes and whispered conspiratorially, "Maybe you will even fall in love." And with a wink and slight skip to her step, her mother continued on forward heading for their little house on the edge of the market square.

Skittering to catch up as her mother pounced through the front door, Wren's mind was spinning with confusion, embarrassment but most of all curiosity. What had her mother meant to do by bringing these ideas to the forefront, had she been joking or had she been trying to provoke her for some unknown reason? It was these thoughts that ran through Wren's mind as she quickly put away the day's purchase from sight and began putting water on the fireplace to boil, rice in the pot's basin with a dash of turmeric for dinner.

As the fire heated up she began to come to her senses once more and noticed that now would usually be when her father would walk through the door. He had only been in the village next door's tavern today, surely he would be home as his usual routine would tell him when she put the rice on. Worrying to herself she decided to call her mother.

"Mother! He's not come home, I've put the rice on, and usually that's the moment he walks through the door. What should I do?"

With a heavy sigh her mother said, "Go and see if you can find him, he might've just gotten lost in his stupor or found someone to buy his drink for him." She looked to Wren through heavy lids, as she drifted between consciousness and the sleep realm. As she slipped once more into her sleep she whispered, "Be careful, Wren, it is dangerous at night, be swift in your return." With that she was back into her slumber. The markets tired her out more these days, as she aged she was unable to keep up with the hustle and bustle of the market and still come home and ready the house for Wren's father's return. Wren took up the slack to allow her mother to rest and had begun in the last years cooking dinner while her mother slept on ready for his return, ensuring that the house kept peaceful and within routine with her father returning from whichever tavern he had frequented that day, eating a meal before slumping off to the bedroom to pass out before repeating the entire sequence the next day.

The front door creaked open as Wren left their home, she had not been out quite this late before, the night's sky had grown dark and the light was dim, throwing shadows against every available surface. The only natural light came from the moon and stars that littered the sky above the city of Ekoni. The rest came from the open windows of people's homes and the open doorways of the taverns across the city's villages. The air was abuzz with the sounds of men in the taverns and down the streets surrounding the taverns, singing old world shanties and songs that depicted the wars of the generations. Wren could smell the pungent odour of ale and sweat coming off the men already stumbling the streets looking for a way home or a woman to warm their beds for the night.

"Why anyone would want to associate themselves with men like this I have no idea. Why on earth would mother ever assume I could fall in love with something so repugnant?" she thought to herself as she made her way from roof top to roof top sliding to a stop soundlessly atop the roof of the house opposite "The Merchant's Arms" where she had seen her father wetting his tongue earlier that same day.

She sat in wait observing the tavern, knees bent double and her ankles feeling like they might break at any moment; atop her perch here in the shadows Wren felt at ease despite her discomfort. The Merchant's Arms was the main tavern in the market village and had been a staple in her father's drinking exploits since she was little.

Tonight things seemed to be exactly the same as it was during the day, loud, smelly and bright. Wren had assumed that she would see her father on her way to the tavern or within a few minutes of arriving but it was becoming slowly clear that she would need to be able to see into the tavern to confirm her father's presence.

Looking to her side at the distance between the perch she had taken up on she knew she would not be able to jump across the street from this roof top to that of the tavern despite the tavern's roof being flat. She would need to find another way to get across but remain unseen. Eyes scouring the streets, she noticed that two houses up the street had a wash line out. She made her way across the roof tops to the house she needed and looked at the line, it seemed secure enough, all she would need to do was walk across it, or perhaps slide along it using some material. She edged towards the line that spanned between the houses across the street, heart beating much quicker now; she took a deep calming breath and put the weight of her leading foot out to test the strength of the line. As she pressed more and more of her weight on to her front foot, she could feel the slight dip of the line before it sprang back up and into place. She would be able to cross here, the real test would be of her own strength and balance as to not fall as she slipped along the line toe to heel, arms stretched out wide like a balancing beam. With one final look down she focused her sights on the peak of a chimney on the roof top at the other side of the line and zoned in as she started her journey. Each step felt like being an earthquake with the way the line shook from the strain of her weight, but Wren never faltered, never panicked, she continued on, with every wind wisp and wobble she took another step, never taking her eyes off the chimney stack in front of her. She did not breathe nor make a sound as she made what seemed like quick work of moving across the line but that felt like ten hours inside Wren's own chest. She stumbled across the edge of the roof and gripped onto its ledge to pull herself over the side letting out a stuttered breath as she came back to herself and away from the determined and zoned in on focus she had adopted to get herself across the line.

 Taking just a second for her heart rate to return back to normal, Wren knew she needed to continue on in search of her father.

 Light flickered into existence blocked by the chimney breast that she had been intent on minutes earlier and as Wren skulked around the corner she found an opening in the rooftop just big enough for a ladder to poke out of and the smells and sounds of tavern wafting up through the hole. Creeping closer she grabbed a woman's wrap that had been pegged to the line nearest the chimney breast and twisted it around her body fashioning it into a dress coverall as she decided to peek through the opening.

Acting on instinct as soon as she saw the room was clear she swung herself down into the room below the rooftop and skipped into an alcove next to the stairs that descended into the tavern's main bar area. She knew that from here she would be able to remain anonymous and get a good vantage point to see all of those in attendance at the tavern that night. She moved forward to scan through the now thinning crowd and could see plainly that her father was not one of the men here.

Jolting back with a quick gasp she noticed that the Landlord was making his way around the bar to ascend the steps to the very room she was in. She knew she would need to retreat back to her rooftop and away before she was caught here. Thoughts of her father's absence caught in her mind she ran silently across the roof, and taking a crouching position mid stride she sprang up and out of the opening in the ceiling with nothing more than minimal effort, too deep in thought to even notice that she had just cleared a six-foot space without a care. Wren ran and jumped, almost flying across rooftops as she considered the whereabouts of her father. Having put a sizeable gap between herself and the tavern she slowed to a halt two roofs away from her own and began descending the building side to make her way home without concerning her mother.

Having decided to tell her mother of her father's absence from the tavern, Wren let her thoughts wander to the conversations of "what if?" she had had earlier that day on the way home from the market. Where would she even be able to go to get out of the city? The wall kept everyone in and only the guard were allowed to exit via the gate to pick up and officiate trade between the merchants importing goods for the city from across the realm, even those had to be sanctioned by the Queen and papers kept on hand to be checked every ten minutes. No, that way would be blocked. There must be some other way out of the city wall.

With that thought in mind Wren came to her front door and quite unlike herself pushed straight open, deaf to her usual instincts that had been on overdrive only fifteen minutes prior. Deaf to the sound of footsteps approaching the door from inside, oblivious to the smell of burning rice and stale ale and blind to the flickering light obscured by a large shadow as the door was wrenched away from her hands and she was dragged forward by the scruff of her neck.

"Where the fuck have you been?" a deep voice slurred at her.

"Out with those boys I hear you've been running about the city with? I hear things you no, things do get back to me!" his voice began to get louder as he spoke.

"No, father, I swear... I—" Wren stuttered. She had never seen him like this, never seen him so drunk he got angry, enraged by anything.

"Shut up! You're a slut, just like your mother! Nothing but a whore, I bet you've been whoring yourself out to all the little street boys!" His face grew redder as he went on, imaging up lies to fuel his own rage, not allowing her to get out more than a word here or there.

"Please father le—"

"I said shut up!" His voice hit a crescendo as his open hand swung out as fast as a snack, hitting Wren square on the cheek with such force it would have knocked her back if he didn't still have such a tight grip on the collar of her shirt.

"You wear men's clothes, you run around town as if you own the place, always with boys, never the girls, never acting like a lady." A shove permeated his words, she fell back now onto the ground cheek already purpling from the slap she had received.

Wren began slowly crawling back in terror trying to get away from her father as she took slow and meaningful steps forward.

"You will change, do you hear me, no more of this blasphemousness in my household." He pushed his finger downwards at her with every word. It was now she could hear her mother hammering at her door from her parents' bedroom, shouting to be let out and calling her name in desperation. "You will look at me when I am talking to you, Wren Lao, or so help me god." A kick this time to beat in what he was saying only just hitting her with enough force to wind.

His moves became sloppy as she carried on, words now too slurred to fully comprehend what he was trying to say. And as he stumbled backwards and fell into a chair Wren's vision blurred out as the exhaustion of the night and her first ever beating settled in over her like a weighted blanket pushing her into sleep on the floor of the living area.

It wasn't until the next morning that Wren's eyes fluttered open, stiff and sore she surveyed the room to make sure she was alone. The first thing she noticed was that the chair she had seen her father fall into was now vacant and the room was cold with the fire having gone out while she was asleep. He must have woken up with the sun and gone to one of the taverns again to top up the drink that was now surely leaving his system. Wren did not allow herself to wonder if he regretted his actions and she slowly made her way to her feet, knees creaking as she went to stand. The room span as she righted herself and memories of the previous night flooded her mind. With a panic she looked to her parents' bedroom door, still shut, as the sound of her mother screaming her name echoed in her ears from the night before. Making it to the door and not hearing a sound she turned the door handle only for the door to jam when she tried to pull it open. Locked. She looked around and quickly went to the kitchen, routing through all of the drawers looking for a needle that she knew she had put back there after mending her mother's dress the week before.

"Aha, found you." She smiled in triumph before running across the room back to the locked door. Using her hair pin and the needle, she slipped them into the lock on the door and twisted them around and pushed against the internals of the locking mechanism until she heard a faint click when moving the needle. She held it firm while she moved the hair pin around until another faint click could be heard and used her chin to pull the handle down while her hands firmly held her two tools in place and the door came free from the frame. Dropping everything she quickly pulled the door open further and ran into the room. Stopping abruptly, Wren gasped as she made out the figure of her mother, scrunched up into a ball in the corner of the room, unconsciously whimpering.

Maggie looked a mess, her clothing had been torn, hair knotted and sticking out everywhere and bruises starting to form on her skin that you could see through the tears in her once pristine dress and Wren knew she had gotten the blunt end of her father's rage when she walked through the door the night before. As Wren sighed she flinched, the pain in her body and face making itself known now, she leant down and wrapped her arms around her mother before lifting her, lip caught between her teeth and she suppressed a moan of pain from the movement. Placing her mother on the bed, Wren moved to re-lock the bedroom door and open the curtain of the window. As she lay down next to her mother she knew today they would not go to the market, today they needed to rest before he returned.

"Nothing will be quite the same again," Wren thought as she slipped back into sleep on the bed beside her mother.

6

Wren

In the months that followed, a new normal descended over the Lao house. Wren would get up before her father, clean the house and put fruit on the table before rushing quietly back to her room to slip on a dress and make her way back out for her father to see for all of a minute as he picked up the fruit from the table and heaved on his coat and left for a tavern. She would then proceed to re-dress herself into her britches and shirt before knocking on her mother's door to check in and see if she was all right from the damage her father had surely done to her overnight. Once ascertaining that her mother was somewhat okay, she would rush around and down to the market to set up their stall of now somewhat crumpled flowers. Once this was done she would make her way back to the house to see if her mother would be coming down to sell at the market, before multitasking between trying to make enough for the day's food and keeping look out for her father down the end of the street. Once Market was over they would run home laden with whatever was left over from the day and hide it within the house before Wren's father would get home and begin ordering them about.

    More days than not now this would lead to some sort of beating, whether it be because she had forgotten to put her dress back on, her hair was a mess, she was too dirty, the house was too dusty, or the food too bland or too spiced. He would find an excuse and she would try and take it for her mother so that she would not have to bear the brunt of his attacks. As time had progressed since that first beating her mother had stopped trying to get in between them, shrinking as soon as he raised his voice, she would not come to the market as often, left in a near catatonic state from the abuse he had committed towards her. Though beaten down, Wren did not lose hope that one day things would change, for now all she knew was that she needed to survive to keep her mother alive, to help in any way she could.

As the change set in and Wren had figured out a manageable routine for her and her mother, everything seemed to become more bearable. Now used to the beatings, having previously never been in a fight let alone beaten by someone they thought loved them, they were able to bandage themselves up well enough to carry on with the day. Maggie tried to keep spirits high most of the time while they were at the market together and they often talked about upcoming events, planning on how to celebrate while keeping Wren's father away.

Wren was due to turn fifteen in the upcoming weeks, traditionally this would mean that she was now open to looking for suitors for the day she turned seventeen. Becoming open to have her parents begin discussions into the arrangements surrounding her future within Ekoni, would she stay in the market village or would she travel across into other villages, what worth did she have, could she raise above her station and marry someone for more standing, perhaps a guard? These were meaningless to her, she had no desire to marry, no desire to better her station in the way that other ladies of the village wished. All she wanted was to stay surrounded by her market with her mother by her side. Her father was a drunk, a war hero but a drunk all the same. No one would be rooting for her in the background trying to get the best arrangement possible on her behalf. She resigned herself to the possibility she may become a spinster, the independence wasn't something that bothered her at this point in time, much rather a life alone than chained to a drunk and stinking man like her father.

They had decided in those weeks on the run up to her birthday that they would save up some of the money made while at the market and have a special lunch during the day while her father was at another tavern. Nothing extravagant just the simplicity that came from having a treat. Wren was looking forward to it and the nearer the day got the more she noticed her mother's smile grow. She was glad that things like this would help her mother move forward, things had been particularly good this week, neither of them had received a single beating, her father had returned too drunk to speak, stumbling through the door and straight into bed each night before waking up with the sun and leaving the house, dirty clothes in trail behind him and crumbs where he had taken the bread and fruit from the kitchen table. It felt as if all their hard work was beginning to pay off, the walking on egg shells was leading to respite from her father's fists and some welcome peace within the home.

And so on Wren's birthday when rather than being the first awake in the house she heard her mother singing quietly to herself in the living area, she slowly smiled and shrugged on her dress without so much as a suspicion that today would be anything but fantastic.

Walking into the living room her mother's melodious tune became clearer in her ears.

"...Silver day, silver dee, won't you bring my love to me, with the ocean spray, may the good lord play, bring my love to me." Her mother danced around the room, skirts swaying as her hips moved in time to the tune she sang.

Wren barely let out a whisper as she stared, a smile gracing her lips, astounded by the sheer change in her mother today. She had not seen her so happy in a very long time, her father was nowhere to be seen and the birds chirped in the background, the sun shining in from the windows. It felt like a dream.

Catching her mother's eye she sang in response, "The ocean chases, the moon rises, still my love comes back to me, silver dee, silver day, and I won't be long, gone away." The song was from the old world, before the Pirate War, before the city wall gate had been sealed to all those that wished free passage. A family lullaby from the Mountains of Lao where her family had immigrated from generations since gone. She had not heard her mother sing that song since she was but a small child.

"Happy Birthday, dear," her mother said softly as she lay down a fresh loaf of bread to the table with some crisp fruit.

Stunned, Wren took a seat at the table, still staring open-mouthed at her mother. This didn't make sense, she must be dreaming. A frown took over her face as she focused in on her mother. "What is going on? How is this happening? I… I don't understand."

"Well you see it's rather simple really, you're my daughter and I wanted to do something nice for your birthday."

"But father…?" Wren whispered.

"Your father is out, exactly where he usually is; today, however, he was just persuaded to leave earlier than usual" Her mother trailed off slightly hysterical, taking a breath before she continued.

"So today you are going to have some fun, be yourself again, even if it is just for one day. We can't, no, we won't, let your father's bad behaviour dictate our lives any longer! We will stand up for ourselves, do you hear me, Wren? We are strong women, we do not need to live like this." Her mother panted as she came down from her emboldened speech. "So today, my dear Wren, seems like as good as any day to start living," Maggie whispered as she tapped Wren's chin with her forefinger.

Scrambling to finish her breakfast she wanted to change back into her britches and shirt; if today was as her mother said she would be making the most of it. She ran through the small house to her room shucking off her dress and donning her newest clothes. Taking a minute to let the small feeling of triumph wash over her she put her hands to her hips and whispered to herself, "Right, you've got this." Before whipping her hair up on top of her head with a leather strap and speeding out of her room back to her mother patiently waiting by the front door with the market stall equipment and flowers.

Grin plastered on her face, she grabbed up half the baskets from her mother's hands, slinging the stall cover across her shoulders, and pushed the front door open with a swift kick of her foot.

Her mother's laughs could be heard, sweet and pure like the trilling of birds behind her as she wobbled her way down quickly to their market stall. She managed to get there only dropping a few flowers here and there on her way across the cobbled street. Setting down her load she turned sharply to look behind her bouncing on her heels eagerly waiting for her mother's arrival. Her mother seemed to be carrying more than usual in her arms. Wren let the thought flit through her and leave just as quickly as it arrived as her mother arrived with amusement twinkling in her eyes.

"Someone's in a rush today, help me set up and then off you go," Maggie's voice bubbled with barely concealed laughter.

"Look, help me set up and then you, the birthday girl, can go and race the Street Children and explore the city," she said as she passed a basket of tulips to Wren's already outstretched hands.

Wren made quick work of setting up the stall, energised by the fact she would finally be able to go and play with the others who she had missed over the weeks and weeks her father had taken over their every living moment. As she finished, she knew she needed to ask as always.

"Mission, mother?" Expectantly waiting, Wren met her mother's eyes with a glint.

Her mother thought to herself, how has it come to this where we have to have missions to play, quests to get by and she cannot just be a child like the others of the village?

Straightening up, she replied, "Today, my Wren, your mission is to enjoy yourself, go and play and forget for a few hours." She cleared her throat once more. "Go now, and be back for when the bell strikes three."

That last reassurance was all it took for Wren to sprint away from the market, wind whipping at the baby hairs that had escaped her bun as she went in search of her friends the Street Children.

Skidding around corners and nearly tripping on the uneven surface, Wren ran through the streets with speed, looking for one of her friends to begin a day of adventure. She had four hours before she was due back at the market to her mother and because of her large breakfast she knew she wouldn't need to eat lunch that day; her energy would last her until the third bell. On autopilot she found herself running in the direction of the abandoned houses that the Street Children called their home. She had not seen them on the streets yet today so she had concluded that this was the most logical place to look for them. Climbing up the side of one of the buildings on the way to her destination she continued on hopping from roof to roof towards where in the distance she could see the wall towering over the roof tops, she had taken the long way in her daze and had automatically gone past one the taverns her father frequented. She looked out across the roof tops and took in the bold colours of deep reds, purples, greens and blues that littered the washing lines of the houses near the market and the other villages before becoming more and more sparse the nearer it got to the Street Children's homes where only scrapped browns and beiges could be seen from the cloth that they had hung up to dry. With a quick sidled smile she barked out a small laugh before racing her way to them, she could see her friends on their roof top crouched looking below into the streets that surrounded their home. Her feet touched down on tile and limestone flat roof as she made her way across the village, crisp and dry air filling her lungs, and she effortlessly floated between houses. As she neared they spotted her and with nothing more than a slight incline of the head allowed her entrance onto their roof top, where she crouched into a squat as soon as she had stone beneath her foot, twisting to face the same way quietly as a mouse as her companion.

"You have been gone," Letta let out, with barely enough volume for Wren to hear, frustration straining her voice.

"I am sorry, my friend, things have changed, you have me today," responded Wren.

"Do we?" With a raise of an eyebrow Letta took in all that Wren was, eyes as old and wise as a bird. "Here today, gone the next. We need you, Wren, you are one of the only ones that look at us with worth."

"Don't be so serious, Letta, you know as you grow things will get better. But for now let's just be children, nothing more," she pleaded.

Letta hesitated for just a moment before smirking across at Wren. "Well I suppose it is your birthday after all. BOYS!" she called out into the complex of houses behind her, voice echoing off of the bare walls.

"They've been practicing, Wren, there is no way you'll win today. But I'll tell you what, win today and we will make it official and you'll be part of the family." She winked as she said this to Wren.

Two boys of eleven and thirteen years skidded ono the roof from the stairwell. Dirty with torn up clothing, they looked as if they could be twins, tan skin and light brown eyes. Wren knew them as Aab and Ber, the same two boys she had raced all those months ago. Standing to attention in front of Letta, their unofficial leader, at sixteen she was one of the oldest Street Children in the city of Ekoni, they awaited their instructions.

"You will race from here, through the village of makers, through the village of writers, around the clock tower and then through to Maggie Lao's flower stand. I will be in the shadows watching. Do not be seen, do not be heard if you can help it. First person to give Maggie a flower is the winner." She looked to Wren and raised a lip in a half-hearted sneer. "Off with you."

Let the race begin, was the last clear thought Wren had before her legs took her away, determination and focus clouding her mind from all other thoughts than the race and the path laid out before her.

Heart pounding in her ears, Wren ran, she had made it to the edge of the market village before she had even needed to release her breath to draw in more oxygen. Flipping her body upwards and across her had bridged the gap between the last house of the market village and she grabbed out for a flag sailing high above the houses that lined the small indistinguishable border between the villages. Touching down to the roof of the first house of the village of makers, she continued her journey barely pausing for a glance back at her rivals, Aab and Ber, keeping up as they might were staring at her dumbfounded as they looked for a way down the side of the last house of the market village to make their way safely to the next village, never having seen the type of vaulting skills Wren had just displayed from anyone before during their races.

Wren shook herself and turned back to the mission at hand, the village of the makers held some odd types and many liked to venture on to the roofs to work on experiments in the sun. She would need to be careful here not to be seen. She took note that the next two house tops were empty, and made her way slower now across them. As she moved she looked down to the streets running in between the buildings. Aab and Ber had levelled with her now, they were moving from corner to corner, watching carefully for any person that may be coming from their houses. As Wren brought her eyes further up the building sides, looking for another way around the houses without being seen, she noticed that the awnings of the houses were not made out of clothing cloth as she had expected but seemed to be woven much like the rice sacks that she saw the market sellers using to haul about their wares.

Theoretically she knew that this sort of material could provide more than enough support to carry her body weight.

With that thought in mind as Wren came to her next jump, instead of moving towards the next roof she allowed herself to fly straight downwards towards the material pulled taut at the side of the same house whose roof she had just been stood upon. A momentary lapse in confidence brought Wren back to reality.

Panicking, she brought her knees back into her body and rolled her head chin into chest to brake for impact as she hurtled towards the awning. As she thought she was surely done for out of her own stupidity, her body slammed into the material of the awning and it began to give, bending. She thought she was sure to break through, ripping the sacking in half, but much to her surprise and just like the washing line when she had bravely stepped out onto it all those weeks ago the awning snapped back into its taut shape and flung her back into the air. Flailing her arms at her sides, Wren managed to remain soundless as she righted her posture and wide-eyedly landed back on the roof that she had just jumped from. She looked further down the street where Aab and Ber had pulled ahead of her by at least ten houses and she soon noticed that each and every house on the street had an awning here to allow them to work outside on their ideas. A new plan formulated quickly in her mind and with a mighty leap she was back off in the air aimed straight back at the awning and this time as it flung her back into the air she propelled herself forward with her arms and landed straight onto the next awning feet first and with such momentum that it instantly bounced her straight back out, and over and over again this happened until her face was wind burnt and she had far passed the two boys she was racing and had made it cleanly to the last street of the village of makers. As the last house came upon her she allowed herself to be flung straight up onto the last roof landing with a wobble on the arm of a flag pole.

Uncontrollable laughter pushed its way out of Wren's chest before she was able to remember herself as she looked round to see Aab and Ber panting mid run a good five minutes behind her now. With a deep breath Wren look back towards her next steps and could see that the village of writers, although very small, was also the most crowded. She would need to use her stealth here more than her speed in order not to be seen. From the edge of the village she could see in the not so far distance the clock tower that edges the village and marked the three-quarter point of the race. From there it was quick work to make it back to the houses edging the hill against the castle and she would be able to roof top run the entire way back to the market from there, the route she was most used to taking when looking for her father as many of the village's taverns would be nearest to the hill and away from the wall lest a drunken man try to leave the city limits.

Taking note of the ivy growing alongside the wall of the building her flag pole was currently placed upon, she came down to grab the pole nearest her feet and swung her body forward and over itself releasing her legs and stretching her body as she once again became vertical pointing her toes towards the floor as she let go of the pole coming to a stop stood straight under the flag pole with little more than a slight pattering of noise in the wind. She crouched down and held on to the ivy that was weaved within the very brick work of the building and dangled her legs down off the side of the building. Slowly she climbed down, knowing that she had enough time but also understanding that if she rushed this part then her head start would be for nothing as she would fall straight into the small alleyway that was underneath her.

Once her feet were safely on the ground she was able to discern what the best route would be to take to stay out of sight here and with that she realised that it would need to be good and basic sneaking. Coming forward she placed herself on the corner of the first building and slowly made her way from corner to corner, ducking down under tables to avoid people's gaze as they lifted their heads from their work. Side stepping into doorways and turning corners with her back pushed up against the wall

Wren was able to make it through the crowded village of writers with little real trouble albeit much more slowly than her preferred pace. As she left the village she walked with more confidence to the clock tower that seemed much bigger now she was looking at it from down below rather than across the sky line. Looking around, Aab and Ber were no longer anywhere to be seen; she hoped they had not been caught by one of the academics that lived in the village of writers, they had a tendency to try and take in any of the street children they found and the rumour was that they would never been seen again, experimented on or at worst eaten. Wren had never paid much credence to these stories but she sure didn't want to find out the truth like this. With a sigh she knew she needed to carry on with her journey. Walking around the clock tower she came upon some detailing in the wall that she knew she would be able to scale easily until at a height tall enough to allow her to jump or free fall onto the roof top of the next building nearest the Castle's hillside.

As she scaled the side of the clock tower she let the events of the last few weeks run through her head and thought about what her mother had said to her this very morning. She had been so quick to believe that things would be changing now she hadn't really taken the time to think about what she wanted now, had things changed for her? Would her father even let up enough to make change a reality? She knew she wanted to never have to see her mother in pain again, that was what she knew was dearest to her heart. It was then that she decided that if she won today she would ask Letta if the street children would be able to teach her to fend for herself, scrap like they did, maybe then she thought she would be able to protect her mother.

She had made it to the top of the tower, perhaps a little further up than she had intended to climb but as she looked out across the villages of the city, higher up than she had ever been.

She had a feeling of rightness and as she looked out further across the wall and towards the tree tops of the forest that she knew to be near her home she felt a pulling that had her letting go of the tower and glancing forward in a swan dive towards the roof top she had spotted earlier. Twisting her body and spinning, she came down hard on her feet. Stumbling only a little as she sputtered to her knees, she allowed herself a minute of shock as to what she had just done and prayed beyond hopes that no one had seen her. Flicking her head up she took to a run to jump across the roof tops on the last leg of her race, homeward bound she could already smell the spices and flowers aromas of the market as she drew closer to her end goal. Two houses away now and she could hear once again Aab and Ber at her back, footsteps chiming on the streets below her. With one last final jump she jumped onto the last house's awning that she knew now would hold her and sprung forward never stopping her legs in their running motion to hit the ground running and slide into her mother as she shouted with joy, "Win." Unable to quite catch her breath she continued to breathe out and say the same word on repeat. "Win... Win."

Taking her hands from her knees she slowly looked up and straight out into the alleyway ahead of her, feeling as if she knew someone was there she was met with two eyes that she knew. Letta. She had won and Letta had seen. There was no way they wouldn't be able to let her into the family now. Straightening herself and tearing her eyes from Letta, Wren looked around to see the boys, heads hung and shuffling off into the alleyways sighing in defeat. Her attention was brought back to the market when a firm hand wrapped around her upper arm, with a flinch Wren turned around somehow expecting to see her father.

"Better, dear, far less prideful than last time, you won well," was heard as she was met with her mother holding out a jug of water for Wren to drink. The water was gladly and greedily accepted by Wren and as she chugged it down not stopping for breath her mother span around and picked something up off her perch behind the flowers lain out for selling.

"Happy Birthday, my Wren," was uttered by Maggie as she held out to her daughter something she had been saving and saving for months for, before the incident with Ryn, Wren's father.

Wren looked down to a beautiful wooden sword, hand carved, resting in the now unwrapped cloth in her mother's arms. She was speechless, the detailed work on the handle of the sword showed little birds Wren could see were that of her name-sake. Ivy spun its way in wooden carving across the handle and the sword length, somehow making faces with their patterning. She was speechless.

And as she came to look at her mother again with adoring eyes she whispered, "Thank you, Mother." A tear escaping as she looked back down to her new practice sword.

7

Wren

Later that very same night, Wren and her mother had gotten back to their little home expecting to have to face Ryn in all his drunken glory but as they approached the house the windows were not illuminated by candle light as they would be if there was a presence within its wall. Perhaps he had stumbled in and not brought flame to the wicks in his stupor, passing out before he could realise their absence.

Pushing the front door open as slowly and quietly as possible they creeped through the opening so as to not wake the man they thought resided within. As the full view of the room came into view they realised that he was not there, the set by the fire place was remarkably empty, there were no sounds coming from the bedroom as they strained to hear even a single snore — as was common when he had passed out drunk — and the house was cold. As this realisation sank in, a smile crept along Wren's face as she knew her birthday would not be marked with the violence of her father's hand. They quickly got to work making sure the house was in order, the candles lit and the fire burning low and steady, warming the house and becoming ready for broth to be cooked atop it. It was as they scurried about readying the house that Wren realised that she had left her sword out in the open on top of the dining table that sat against the wall just by the front door. Knowing that this would need to stay hidden to be safe from her father's hands she began to search for somewhere that no one other than herself would be able to find it. Looking within the cracks of the living room as her mother chopped away at day-old vegetables she wiped at the dust-covered sweat on her forehead and began to gnaw on her lip in worry. She could not find anywhere that would house her sword; she would need to look in her bedroom. Walking across the way and into her room she looked around at the bare limestone walls and the singular bed and small table that made up the contents of her room and knew that she would not be able to keep her new gift for long. Walking dejectedly across the room to sit on her bed she heard a creak in the floorboards as she moved.

Freezing at hearing the sound, she shifted her weight back onto her heels and then rocked forward with a swift motion onto the balls of her feet. There it was again, another creak, louder this time. Her heart raced with excitement as she repeated the action two, three more times to be certain that it was not just her imagination torturing her. But no, surely enough with each repetition there the creak was again. Stepping to the side, Wren lowered herself to the floor to inspect the floor board she had been standing upon. As her eyes scanned across the wooden panel they came to rest on a slight crack the size of her index finger along the side that ran parallel to the next wooden floor board.

Carefully she ran her finger along the crack and managed to fit her fingertip just inside the alcove it created. Using the side as leverage, she pushed sideways with her fingertip and pulled upwards as she felt tension. Heart racing now and clammy with hopeful anxiety, she pulled; the panel seemed to be lodged pretty tightly but with one last jerk of her hand it came loose. Relief washed over Wren as she looked down at the space left under the floorboard just big enough for her new sword to be stashed. Taking one last look at her prize she wrapped it back up in the linen her mother had given it to her in and placed it carefully into her new hidey hole. Grabbing onto the floorboard she slotted the panel back into place and as the satisfying creak of it falling back in perfectly hit her ears so did the slam of the front door opening and the frightened gasp of her mother.

Father was home.

Wren looked around moving quickly toward the bed again to hide what she had been doing as she heard the heavy footsteps of her father in the living area of the house. Fighting with herself she was torn between going out and ensuring her mother was safe with him and hiding away in her room to ensure she did not have to face the wrath of his drunken anger. Too many times in the last year had she seen the results of his fists imprinted on her mother's ribs, arms and legs coloured in blues, purples and greens showing their age and renewed presence. A fast-paced beating in her chest caused her lungs to constrict as she fought to breathe steadily, looking across her almost barren room to the door, the edges of her vision blurring as the weight of her indecision pulled at her very life force and her inner eye began to drift, imagining what her life would have been like if Ryn had never been injured.

Her room faded out and was replaced by the scenes of a little girl running, bathed in golden sunlight giggling as she runs straight into her father's arms, his smiles brighten the already golden glow of the morning, a thick lustrous beard, eyes that crinkled at the edges from the sheer joy that had been his life and family. Laughing as he picks up the small girl and spins her. A brush of his hand to her hair and the squeeze of love and adoration as he puts her back to the floor. Holding her hand and walking across their gardens. The property that surrounded them was not the one she had grown up in, she noted that marble ran more strikingly through the walls of the limestone house she was looking at, the gardens thick and green with bright colourful flowers dotted between paths leading to a large marble fountain. This type of luxury she had never seen before, but as she watched the little girl let go of her father's hand and run towards the water, she knew that the little girl was really her. This is what her life would have been like if her father had never injured himself during the Pirate War. Happiness, joy, no drunken displays of withheld and misdirected anger. A father whose career would have led him to the highest ranks of the royal guard. As she continued to look out at the scene before her, her eyes wandered across the house to the balcony above and there stood her mother smiling down at her. Not at the little girl but her as she looked on. Wren's vision flickered back to the bare wood of her door as she shook herself out of her musing of what ifs as she thought of her mother. The tightness in her chest began to abate as she realised that everything around her had gone quiet yet again, she had disassociated through it all and her decision had been made for her, she would not intervene. She strained to hear what was happening. She could hear the mumbled voice of her mother singing to her father. Wren crept forward towards her door that she had been staring at during her musings, slowly pulling it open to peer out trying to see if there was anyone in the living area. Candle light flickered across the floor of the hallway, shadows of her mother and father being thrown out of the small opening of their bedroom door. She must have been out of it for some time, she thought to herself as her stomach rumbled and confirmed to her that yes she had been gone for quite some time, enough even to become rather hungry despite a day of treats from her mother. The smell of the broth she had seen her mother cooking wafted towards her as she opened her door further and quietly moved forward to go and get some food and check on her mother as best she could.

Coming up to her parents' bedroom door, she peered through the crack, lingering in the shadows so as to not be seen, looking in she saw her father splayed out across their bed, half covered by the crimson sheet laid out on the mattress and half on top of her mother who was for all intents and purposes trapped under the weight of him, looking rather resigned to her fate. Her face was perfectly unmarked — he knew now not to touch the face — but on her arms and legs that were visible and not stuck underneath Ryn, Wren could see the beginnings of new bruises, red and puffy areas, and stark red bites marks on her shoulder — this was new — she knew that she needed to do something soon as it looked like the beatings were going to get worse. He always was harsher with her mother, the enabler, he blamed her for the way that Wren had turned out, the fact she was so free spirited and independent. A starkly different idea of what a girl should be like than his traditional and outdated views.

Understanding that there was nothing more she could do today after her inability to intervene earlier, in time to stop the beating, she moved forward and onwards to the living area to quieten the beast that was now dwelling in her gut.

That night Wren ate her broth cold, too worried to re-light the fire that had been let to go out with the distraction of her father's entrance. Upon plodding — as quietly as one can plod — back to her room, Wren sat back down on her bed sleepy from the food in her belly. She looked once to the floor where her new sword was hidden and yawned to herself before drifting off into dreams of protection, training and never having to be scared of anyone again.

The next morning with her dreams still running through her mind she was keen to wake and get ready for the day to go and share her half-made plans with her mother and see if she could help her scheme and improve on her plans and she usually had a better understanding of how the world worked and ways around the systems in place that usually allowed for Wren to bend the rules — as could be seen with Wren's different style of clothing, not many could get away with wearing britches as a girl. Rushing through her daily chores, she was able to get things done in half the time that she usually allowed for setting up the fire to warm breakfast, clearing the mess from her father's entrance from the night before and setting the table for her and her mother who she knew after last night would need a little extra help today. Upon finishing she looked out across the living area and nodded to herself, yes she had done a good job. It looked as good as new — if a little worn — her mother would be happy to forget the events of last night, even if for just this morning. As this thought left her mind a new one replaced it like lightning, where was her mother? The sun had risen now at least an hour previously, she was usually up by now, especially when she could smell the food Wren had warmed for breakfast, even if it was to sleepily totter in from her room rubbing her eyes and still in her night dress. Frowning deeply, Wren slowly approached her parents' room to look for her mother and wake her for the day so they could go to market.

"Mother?" Wren whisper-called as she brushed her fingers against the door of their parents' room that had been closed firmly since she had awoken.

Having not received a reply she placed her palm against the wood of the door feeling its rough surface and pushed forward. With a jerk, the door opened slightly letting in the light of the day through the door way as the curtains at some point had been drawn across to block out the sun.

"Mother?" Wren queried just above a whisper now as her worry began to take hold pushing the door fully open.

The red sheet covered her and Wren moved across the room with a sigh to open the curtain blocking out the rest of the sun from the room. As she drew the curtains back she looked around and could see that her mother was unmoving under the sheet.

"Come on, Mother, get up. I know it was a hard night but we must eat and get across to market before our spot has been taken by the spice merchants," Wren exclaimed as she went about tidying the room.

Still with no reply she grabbed for the sheets intending on wakening her mother up a bit more forcefully as she had been ignored.

As she removed the sheet a strangled cry came from her mouth as she fell to her knees. What she saw was not her mother. It was the body of a woman who looked exactly like her mother but without the warmth in her skin; the love in her eyes and softness that emanated from her was void. Bruises littered across her arms and legs and as Wren looked across her unable to fully take in what she was seeing a bruise larger than all the rest became noticeable across her stomach, black with blue and purple pooling through it spanning the entirety of her waist. Her mother could have been asleep apart from the blank stare of slightly clouded eyes that could only be reminiscent of the dead that lay across her face. Wren could not bring herself to touch her mother in that moment but let out a strangled whisper "Mother" as she got to her feet and frantically backed away and out of the door.

What was she going to do? Where was her father? Had she

been dead when she looked in on them last night?

This was her fault, Wren felt it in her bones, if only she had stood and intervened rather than getting lost in her thoughts and day dreams of a father who loved them.

Tears streamed from her eyes and she looked about their small home, she flung her head back and cried out, "Why, Why must you do this to me, what more do you want?"

Bringing her head to her hands she let the tears slow as she kneeled there in their broken home, hours went by as the sun rose to its peak throwing reds and oranges across the room and began to set again bringing out shadows in every corner of the little house and she sat there fighting internally to process what had happened.

Raising her head with a steely eye she knew then that she must not let her father get away with this, she would report it to the guard, there was no way that they would let him walk free after this no matter what he had done in the war. No matter who he used to be, there was no other explanation other than him as the cause for her mother's death, she was sure of it.

This would be her vengeance, justice.

And with that last thought she stood strong as she marched out of her house with the full intention of having her father jailed as she reported her mother's death to the guard.

8

Wren

Death has a funny way of changing us and in those first few hours after Wren discovered her mother's body she became irrevocably and irreversibly changed by the events of her life. Always hidden in the shadows, trailing her father, finding out the gossip and events of the villages along her way, never to be seen or heard, learning with the Street Children and eventually besting them, Wren now felt like steel, able to stand and be seen. She had stormed to the guard house, passionately condemning her father, explaining the beatings that both her and her mother had endured all of the these months, while he went and drank every day, she ranted and raved about everything he had done to them until she came to a grinding halt and whispered his worst sin. "He's killed Mother." Just like that she crumbled as she voiced aloud for the first time that her mother was gone, dead, never to return.

This, of course, was the only thing the guard heard as he looked down at her in his shining uniform. The guard had a kind face, childlike, with cheeks that could still be tugged upon by an Aunt if she so wished. He looked at her then with a twitch of his eye and shouted for his superior.

"Sarge, you better come through, this one says she got a dead mother back at her house by the hand of her father." His accent was common but as he spoke his tone changed the way she viewed him, gone was the image of an innocent and kind young man only to be replaced by the patronisingly kind tone of a man that did not believe a word she had said.

Trudging through the open doorway to the back rooms of the guard house came the Sergeant, white hair and wrinkles lining his face in full uniform. He looked Wren up and down taking in her stature and determined posture.

With a frown he spoke, "You're Ryn Laos kid?"

This made Wren stutter, "Y-Ye-Yess... I am, sir." She had not expected to see a guard who knew her father and some of her confidence knocked out of her like the wind being blown through a window. A picture of her mother's dead face came to mind staring into the abyss and that same confidence sucked back in to her chest.

"Sergeant, my father has killed my mother, you must come and arrest him! He cannot be allowed to get away with this." She puffed her chest up and set her steely gaze upon him, looking him dead in the eye as she said this, taking in the way that his bushy white eyebrow rose into an arch on his left eye and the sucked in cheek that showed that he was gnawing at the side of his mouth as he took in what she had said.

"You must be mistaken, my dear, your father Ryn is a war hero. The man is beloved by the guard; he would never do this." He spoke down to her as he said this, still frowning so deeply that Wren could barely see his eyes through his eyebrows.

Wren continued with a raised voice, "I assure you that he has done this. The man is no longer my father; he has gone too far, he has laid hands on myself and my mother for too long and now she is gone. You must come and see for yourself."

The rest of the guard took notice now at the raised voice as Wren had intended. The pressure she hoped would break through the fact the Sergeant knew her father and she hoped it would be enough to get him to come with her and see her mother. She was sure if only he saw her then he wouldn't be able to brush off her accusation and would help her bring her father to justice. The slight tilts of heads and turning of bodies to face further towards them as they spoke didn't go unnoticed by the Sergeant and with a huff he said, "Fine, yes I will come with you. But so help me god if you are lying, child, it won't just be your father that you have to be worried about."

Taking this, Wren span on her heel and led the way back to her home, hearing shouts of, "Kid you're coming with me! Button, keep an eye on the house. You two, on patrol now, locate Ryn Lao this instant."

With a pre-emptive and half-grimaced smile, Wren continued on down the cobbled road toward her house on the other side of the village that led to the market. The guards followed behind her in a march that felt all too casual for her liking but still she strode on until they reached the front door to her house. Spinning on her heel to fix a glare back upon the Sergeant, Wren firmly said, "She is in their bedroom, this is as far as I go." Stepping to the side to let the Sergeant and his men through, they hesitantly made their way through the doorway and into the house in search of Wren's mother.

Wren leant against the wall to the side of the front door of her house and breathed out, letting the air out of her lungs, like a breath she had been holding since she found her mother that very morning. They had to believe her now, they just had to. Her senses felt as if they were on high alert, the wall felt too firm on her back and the cloth of her britches seemed to become harsh and itchy as she waited for the guards to return with their verdict. The afternoon sun was high in the sky and she could feel it as her skin became too hot and burned slightly in the heat of the rays.

Squinting, she looked up and around as she noticed the side eyes of her neighbours looking at her and the house trying to listen in and find out what was going on. She was sure there would be lots of rumours and the market would be hell the next day. She had never been the subject of the rumours and the harsh words whispered around the market by the sellers and the women who went to buy supplies for their households and employers before. She had only observed as some people had been shunned for a week or two and then brought back into the fold by the gossip mongers as new meat appeared with the next big rumour of scandal. It was a dark side to the market that Wren usually liked to ignore and shy away from, not wanting to ruin the colourful and wonderfully smelling adventures that made up her market days. What would her mother think of all of this? Shaking the thoughts of her mother back away and focusing on the task at hand, Wren pushed herself off of the wall and turned to peer into the house to see what was taking so long. As she did this she was met with the scene of two guards carrying a shrouded body out of her parents' room. No skin on her mother could be seen, nor her face. Completely covered, it could have been the body of any woman. Except it wasn't, it was her mother and she felt a small part of her break away as they carried her further out of the house and began walking up the street back towards the guard house.

"Wait, where are you taking her?" she called out taking a stumbled step forward.

"No worries, Miss Lao, they are taking her to be examined by a doctor to confirm the cause of death," the Sergeant spoke softly to her as if she was a deer that might startle at any moment.

"What are you going to do? It's clear that she has been beaten to death, surely you see that. Bring my father in, he is responsible. I beg of you," Wren pleaded with the man as he looked down at her with the same soft look.

"We will bring your father in for questioning, I promise." The Sergeant said this with such finality that Wren almost believed him. As she thought about his words and the lack of confirmation of intent to arrest she saw his eyes change back to that hardened gaze she had seen previously.

"If that'll be all, Miss," he said as he turned and began his short journey back to the guard house.

In shock, Wren stood there staring after him, mouth hanging open in astonishment. He had just dismissed her like that, she knew she would have to wait it out and see what would become of her father; there was no questioning the higher ups of the guard once they had made a decision and if the Sergeant said he was going to question him then surely he would, despite their connection. Unable to fully come back to the present, Wren walked back into her house, slamming the door behind her and taking a seat at the table she had set for her mother's breakfast that morning. She would just wait here for now, until she knew what to do. Her father did not come home that night and she took it as a sign that things were going well, they would have arrested him and her mother would have justice for what had been done to her. With that, the anchored feeling in her chest let up slightly and as she sunk into her bed that night she let out all the emotions she had been keeping shut up inside of her, sobs wracked her body causing her to shake and convulse with the power behind them, her tears not letting up until the moon was high in the sky and she had run dry of all the water in her body. With sniffles, she fell asleep in utter exhaustion of the emotion that had ripped out of her.

Waking the next morning with a pounding headache from her night of sorrow, she swayed in place as she sat up holding on to her head, still feeling marginally foggier than was normal for the morning time for her.

Stumbling up and making her way through the house to the kitchen to grab some water to wet her parched mouth that felt rough and cotton-like she felt dazed, re-processing the events of the previous day. Leaning against the kitchen side she gulped down the water in her glass, still dirty from the day before. As the fog began to clear she thought on the things that would need to be done — her mother would not want her to lose sight of life because of her death, not after everything she had done for her. First things first she needed to go across to the guard house and find out what had happened with her father and ensure that they had done the right thing. Kicking off the side, Wren took long strides across the room to go and change into her day clothes, the best britches and shirt she owned were in order for today, she needed to be seen as a calm, mature and imposing adult despite her being only fifteen. She knew she would need all the help she could get. Tying the last of the laces on her shoes she stood back up and raised her chin and spoke firmly to herself, "I am Wren Lao and you will listen." With those words of determination she made her way out of her family home and up towards the guard house, garnering side glances from the villagers both who were in the know and those who weren't. She paid no mind as she made her way, not stopping to knock on the guard house door before marching straight through onto the front desk and slamming down a fist to its wooden surface.

"I am here to enquire as to the result of my father's questioning," she stated clearly and with authority in her voice.

The guard behind the desk raised an eyebrow with mild disapproval at the young girl before him, staring her down he replied, "That, Miss Lao, is no way to speak to a member of the guard and you best not forget it." Looking slightly to the side to imply he was thinking about the other guards in the back room, he continued, "As to your father, he has been questioned and released this morning, and that is as much as I can say on the matter." Going back to his work he did not expect what came from Wren next.

Her face turning crimson and eyes wide she raised her voice with indignation and said, "I demand that you bring the Sergeant to me this instant! This is completely unacceptable, I gave you everything you needed!" Beginning to charge forward, the guard on autopilot stepped into her way putting his hands on her shoulders, one of which she instantaneously gripped pushing her thumb forcefully into a pressure point on his palm causing his legs to wobble and begin to slightly give as the Sergeant charged out of the back room.

"What in tarnation is going on here?" he exclaimed, eyebrows knit together and anger in his tone.

As he said this Wren released the guard in front of her with a flourish, noting the embarrassed and somewhat shocked expression as she stumbled back and away from her, righting himself as quickly as he could to not lose face in front of his colleagues. Stepping forward into the space made by the guard falling away from her Wren smirked as she addressed the Sergeant, "Why has my father been released?" she asked in an eerily calm and detached voice, the smirk on her face only went to disturb the Sergeant more as he looked down on the young woman.

"Now, erm, see here, Miss Lao, I have questioned your father and it has been determined that in the case of your mother it was an accidental death, nothing sinister going on here, yes that's right, yes. Hmm," the Sergeant blustered out red faced.

"So you're telling me that you found my mother, beaten black and blue, dead in her marriage bed." Her voice hitched, clearing her throat she continued on, "And with my eye witness account of having seen my father on top of her passed out late the night before, you are unable to make the logical and small leap to it having been him that killed her? Despite knowing full well the man has been beating her and me both for the last year!" Wren's voice raised to a crescendo as she concluded, arms flailing outwardly as she finished, panting and red faced as she lost the detached coolness that she had been holding on to.

Stuttering, the Sergeant floundered for a moment before something switched in his head and he clicked his heels together coming up to his full height looking down at the young woman and aggressively asserted himself and his position by stating, "Look here, you are nothing but a child, I am the Sergeant of this guard house within the city of Ekoni, my word is law and it will be listened to, respected and left unquestioned!" Wren felt her confidence waver as he became progressively more agitated looking away slightly to avoid his eye jumping as he bellowed, "DO YOU HEAR ME, GIRL?" A slight incline of the head was all he received before Wren stormed from the room barely able to contain her own anger and frustration at her inability to do anything.

Wren continued on through the streets mindlessly walking, trying to keep the tears of her frustration at bay as she moved forwards. As the first tear fell through she began to run, not caring where she was going. The villages passed on by her as a blur of monochrome grey hues and then the sky and the rooftops seemed to be never ending as she scrambled up upon them trying to get away from the people, needing to be as alone as you can be in a walled-in city. She moved faster than she had in months as she ran and jumped and flew, still as quietly as if she was hiding but unable to stop herself from continuing. As her tears began to once again dry and the ache in her chest grew faint, moving deeper into her chest and away from the surface, her toes snagged on the edge of a rooftop as she went to make one final leap. Eyes widening in terror and arms flapping out in front of her she silently screamed as she fell forward. In that moment it felt as if her soul left her body as she watched from above as she fell, jaw hanging open. She saw herself twisting her body and rolling forward just in time to roll across the landing upon another roof and land, legs sprawled and head hung to chest as her reality snapped back into itself and once again she was within her own mind sat in shock at what had just happened to her.

Looking around her as she came out of the trance she had been in, she began to take in where her own legs had carried her. Limestone roofs lined the outer wall of the city, as it towered over them she could see the bare windows of the upper levels of the houses and the way the linen slung across wash lines was ragged and torn. She stood on shaky legs as she made her way towards the edge of the roof to get a better vantage point of the roads below to confirm her belief. She had run straight across the villages and into the boundary of the Street Children's territory. With a laugh she realised that no one seemed to be home and despite her having earnt "family" status she was not quite comfortable enough to simply stroll into their homes unannounced. Making the decision to wait she slumped down, back rested on the ledge of the roof as she began to dwell on the events of the last couple of days.

It occurred to her then that she most likely could not return home, at least not while her father was about. She would need to find somewhere to hide out during the waking hours in between

Market and sleeping time. She would definitely need to continue with the market to some degree to provide for herself; it was lucky that her mother had been getting her to deal with the other merchants and sellers over the last few months so they had already become accustomed to dealing with her in that capacity and she would not have to worry about gaining a semblance of respect from them as she already had it, to a degree. She would need to figure out a way to safely get the things for market in and out of the house in the early hours to set up for the day, her father would need to be monitored. Sighing she ruminated on how she could possibly go about these tasks alone, without being caught. Resting her head back and looking to the sky, she mumbled to herself, "I really am all alone now, aren't I?" Closing her eyes, letting out her breath, Wren's thoughts wandered to her mother and her fifteenth birthday that had been so special, it seemed like a life time ago but in reality she knew it had only been three days now since she had awoken to a singing and laughing mother. Loved and warm, how could things have changed so drastically in such a short time? As she tried to remember every detail of that day, the tones in her mother's voice and every crinkle in her face, her eyes snapped open as she remembered the wooden sword under her floor boards. This remembrance reignited the determination in her heart as she realised she would need to find a way to get it back, she could and she would do this, she would survive.

With renewed vigour she jumped up from her seated position and went to turn around. A small yip left her lips as she jumped again but this time in shock as she was met with the faces of three people she knew staring straight at her with curiosity and mirth in their eyes.

"Did you know you talk to yourself?" said Letta, voice

coloured with amusement and eyes twinkling with laughter.

The leader of the Street Children had her head rested in her hands idly watching Wren from her own roof top in their territory, leant against the roof's ledge a smile on her face as she teased her. To either side sat Wren's own little competitors Aab and Ber, sat in the exact same position perched on the roof ledge feet flat and knees bent down into a crouch they let their hands hang and their heads tilt as they observed Wren and her interaction with Letta. As Wren looked back at them a plan began to form in her head, perhaps she did know a way that she could monitor her father. She would just need to make a deal with the Street Children, after all wasn't she supposed to be family now?

To test this, Wren brought herself back to the present and took in Letta before making a run and jump across the roof top with a spin, she landed just behind her with a rather loud thump to only smile and say "Hello" so quietly you would need to strain to hear.

"You are getting confident, my friend, it is a good thing that you won that last race, no?" Letta jutted out her chin as she said this.

"You have my allegiance. Family looks after family." With a wink Wren turned to the boys. "I've got a job for you two if you don't mind my asking?" The boys looked to each other and then to Letta with uncertain faces. Wren knew she needed to address Letta with the way they were looking at her and turned back to the young woman and continued, "As I am sure you know, as you know all of the goings on in all of the villages, my mother has been murdered at the hands of my father. Having reported this to the guard they have dismissed my claim and announced it to be accidental. I will need to stay away from my father whilst still using the house to store goods etc. and sleep."

Wren said this matter of factly and paused to take in the way Letta was looking at her expectantly before continuing on. "I understand my part in this family will only extend so far, having only been initiated days ago, but I was hoping that I could use Aab and Ber to monitor my father in the mornings and in the hours before the sun sets to safely enter and exit my family home." Having said this, Wren realised that Letta did not seem convinced so moved on quickly so as to not let her speak and pass judgement quite yet. "This will allow me to work in the market and the money I earn there will allow me to stay in food and clothes but I intend to then also use this money to provide more for the family here. I can buy cloth to make shoes for the children, I can buy spices that you wouldn't not usually see, I can provide the money directly for whatever you see fit." Wren rushed this last part out so quickly that it hoovered almost into the area of begging, her eyes, however, couldn't be mistaken. They held the same glint of determination that she had begun with; now, however, they also showed a degree of respect that she knew Letta would appreciate. With bated breath Wren looked to Letta and waited for a reply.

 Letta considered Wren, looking her up and down and evaluating the benefit to her family here. Aab and Ber she knew already enjoyed the spying and missions that Wren went on for her mother and had been following her for quite some time before the race to learn this skill to use for the family already. The money and access to materials was something that she knew Wren knew was something they needed desperately; the sellers at the market would not sell to the Street Children, not trusting the money and trades that they offered as honest. It would see her family safer as a whole and she knew this. Her worry came from the violent nature of Wren's father, having already killed a peaceful woman and beaten Wren herself, Letta knew there was a high degree of danger involved for the two young boys. It wasn't that she didn't think they could take care of themselves — they were the fastest of her older ones and the most skilled in a scrap — it was that she worried what would happen if they were caught as the guard would not protect them and who's to say the large and imposing man that Ryn Lao was wouldn't see fit to bestow his own punishment on them? Fact was fact, however, and the good would outweigh the day and with a slight sideways tilt of her head to the boys and a barely noticeable incline back from them she sighed and looked back to Wren.

"Very well then, look after them, Wren, I expect a report every night as the moon rises in the sky." With those few words of acceptance she turned and began to make her way back towards the stairway leading down into the heart of the building leaving them to their planning.

9

Wren

Their plans were put into process the very next day, it had been rather simple to carry out the monitoring of Wren's father because of this commitment to going to the tavern, and the difficult bit had been ensuring that Wren was warned with enough time when he was returning to the house due to his going to different taverns every day. It all worked out in the end though and within days things began relaxing slightly into routine as she became closer with the boys and them her in turn. Her money from the market each day was divvied up and everyone got a fair share, and she knew it wouldn't be long before they began requesting she make them clothes and shoes like her mother used to for her as they became more confident in her loyalty to them.

  Her reports to Letta had grown into more conversational pieces — off topic and yet still slightly strained — Wren was sure this was because she no longer knew how to interact with people closest to her own age. Looking after the city of Ekoni's Street Children — who ranged between five and thirteen turns — she was now allowed in the heart of the territory and was in awe of what she had discovered. They had built themselves a village within a village in the houses by the wall with linen hung from strings spanning across each room, dividing it into smaller rooms for privacy and space for each child. They had kitchens that seemed to be run by the middle children, big baths of broth on the fires and a holey dining table taking up room near the outer wall. Another house contained room for storage of broken clothes, shoes with holes, rags that though worn might be used for other projects. They had saved everything they might use again or that might be fixed if the skill was learnt and the materials found to do so. Another house furthest from the central hub had been cleared out and remained bare, in here they had children learning to fight with each other, punches and jabs thrown, swishing of legs as they pull another's from underneath them. They also seemed to be strength training, doing routines that pushed their muscles to the brink or exhaustion before then pushing further to spar once more. Letta had explained to her when she mentioned it in one of their meetings that the children must learn to fight at an early age here, if someone with ill intent wandered into their area and tried to harm them they would need to be able to defend themselves and others, especially the younger ones who are too small to fend for themselves. It is the same that when they eventually get to the age where they can go out and do those tasks that must be done to keep the family going they must be able to be prepared for anything, drunken men, entitled guards etc. It was with this that Wren realised that though she was fast and nimble she didn't know how to fight, she would need to learn this and build her strength in case she was ever met with her father again. Her mind went back to her wooden practice sword again as she envisioned herself moving with grace as she fought an opponent.

One day she ventured to ask Letta why they did not train with weapons and her simple reply was that they had no need of them.

This had confused Wren deeply and she knew that although she would commit to learning to fight she needed to learn with the sword that was the last thing her mother had ever given her. She needed to find some meaning in her death and above all she wanted things to change for the better for not only herself but all of the mistreated children in the villages. It was as if a lightbulb had gone off in her head in that moment; she would need to master the sword, the fighting and become strong enough that they couldn't dismiss or deny her. She would have to become one of them and not only one of them but eventually go all the way to the top, becoming not only the first female guard but if she became the head of the Royal guard she would be able to enact actual change within the villages. Wren slowed herself down in that moment and knew she was getting ahead of herself and that she needed to slow down and take it one step at a time. Step One would be learn to fight. Step Two would be find somewhere to learn to sword fight and then it would be a case of practice and self-discipline. With this she went off in search of her two boys, Aab and Ber would be around here somewhere and she knew they'd know somewhere to practice.

As it so happened the boys did know of somewhere that she could practice and teach herself the art of the sword safely, it was just not what she had been expecting at all. As she followed them down into the fighting house — as she now called the place where the children sparred — they came to a bookcase, which loomed large and empty against the wall of the back of the house. Confused, Wren went to ask Aab what exactly was going on when Ber began pushing on the bookcase's side, with a bit of force it swung over and onto its side. Astounded at the strength Ber had shown by pushing the bookcase over alone she failed for a moment to see the little piece of cloth that hung against the wall or the slight breeze that seemed to be making the same piece of cloth flutter and send a chill up her arm. That was until, with a grunt, Aab gestured his arms with an exasperated look towards it and proceeded to grab at her hand dragging her forward towards the exposed hole in the wall.

Reluctantly, Wren shook off Aab's hand and followed him of her own free will, she had always wanted to go on an adventure, why should she stop now that one presented itself before her? Slowly moving forward to follow Aab who had now disappeared behind the cloth that hung loosely on the wall she descended into the dark tunnel ahead. Hearing a low click, Wren chanced a glance behind her only to be met with darkness and the slight glow of white from Ber's eyes as he followed them down the tunnel. He had blocked the path somehow so that no one could find it as they explored. A thrill made its way through Wren as they moved further into the tunnel, not speaking to each other as they continued on. After five minutes Wren could swear that she could see light ahead and begin to feel the breeze more strongly upon her skin. She thought her mind must be playing tricks on her before the tunnel began to open up and lighten as she began to make out green vines wrapping the walls of the tunnel in colour and the streams of light coming certainly from ahead that could mean only one thing. They had made it to the other end of the tunnel.

She had no idea where the boys could have possibility taken her, and couldn't understand why they had not shown Letta their discovery. As she walked up to stand beside Aab, who had over the last week had had a growth spurt, miraculously he now stood almost as tall as her at five feet six inches, she noticed that he was beginning to really become a man, no longer the small child that teared up when tripping over the stones during their races. As Wren looked around she saw that the tunnel widened significantly here and the wall ahead of them was simply made of thick bushes and vines casting a green luminescence across the small opening in the tunnel. As she wondered at the sight before her, Ber came to stand on her other side, he too had grown, standing as tall as her now, with thick muscled arms and stubble beginning to form on his upper lip. Two young men, she realised, they would become easily the next protectors of the family. She had unknowingly taught them everything she knew and they in turn were now showing her one thing they had kept to themselves — a secret — for there was no knowing how long.

"Wren... This is the furthest we've been, but if you go out through the vines you'll be on the other side of the wall near the forest," came Aab's scratchy high-pitched voice. He was looking down towards his hands where Wren could see that he was picking at the skin on his fingers — a nervous habit he had picked up in recent months — this nervousness was far removed from the young man he was becoming and the one who had led her down here just moments ago.

"Aab, you do realise that I am not annoyed at you?" she laughed out. "I am just relieved that you have trusted me enough to honour me with this knowledge! It's beautiful"

This seemed to brighten him and as he looked up and smiled at her Ber picked up where Aab left off, getting down to business. "Look, we like you and as Letta has said you are family, more so to us than the others, but you see our meaning." He stumbled to find the words for a moment as he said this looking around wide eyed. "We haven't gone out through the vines but we have investigated enough to know that there is a river or stream before you can reach the forest and the guards have line of sight from on the wall."

She took him in in that moment and saw the worry in his eyes as she understood his meaning, he was worried for her. That she'd be caught by the guard and more than likely killed for her effort.

"Ber, there is a risk to everything and if I were not sure of this and its worth I would not attempt to do it. Please, just trust in me, I can do this," she pleaded with him to understand.

"…If you're sure, but, Wren, you must tell us when you are going out so that we at least know where you are," Ber replied.

Hearing the implied "and are safe" in his tone, Wren could not help but let out a breathy laugh as these young boys tried to mother her. They would make great men one day.

With a nod she advanced towards the vine curtain that covered the exit of the tunnel, she closed her eyes briefly before pulling them open to, for the first time, see outside of the wall of the city of Ekoni.

As a young girl she had always dreamed of the world outside of the wall, her mother had taught her to dream and often her play would turn to the Pirate Wars, the lands beyond the wall that she and her mother had only ever heard about but never seen. The stories she grew up with spoke of the forest of Kasia and all of the magic it held, the Fae that lived there invisible to the warring world of the humans. It had been said that their very own Princess was Fae touched, named Faeryn for their sake and honour. The games she would play, she would pretend the Princess was her friend and that they would go and play with the Fae together in the forest. But that was before the weight of reality hit home and the days of imagination turned into tasks and missions, learning to succeed the hard way with scraped knees and bloody noses. Before she realised that no one had seen the princess other than small glances in years and even still if she came out of the castle, why would she want to be friends with a commoner such as herself?

The feel of sunlight warming her face and the smell of pine hitting her nostrils brought her out of her reminiscing. Opening her eyes Wren looked out onto the world outside of the wall, never having felt so free as she did in that moment, a grin stretched across her face and she took one step and then another out past the wall.

"Wren, the guards!" was hissed out from the opening in the vines. Pulling Wren back to the present moment she dived into the bushes next to the opening so as to not enter the tunnel again.

Looking around she saw that the river was in fact a small stream with a small current running through, there were also three rocks protruding out from the fast water. Wren knew she would be able to cross the stream easily with the roof jumping she had been doing for the last few years.

From the other side it looked like a straight run into the thick trees that lined the edge of the forest of Kasia.

Feeling it in her chest she knew she would be able to get across to the forest unseen even with a pack on her back.

Taking a look back at the boys she smiled lopsidedly at them before making a run for it, sprinting towards the river. Aab and Ber could not shout out for fear of bringing the guards' attention down on Wren but they gripped onto each other as they watched her sprint to the stream's bank. With a leap, Wren landed her first foot onto the first rock and went to swing her other leg around with speed to leap straight across the next. As soon as her other leg came within an inch of the next rock she could feel herself slipping, she had severely underestimated how slippery these stream rocks would be. With a splash her second foot landed straight in the water, her body lying half over the rock she had been aiming for and her foot that had been on the first rock having come out from underneath her. Wren knew she would have to act quickly and used her arms to pull herself across the stream and onto the final rock where the water was shallower. Sodden, she scrambled up the bank of the stream and made one last sprint to the forest's edge, luckily it seemed as if the guards were too high up to notice a splash of water or the squelched step of her sprint as she collapsed behind a bush to regain her breath.

Still out of breath, she pulled herself up to look out over the bush back to where she had started her mad sprint for freedom. Peeking her head out she could see the boys, brave enough now to at least peer out of the vine curtains of the tunnel. With a little giggle she waved haphazardly to them as they stared dumbfounded at her. She could see them mouthing the word "Crazy" at her.

Maybe she was crazy, she mused to herself. As she turned, still soaked through, to look on into the mass of trees that made up the forest.

Knowing she would need to find a clearing of some sort big enough to train, Wren began her hike forward into the forest to seek out her new training rounds, making sure to take note of the way so she would be able to get back to the tunnel later.

Wren had never seen so many trees before, she looked around as she made her way through the forest. There were trees that smelled of the pine scent ladies wore in the markets. There were trees so tall she could not see the end of them as she looked up into the green that made up the canopy of trees above, blocking out the sky. There were even trees whose trunks were different colours to the usual brown that she knew of: red ones that spanned out so wide that she could not wrap her arms around and silver ones thin enough she could hug them. The floor was littered with little plants, bark and mushrooms and she could hear the trilling of birds everywhere around her — she was sure they were discussing her arrival — and as she thought she could not be in any more awe of this new world she found herself in she came across just what she was looking for.

The clearing was large, surrounded by the silver trunks of the trees she had just discovered and had a small opening that you could see the castle through. It seemed as if the clearing was on a hill and the wall came into her sights below her level and the castle towers just towered about her. In one of them she could even see an empty window in her line of sight. The opening was just big enough that she knew that the guards on the wall would not be able to see, and she was certain that even looking from that window no one would be able to see into the clearing itself. Moving back into the centre of the space she span herself around looking up into the clear sky.

"This is where I am meant to be," she sighed out as she came to a stop, feeling relaxed for the first time since she first dreamed of the forest as a child.

It felt like home.

It wasn't long before Wren got into a steady routine with her training, sneaking out to the forest every night under the watchful eye of the moon to practice with her sword in her clearing. Some nights she would sleep out under the stars knowing no one would miss her other than the Street Children and Aab and Ber knew where she was, so it was all right. They were still too frightened to come out here with her but she was all right being alone. Every night she trained until she could barely stand, going over the movements she knew from the guards that would fight in the streets or teach their own children, she became stronger slowly but she knew she already had a good base of muscle to build from. But she couldn't stop herself from time to time going out and standing in the opening of the clearing to peer out across at the castle's window and wonder.

10

Faeryn

Faeryn had been isolated now for weeks, it was unlike her mother to let punishments such as this carry on for extended periods like this. Since hurting her ankle she had been unable to fill her evenings with exercise and had taken up most nights in residence on her window seal looking out across the village and across the wall to her forest. From her tower she could see out along the side of the wall that enclosed the city, having had enough time to examine the wilderness that grew across the edges of the wall she could see that it differed slightly from the forest itself, patterning along the limestone in intricate vined patterns. She assumed that this was because of the stream that ran parallel to this portion of the wall, it ran white in places showing the strength of the current and Faeryn wondered if it was anything like the feel of letting the bath run cold, submerging yourself in it. Looking further to the forest she could see that it was only a small distance to the tall looming trees that ran along the edges of the forest.

    Two nights ago she had been lucky enough to see a deer here coming out from the tree to go and take a drink from the stream. She had tried to follow the deer with her eyes through the forest but it was too thick with trees to see much further than a few trees in. In fact the only place she could see any further at all in the forest was slightly further to the north where a small opening on a hill within the forest allowed her to see further into the trees as it became illuminated with the moon. It was one of her favourite places to watch and always brought a smile to her face through the boredom she felt. Every night the same pulling in her chest led her back to that view, and for hours she would get lost in the beautiful magic that is the Forest of Kasia.

It was on one of these nights that as she was looking out towards the stream, something caught her eye, there was someone out there! Heart racing, Faeryn focused in on the girl, shifting her body to face further towards the stream. It was twilight and from what she could see this person was running from the greenspace in the wall, seemingly from nowhere towards the stream! "Who the fuck is that?" Faeryn thought to herself. The person was dressed in red britches and a dark blue shirt, fairly common colours from what she could see of the village from her window. Faeryn gasped as she watched the figure jump athletically from one rock to another to cross the stream. They did not stop there, sprinting into the forest trees as if they had been doing this their whole life.

She had thought that the wall was inescapable.

In shock, Faeryn slumped down as she lost sight of the runner, an ache in her chest began so abruptly as she let out a shaky breath. "I can leave, I don't have to be here any more," she said to herself as she looked to the tapestry above her bed. "The passageways must have a way to the wall, a way through the wall. They have to. I can't live like this any more." The ache in Faeryn's chest got stronger and stronger the longer she spent looking away from the forest. And as the ache got stronger so did her agitation.

Throwing her hands to the ground to propel herself upward she growled out in frustration. Being locked in the castle had been one thing but having been locked inside her room for weeks now with no reprieve had been hell on earth. Dark thoughts had been swirling around in Faeryn's head for too long and she felt as if she was at the tipping point, she needed to get out before she couldn't come back from where she was.

Tears threatening to spill over, the ache in her chest brought her back to her window. Sat back upon her window ledge her eyes cast not to the stream or the forest where she had seen the figure disappear but into the opening that always made her smile. Lit up by the moon today it was different and a frown cast over Faeryn's face as she looked on. There were shadows being cast in her clearing, but not still and tranquil as she was used to but fast and slashing shadows, cutting through the opening every few seconds in a different arching shape.

Caught up in the oddity that this stranger had brought to her usually calm night, Faeryn had lost all sense of time, far surpassing her usual time for sleep she realised as the sky to the east began to be flecked with the reds and oranges that signified the sun would soon be saying hello again to the city of Ekoni and its people would soon be waking to begin their duties. Shocked at this revelation, Faeryn looked around and whispered to herself, "The guards didn't come." This had been the first time that she had not slept through the night and she had been under the assumption that the guards were checking her presence throughout the night as her mother, the Queen, had demanded. Her mouth hung open as the first servants came through her door, eyes widened in shock to see their Princess up and about rather than tucked up in bed as was usual for this time of day. As they began bustling around her one thought came to mind as Faeryn followed the motions — "I can sneak out at night."

It took two more days for Faeryn to build the confidence to venture out of her room through the secret passageway that hid behind her tapestry. Both nights she had clung to her window ledge and looked out at the figure who she realised returned each and every night, at different times, and took the exact same trip across the stream to the forest. She had grown accustomed to this unassuming stranger, feeling a companionship as she would watch them leap across the stream and sprint. Her eyes had grown accustomed to the squinting to make out more features of her stranger and was pleasantly surprised when she discovered that the figure was in fact a girl.

From the little that she could make out, the girl was lean, hair black as the night, she was athletic in build, strong enough to bridge the gap of the stream's bank with complete ease and as elegantly as one could imagine. The way she moved enraptured Faeryn and as she made the journey each night she could not keep her eyes off the girl moving. Never before had she been as fascinated by another. This girl seemed to have so much freedom, she certainly hadn't seen anyone else make it outside the city's wall. The sense of adventure Faeryn got from just watching her ignited another part of her soul and the longing within her chest for the forest became a burning and the ache within her heart weighed her down begging for her to move.

On the third day the longing moved to become a lump stuck in her throat, gagging her and threatening tears every time she tried to speak. That night as soon as the moon hit the sky she tore through her opening to the passageways feeling her burden ease with every step. On autopilot, Faeryn ran through the passageways towards the guard viewing window that she knew was the closest to the wall, the ache pulling her faster with every step. Heavy breathed and sliding to a stop as she met her target, she looked wildly around, she had not made it past this point before, which way to go, how to get out?

Frantically she mumbled to herself, "Buggering, tit wank, where the fuck am I supposed to go? ARGGHH." Slamming fists to walls and letting the first tears spill she angrily began down another passageway, an unknown, feeling along the walls as the ways got darker and seeing became almost impossible.

After an age the barest glimpse of light began to lighten the passageway back to make it semi-visible to Faeryn's own eyes. As she moved on forward, fear took her as she realised that the light was coming from three thin lines shaped as a doorway in a wall ahead. Heart pounding in her chest and ache barely a whisper she crept as quietly as she could towards the doorway, fingers brushing against the wall. She came to the light at one side and brought her eye to the gap.

Looking through the line she could see that in front of her lay the sitting room to her mother's chambers, creams and golds fashioned on the walls, furniture more for show than comfort and flowers in vases on every surface. The fear dwindled as she realised that there was no one in the room. "How did I end up here? This is all the way on the other side of the castle, and I don't remember climbing steps?" Faeryn was bewildered as she turned herself back around and made to go back into the darkness of the passageway. "Perhaps it was the other ruddy passage?" she huffed as she picked up her pace to get back to the guards' viewing window quickly.

As she found her way back to her original spot, Faeryn took a minute to look out across the guards' training grounds, there were two men hard at work with their swords sparring and dancing around the ring. She loved to see the way they moved. Sunlight glinted off one man's sword and Faeryn's eyes bulged. "Sunlight, oh fuck, I need to get back to my room, how in the hell did the night go so quickly?" Sprinting and sweating, Faeryn ran through the passages she knew before diving through her tapestry hole trusting no one to be there. With a slight slam she landed on her bed, rushing to get under the covers and feign sleep. As she closed her eyes, yawning in sudden exhaustion, a maid entered her room with a tray laden with fruits for breakfast, a curious look on her face and Faeryn rolled her eyes as she realised she would not have time to sleep before her tutors would come striding in to teach her once again.

The day wore on slowly for Faeryn and as night came rolling around she was so sluggish that she could barely move. As she approached her bed to climb through the hole she was pulled down into the softness of her own pillow as her eyes closed involuntarily.

"Tomorrow, I'll find her tomorrow." the last whispered promise that could be heard as the world descended into night.

11

Faeryn

The sun rose the next morning and the birds chirped as Faeryn slept through the day break. Her maids came and went, tidying and cleaning the room, laying the new fire and hushing away any signs of cobweb as she lay soundly asleep. It wasn't until a girl shook her shoulder — rather firmly — that she began to stir from the depths of unconsciousness. Blinking away the sleep in her eyes, Faeryn looked around confused as the sun flooded her room and it was plain to see that it had been cleaned and tidied, how long had she been out for? She sat up and stretched out her arms as the girl backed away towards Faeryn's closet where a new dress was hung against its door.

As Faeryn went about getting ready with the maids she could barely contain the buzzing of energy that was within her chest. She knew the way out now, there was only one passage she hadn't gone down and surely that would be the way to the wall, to the girl who so represented freedom in Faeryn's mind. She only let her thoughts linger on the pathway that she had discovered to her mother's rooms on her previous adventure before bringing them back to her day dreams of meeting the girl in the forest.

With the excitement welling inside of her the day went relatively quickly for Faeryn. Once her tutors had left for the night and her dinner had been brought to her, she knew it was just a waiting game. The dinner that had been brought to her that night was a mix of dried meats and breads, perfect for her, she wrapped half of it into her handkerchief and slung it on to her bed to take with her on her adventure that night. As she waited for the night to turn to twilight she found herself taking residence on her usual window ledge looking out, first across the market village below, then out across the wall and over the stream to the edge of the forest. She knew that by the time the girl came that night, and she had all the faith in the world that she would as she had done every night that week, Faeryn would already be deep in the passageways journeying outward to go and finally introduce the girl that had stolen so many nights and dreams from her. The trees stirred and blew in the window, so many different depths to the colours in their leaves, the breeze came across the forest edge, whirling through the village and straight up to her window, bringing with it the scent of pine and spices from the village. Faeryn breathed deeply as goose bumps spread across her skin and a shiver went up her spine, a sense of calm and pleasure washed over her as she took a last look out before moving her gaze inward to the tapestry as the night darkened and she knew it was time.

  Tying up her skirts to just above the knee, fingers slipping in her haste, Faeryn thought how much easier it would be if she could just wear britches like the girl in the forest; maybe she could ask her for some. With a sigh she picked up the wrapped breads and meat and stuffed them down her brassiere before gathering up the rest of her now puffed skirts and climbing up and through the hole in her wall. Dropping down with a slight grunt she straightened up and with a nod of the head began to make her way back to the guard viewing window where she knew the right path would lead from. The passageways seemed less dark today, almost as if they sensed the happiness and anticipation in her every step and were lightening her way for her. Faeryn quickly made it to the guard viewing window and watched for a second making a dramatic twirl and lunge mimicking movement of the guard out training before giggling brightly and moving on down the unexplored passageway.

The passageway felt colder the longer she walked down its twisting paths, there had been no golden lights coming through the walls of this passage as there had been in the one she had run through previously. Faeryn moved slowly but surely as she made her way through the darkness, waiting for any sign that she was going the right way. After what felt like hours she was nearly ready to give up and go back to her room, and go back to the drawing board on how to reach her girl when a slight breeze came whipping through the passage, picking up her hair, making it dance in the air. The breeze smelt of the pine and spices that she knew was of the market and forest, her heart skipped a beat as she realised that this was the sign that she was looking for, she could cry for the joy of it — she was going the right way.

With renewed vigour she carried on down the passage at double speed. She could feel it as the passage veered slightly downward making her feet skid and her body lean back as she went downhill now. As she moved now she felt the same pulling as the very first day that she had found the passageways taking over yet again. Her feet of their own will began to run at full speed, the passage blurring as she made her way impossibly fast towards what she could only see as blackness, an abyss. She thought that she should feel scared in this moment, but all she could feel was the pulling, the intense feeling of something missing that she needed to get to. As her feet eased their pace and the pulling, although still present, quietened slightly, she came upon the end of the passage. On the wall of the dead end was a door made of limestone, not the usual limestone running with marble that she was used to seeing but the dull grey that she knew the wall and the outer villages were made from. Taking a step closer she placed her hand on the door and looked closer, now seeing the engravings of vines that littered the outer edges of the stone door, the leaves facing inward, and then the handle, thick rope dyed again to look like vines. She wrapped both hands around the vine rope and braced herself against the floor with her feet and pulled. The weeks of strength training locked in her room seemed to pay off as her toned muscles tightened and bulged as she tensed pulling at the stone door. As a groan ripped from her mouth the rope slacked and the door shifted open to reveal… a wall of green.

"What the fuck…? It can't be?" Faeryn whispered to herself as she moved forward, arm held out to touch the green wall that had appeared on the other side of her passageway door. The first thing her fingers felt was wetness. Unable to fully take in and understand what this was, she moved forward once again coming a nose width's breadth from the wall. She could now see that it was made of damp vines entwined one over the other just as they had been engraved on the door itself. Raising her other hand she brought it next to the other one on the vines, fingering the details of the stems that ran across the greenery and began to push them forward through the knots the vines had created. By some strange force the vines began to melt away from the doorway. With every push another vine sank back into the others, until Faeryn was able to put her forehead to the vines and simply push through with her body to move across the threshold and to the other side of the wall.

In disbelief, Faeryn felt the tingle of the forest wash over her and run through her fingertips. "They always said the forest was magical." And she wriggled her fingers and looked forward.

The vines that had made up the barrier she had just entered through continued on in tangled bushes, from what Faeryn could see, she was at the bottom of a hill at the base of the wall and the vine hill was the only thing separating her from the forest itself. She was sure she would just need to get to the forest and then she would be able to find the girl. Looking upward she could see the moon had now taken its place high in the sky; she would need to be quick if she wanted to spend any time at all with the girl.

Making her way forwards, Faeryn found that the vines were not as tangled as they seemed from above, she would be able to crouch and crawl through them to reach the top of the hill without being seen quite easily and without being seen from the guards patrolling the wall of her city. The climb up the hill was somewhat strenuous for Faeryn, despite her exercises, her ankle was still sore from her fall and she had not moved so much in weeks due to her confinement. It had taken her at least a half of an hour to get to the top of the hill through the vines, sweating and somewhat dishevelled she looked back to inspect where she had come from. In shock she realised that she had turned up opposite her own tower, her window stood out and she could see over the wall itself into the village as well. Whizzing around she knew that this meant the opening in the forest that she had stared at night after night must be close; she took her first step into the trees of the forest to look for her girl.

On a mission Faeryn stormed ahead, not thinking of the consequences that could possibly arise from her actions. Not even taking a minute to take in the beauty of the forest around her, she was single minded in her pursuit to get the girl. She went from tree to tree just within the forest in the direction she was certain was where the opening must be. It wasn't long before she came across an area thicker with trees and bushes, stopping to look at the bushes she was sure she could see them swaying of their own volition. Confused, she began to walk more slowly now towards the bushes.

A loud "THUNK" could be heard from the other side of the bushes and Faeryn's entire body jumped as she heard the first one, heart thundering in her ears and she crept forward to investigate the source of the noise, only now realising that she and her girl may not be the only people or things in this forest. There would be animals too, there could even be bears. Frozen for a moment, freaked out by her own thoughts, she had to shake herself to refocus in on what she had come here to do. Taking a few deep and calming breaths she felt her heart steadying once again as she took her next step forward, the thunking had now become louder and came more quickly after each other and a slight grunting could be heard with each one.

Unable to tell if another step would reveal her or not, Faeryn raised an arm to adjust some of the branches to the thick bush she now resided in. All it took was the moving of a few branches and movement caught her vision, she could see into the clearing.

The first thing Faeryn saw was the flawless movements of a figure she knew only too well. Strong legs covered by the dark blue colour of britches met a small waist wrapped in the deep red cummerbund of a clearly handmade shirt swaying with the movements of raised arms. Faeryn's eyes came to the back of the figure's head, her hair was thick with deep black luxurious curls shining in the moon light that bounced with every swing of her raised arms. She imagined what the girl's hair would smell like, how soft her skin would be that with the glimpses she could see from her ankles was lightly olive in complexion. She wished the girl would turn around so she could take in the face of the person who she had been pulled to.

Faeryn stayed still, silently watching and admiring the back of the girl's body and the fluidity in her movements as she shifted her legs forward and backwards in shuffled movement so similar to the way the guards would train in the castle grounds. The girl swung a short wooden sword back and forth across her body and head to hit the tree in front of her. Time and time again Faeryn watched as the sword hit the tree and the girl's hands would slightly loosen their grip before grasping the hilt of the sword again and swinging harder and harder she shuffled her feet again forward. Faeryn's frustration with being unable to see the girl's face grew strong as every hit of the sword on the tree sent a jolt down her body. As she strained to hear the way the girl's throat would release a small high-pitched grunt as she swung, she noticed that the girl was also letting out soft whimpers with every step back before the barely audible groan that led to another swing and hit of sword upon tree. Faeryn realised with surprise that the girl was crying, and she began to feel the need to step forward and comfort the girl.

For the first time Faeryn began to doubt herself, her lip worried in her teeth as she began to overthink.

What if she doesn't like me? What am I even doing, what am I going to do? Just walk over to the girl with a wooden sword in her hands and tap her should and say, "Hi, I'm Princess Faeryn, what's your fucking name?" Or maybe, "Hi, I've been eye stalking you every night as you sneak into the forest, let's be friends?" Because that sounds like something a sane person would do. Oh stars what am I doing?

Panic began to rise up in Faeryn's chest as her anxiety continued to talk her into running away, she looked to her hands as she began to shake and sway, her body jerked forward and a loud "SNAP" rang out through the forest trees. Faeryn's mind went completely quiet and the forest became silent in the seconds that followed.

Heart pounding, Faeryn winced slightly before raising her eyes back up to the clearing and landing right onto the face of the girl, staring straight at her.

"…Oh shit… She's beautiful," Faeryn breathed out as the world stopped around her.

12

Wren

The time since her mother's death had been relatively quiet, Wren and her father avoided each other like the plague, only coming into contact in passing on the odd occasion as Ryn would leave the house to go to a tavern without even a mumble of a hello or goodbye. That's the way that Wren liked it. She could barely bring herself to look at him and felt almost sick to the stomach knowing that he was her father. Ryn himself had become quieter since Maggie's death and had stopped eating in the house at all, only stopping in for a few hours to sleep before slithering back out for more drink. Beatings came sparingly and only on the drunkest of nights where her father would come in in a blind rage and drag Wren from her room slurring out obscenities, mentioning Maggie on more than one occasion.

Last night had been one of these occasions and it had left Wren bruised and sore, she was sure that the ribs on her left side were at least a little bruised as they ached something awful when she breathed deeply. Injuries were now commonplace for her, between her father and her training she knew how to carry on as if she was fine and understood the necessity of building resistance to painful and pulling muscles. This time it was proving somewhat difficult to mask the pain she was feeling as she lugged her stall cover and baskets, over flowing with flowers and buds, across the cobbled streets to the market for the day.

Wren had hobbled all of fifteen paces, resting every few steps when Aab and Ber came up from behind her silently taking up half her load between them.

The boys had been a godsend in the last few months and she had definitely missed multiple beatings in the weeks following her mother's death with their interference and observations of her father ensuring her timing was perfect and reducing the amount of time spent seeing her father to an absolute minimum. They had gotten into a great routine of the day and had even begun to help out where they could on the market. Oddly it was beginning to feel like they had a created a small family unit between the three of them.

"Wren, the tulips are losing their colour, what should I do?" Ber asked her in a soft voice that barely matched his growing figure.

"Right, can you just run across to the spice man and buy a handful of paprika?" she asked him.

She watched as he took the coin she held out to him before scurrying off towards the spice sellers to do as asked. She turned her head to look to Aab as he sold some of the other flowers to two young women adorned in bright robes and glinting yellow jewellery. The girls were giggling as Aab spoke softly to them, describing the meaning behind the flowers and handing one to the girls with a cocky smirk. Wren nudged him with her foot as he did this. She knew that the woman had no idea that Aab was actually so young. He had grown into himself over the last few months, his brown skin darkening and muscles becoming more built upon with the work that Wren had him doing. His facial hair was even beginning to thicken out. It was the only real defining feature Aab had over Ber now who despite being his senior still had sparse facial hair on his upper lip and chin.

Rolling his eyes, Aab took the girls' money and sent them on their way before turning back to Wren. "Why did you do that? I could have gotten them to buy at least another bouquet!" he said with a lopsided smile that showed his youth.

"It's dishonest, Aab, now what do we always say?" admonished Wren.

"Maintain humility, retain dignity and always show kindness," drawled out Aab as he leant his head to her shoulder and looked past her to Ber's returning figure.

Grinning like the cat that caught the mouse, Ber came bounding over with a small pouch of paprika clutched in his hand. "Got it, Wren! And look, I even manged to haggle him down so we have some money left over!"

"Well done, Ber! Now pour half of the paprika into the water for the tulips and before you know it the colour will return to them! We can use the rest to spice the dinner." Wren patted Ber on the back as she spoke, proud he had managed to haggle with the spice seller who was notorious for his stubborn attitude.

The rest of the day went by like a whirlwind with Wren's focus blurred by the ache in her body and despite her determination to stay positive she could feel herself losing faith that things would get better. She warred with herself internally. Was all the training worth it? Could she really be bothered to go out and train while she was in this state? She had to be stupid, they would never let her, a woman, into the guard. Sighing, Wren looked up to Aab and Ber who were packing away the market stall with smiles on their faces, gently shoving each other in jest, not knowing the turmoil she felt, and she smiled sadly as she hoped that they would never have to feel the pain that had latched onto her heart.

Running ahead, the boys went to check that the coast was

clear as they had been doing in intervals across the day, they wobbled up the hill to the house to put away the market stall cover and baskets of flowers for the night. Silence met them as they entered the house, the boys' sight was true and Ryn was nowhere to be found. They moved quickly to put everything away and before Wren could even say that she intended to stay here in her room for the night the boys had grabbed onto her hands and pulled her from the house, stumbling behind them she felt confused as they dragged her around another corner. The boys stopped then and edged to the corner looking around and beckoning her to do the same. Raising an eyebrow she did as instructed and let out a gasp as she saw her father's drunken form ambling down the road towards the house. Wincing as her ribs sent a sharp pain through her body, she leant back around the corner to safety and looked at the boys.

"How on earth did you know he was coming?" she gasped out through the pain.

"Simple really…" Aab started.

"We just had some of the other Street Children set up at posts across the village, they needed training you know, turning to the age you need to know the ways," Ber continued.

"Anyway, they know that when they see Ryn they have to let out a low hooting sound like this," Aab went on and clasped his hands together, thumbs pushed closely, and put them to his lips and blew out a gentle hooting sound.

"This is the first week we've had them posted, and only the second time we've had them watch the way home, trying to mix it up and everything. Good job really," Ber rambled.

Wren looked at them both astonished. Her mind racing at the implications. She knew she was family but this level of protection and care was unheard of from one not born to the

Street Children. Letta. Oh dear, Letta, did she know?

"Please tell me you told Letta you were going to use the babes for this?" Wren said exasperated.

"Of course we did, Wren! We don't have a death wish. Plus even she had to agree this was perfect training," Ber stated with a finality Wren did not know he possessed.

Shocked, Wren followed them as they climbed up onto the roofs to make their way back to the Street Children's hideaway. Jumping from roof to roof, Wren reflected on her new found family and the level of respect and admiration that they seemed to give her and she couldn't understand why. She would need to speak to Letta and understand the implications of this further, she did not plan on becoming their new leader. That job was for Letta and Letta alone. Arriving back to the hideaway, Wren went through making the family dinner on autopilot looking out for Letta and only half-heartedly making low conversation with the boys as they explained the reasoning for the different types of training the babes should be doing already at their young age. As Wren ate, her frustration only grew at not being able to find Letta, so much so that she decided that she could not and would not miss her night's training as she would need to work out her anger from the day, her Father's beating and this strange new dynamic, with her sword.

Groaning to herself, Wren pushed herself up from the ground, unable to ignore the pulling in her chest that made her yearn for the forest and bid farewell to Aab and Ber before walking down to the room that held the hidden tunnel entrance that would take her out of the city wall and into what she now thought of as her forest to train. The fact the forest was forbidden in the land never crossed Wren's mind as she pushed back the bookcase that covered the entrance and slipped in before turning back and replacing the wooden shelves over the entrance and letting the burlap sack fall back down to fully cover the doorway. Continuing on, she marched quickly through the tunnel before coming to the hollowed-out cave-like exit that, through the vines, led to her forest. She had taken to hiding her practice sword here as it was only herself, Aab and Ber that knew about the tunnel and she deduced that this would be the safest place for her most prized possession.

Parting the vines and looking out across the small field, the call of the forest pulling at her chest, she saw the stream that stood between her and her forest; she was always caught by how immense the world outside the city wall was. Just seeing this tiny part of it made her wonder what was out there further, and she supposed that she would go out and venture further from the city if she didn't have the boys and her small family of misfits back behind the city walls. Coming out of her musings she took a breath and made a dash for the stream, setting her eyes on the first rock peeking out from the white rapids. It had taken her weeks to build the strength and stamina to hop across the water's rocks without slipping on the wet algae and moss attached to them but now she skipped across almost elegantly with her toes barely hitting solid surface as she moved. Once across — and mildly damp — Wren continued on with a short run from the stream's bank to the forest edge before taking a moment to rest behind the first bushes of the forest.

It was only a short journey now from the forest's edge to the clearing she used to practise. Pushing through the thick bushes and moving past the tree branches that seemed to reach out to her every time she made this journey, she came to her clearing and came to a stop by the opening that looked out upon the castle. Not for the first time she thought about the Princess that she had imagined playing with growing up. As she looked to the tower she saw that the candle light lightened the only window on this side of the tower. The room looked empty from what Wren could see and she wondered who had lit a candle only to leave it burning alone and unattended.

Shaking her head and turning back to her clearing she shook away the distracted thoughts that had invaded her mind. Looking down at the wooden sword in her hand, worn with use, she put it down on the forest floor and stepped away to begin her exercise routine that would lead up to her sword practise. As usual she began with a series of movements to stretch out her tired limbs, pulling her arms wide and overhead to loosen up her stiff shoulders, lunging her legs forward and sideways to stretch them out and massaging her thighs to work away the soreness that had built up from the hard day's work. As she brought her arms over head in an arch she winced and fell to the floor grasping at her ribs, face reddening in the pain that had shot through her entire body at the movement. On all fours she hit the floor in anger at her weakness.

Hissing out, "How can I have been so weak as to let this happen to me?" Wren began to push against the floor as she continued. "How could I have let my indecision and cowardliness cause my mother's death?" She hit the ground once more as her voice broke. "It's my fault she died… It's my fault," Wren croaked out as she ignored the pain in her ribs and jumped to her feet storming across the clearing to her sword to lash out in anger at the nearest tree. Pounding her sword into the bark of its trunk.

Tears rolling down olive cheeks and the pounding of her sword became more rhythmic as she began to work out the anger and hurt she had been feeling, continuing to ignore the pain in her ribs, almost numb to it now as she let her emotions take over and sooth her mind. Before long she let herself fall into routine, no longer hitting the tree simply for release but working in her training skills, moving her feet back and forth, parrying against the tree and thrusting forward as if to make a stab to the heart. The work came naturally to her and she began to take in the smell of the trees, the sounds of the birds. As she became more aware, moving away from her emotional state, she felt the way the hair on the back of her neck began to prickle and rise, and she knew she was being watched.

Loosening the grip on her sword slightly she carried on with her training, not wanting whoever was watching her to know they had been caught. It could after all be in her mind or maybe an animal she had not yet encountered here. Once again re-wrapping her sword and continuing her practice, her movements became sharper, the hits against the tree less forceful as she readied herself to turn and meet a foe at any moment. She strained to listen over the sounds of her training and the chirping of the birds and the now loud wind in the trees. Minutes passed as she listened and her movements slowed, the feeling still there. She began to ignore it, she thought to herself she must be going crazy. Sighing, Wren stepped forward, sword now by her side, she shook her head lightly and went to lean her forehead against the tree she had just battered.

The "SNAP" of a branch echoed out across the clearing.

13

Wren

Heart pounding, Wren jumped up and twisted around remembering her training with the Street Children — you must never turn your back on the unknown. Righting herself she creeped forward to where she knew the sound had come from, being careful to not let her foot falls make a sound. The bushes in front of her now were thick and she knew that they would make a great hiding place for someone. She would need to get right up to them to see if there was someone there.

As Wren came up to the bush she could see it move slightly and began to hear the harsh breathing of someone panicking. Taking a step back again, sure now there was someone here, a slight movement of an arm made the bush part slightly revealing a girl, eyes tight shut, looking down to the ground. In shocked silence, Wren stood her ground; not recognising the girl from the market, she raised an eyebrow and smirked to herself, "Looks like I'm not the only one who wanted out of the city." And that was when the girl looked up, big green doe eyes met hers and Wren lost the breath from her lungs.

"Princess?" she squeaked out, losing the composure she had been filled with only a moment before.

"Oh for fuck's sake not you too?" the Princess shouted. "Let's get one thing straight, my name is Faeryn, not Princess, we aren't using that bloody word here, do you understand?" the

Princess exclaimed while pacing about in front of Wren, spinning round to point at Wren with a finality to her words.

"Right, um, well then, Faeryn, yes okay. Yes, Princess, I mean, yes, Faeryn," floundered Wren.

Wren had absolutely no idea what was going on, she couldn't understand how her day had gone from training to this, the Princess Koni standing in front of her, swearing and asking her to call her Faeryn. It was madness. As she took in what was happening, she began to get annoyed. Faeryn had come in and she had disturbed her forest, her place!

Narrowing her eyes at the Princess who was now standing rather awkwardly in front of her, Wren asked, "What are you doing here? Shouldn't you be up at the castle?"

"I do as I please! It's not really any of your business anyway. But I actually came to meet you." Faeryn tapered off wistfully. "Why were you crying?" she asked, looking at Wren in the eyes through her long lashes.

Wren stopped and started to speak a few times before she gave up and let out a huff. She had not intended for anyone to see her break down and was used to only letting people see the tough and in control front that she usually displayed throughout the day to get by. The forest was supposed to be a place for her to let loose, train and not have to live up to the expectations of her day-to-day world. Looking at the Princess as she moved to sit down in the opening of the clearing, she tapped the floor beside her beckoning Faeryn to come and sit with her.

"Oh! That's my window!" Faeryn excitedly said as she took the seat next to Wren on the floor.

"So that's how you've been watching me, Princess," Wren stated with a slight cold edge to her voice. She did not mean to be rude but she was still annoyed that her peace had been disturbed even if it was by royalty.

"I told you don't call me that!" Faeryn exclaimed, bumping shoulders with her.

Wren let out an amused chuckle in response, looking out across the city.

"What's your name?" Faeryn asked in a whisper.

"Wren. My name is Wren," left Wren's lips before she could stop. Sighing, she looked at the Princess once more and took in her deep green eyes and auburn hair. "She's pretty," she thought to herself as she waited for Faeryn to speak.

"Are you going to tell me why you were crying…?" Faeryn said expectantly.

Wren considered for a moment before responding, thinking to herself, what could be the harm in sharing this with her, they may never see each other again? Faeryn knew none of her friends and no one would believe her if she started speaking of the girl she met in the forest. They would be a secret.

"It was nothing really, I let my emotions get the better of me. My mother died recently and I am still processing being without her." This came out like word vomit, Wren had not meant to mention her mother at all and the last thing she wanted from the Princess was pity.

"That sucks, I get it though, or at least I think I do. My mother's been kind of absent since I passed my tenth turn, I've actually been locked up in my room for the last few weeks. Bad behaviour and stuff. But I haven't been able to process the whole I'm a Princess, I can't have friends, all is for my duty, shtick that they've got me on," Faeryn rambled out, taking in a deep breath before continuing on, "That's how I found you actually. From my window up there." She pointed towards the window in the tower, Wren had been looking at earlier that same evening. "I can see down and across to the stream, along the edge of the forest and then up to this clearing, only the opening mind, usually you're just a bunch of shadows moving about, but I knew I needed to find a way to come and meet the free girl, that's you, Wren, the free one. So here I am." Catching her breath again Faeryn let out a soft hum, examining Wren's face with her eyes before looking back out across the city.

Wren didn't really know what to say to that, she had never intended to become someone's freedom, or sign of hope, just as she didn't want to become someone's leader — she reminded herself that she still needed to speak with Letta about that. Letting the silence hang between them once more, Wren had no idea what to say, scrambling in her mind for a topic to discuss that Faeryn would find interesting and move away from Wren's own life. She was saved from this when Faeryn spoke again.

"Do you think you could show me how to use that sword? Watching you earlier was magical in its own way and if I am ever going to be truly free I'll need to learn to use one of those," Faeryn said with a nod to Wren's wooden sword.

Wren had never let anyone else touch the sword her mother had given to her before she died. It was her most prized and beloved possession but there was something she couldn't explain pushing her onwards and before she knew it she was pushing off the ground mumbling "Come on then" to Faeryn as if they had known each other all of their lives and as if she trusted her implicitly. It wasn't hard to recognise the pulling in her chest to be the same one that pulled her to the forest and she knew that she would have no real choice but to follow on with the pull and do as it bid.

She found that the Princess had a decent amount of muscle to what she had expected from someone living in luxury and it was clear she had at least been paying attention to the guards and how they handled their swords.

Wren showed her a few movements, advances, thrusts and parries and soon she was moving quickly around the forest swinging Wren's sword and awkwardly calling out "En Garde" to the trees, laughing wildly while Wren watched on, a quiet amused chuckle leaving her chest lowly. She found herself thinking that she could get used to this, having someone be a part of this part of her life. The boys were too scared to come out here and this girl, a Princess, was nothing like any other person she'd ever met.

Lost in thought, Wren did not notice the girl slowing to a stop in front of her. Looking up, she was somewhat shocked to find Faeryn staring at her expectantly with a slight tilt to her head.

"We should do this again," rushed out of her mouth before she could stop it.

"I was hoping you'd say that," came Faeryn's bright reply.

At that, Wren's chest felt like a weight had been lifted and a smile crossed her face. She knew then with the awkwardly big smile that had appeared on Faeryn's face that she had made a real friend here, not one of necessity but a real friend.

"How often do you think you'll be able to get away? I come most nights, but that's to train mainly," Wren asked.

"I think once a week is probably wise, any more than that and they might get suspicious. I have to sneak out through the passages to get here and if they found me missing shit would hit the proverbial fan," Faeryn explained.

"Once a week it is, just set the candle in your window and I'll know that you're on your way down." Wren smiled.

With that agreed, the girls carried on their practice, new energy boosting their movements. It wasn't long before the moon began to sit lowly in the sky and the birds began to sing and they knew it was time to leave the forest and each other behind. A sadness settled in Wren's heart and when she looked to Faeryn she could see that same sadness reflected in her eyes. Neither of them wanted to leave the other and as Faeryn handed over Wren's wooden sword they both hesitated.

"I'll see you next week then?" Faeryn asked.

"Yes, next week, I'll be here. I promise," answered Wren quietly.

Wren watched as the Princess began to walk away, crossing the clearing to stand in the opening, she looked back to her and winked before making her way down the steep hillside to the wall.

Wren watched her go, walking to the opening itself when Faeryn had disappeared from view down the hill to ensure she got back to the wall safely. And as she watched the Princess get to the bottom of the hillside, she whispered out, "See you soon, Fae." Before turning herself back towards the forest and making her way home.

14

Wren

Time went by quickly for Wren after meeting Fae, the pulling in her chest began to calm down with each week that they met and an odd sense of peace had washed over her. Their training had taken leaps and bounds, Wren had taught Fae everything she knew and was constantly surprised at her eagerness to learn and determination to perfect everything Wren taught her. They would often spar or condition their bodies until they were both exhausted, dripping with sweat and falling into each other to relax for just a little while before having to say goodbye once again.

 Wren wished that Fae was able to sneak away from the castle more often but understood the necessity behind the restricted meetings and did not bring up her yearning for more time as she knew Fae would try to do more to make her smile but would most likely end up being caught and then there would be no more meetings and that would be unacceptable. It did leave more time for her to spend with the Street Children and Aab and Ber had grown so much over the last two years, they were well on their way to becoming strong, grown men and would no doubt get to a point in the next few years where they could go out on their own. Perhaps even do as Wren was doing and open their own market stall or together they could expand hers. Letta had grown more used to Wren over the years and now when she saw her a small smile would form on her face and a slight inclination of her head would greet Wren back to their hideout. Despite her insistence, Wren had made the decision to still live at her father's house; she was unable to let go of the place she had grown up, where the memory of her mother was around every corner and regardless of her father's violent behaviour this was her home and she could make it work for her and had since her mother's passing. The market place was close by and in the many months since she had fully taken over the stall and introduced her helpers — Aab and Ber — to the scene, she had become a well-respected and liked stall seller.

Life had become comfortable in its routine and Wren lived for her meetings with Fae and her responsibilities to the Street Children. She was as happy as she thought she could be. She thought back to her sixteenth birthday and smiled to herself as she mused. She had been due to meet Fae in the forest, they were going to explore away from the clearing and see what was out there; they had often argued over the belief that the forest was magic and this could prove to end that argument and provide an adventure for the two. Wren had not told Fae that it was her birthday that day, she did not want the sadness to take over, remembering her mother and that she would not be there for any more of her birthdays. She had put her best smile on and made her way to their clearing. Fae had taken one glance at her on arrival and tilted her head in that considering way that she did and said, "You're sad, what's wrong?" As if it were that simple. She had looked straight through her walls and gotten straight to the point. Wren had stood there, mouth hanging open, as Fae walked straight up to her, wrapping her arms around her and lowered them to the floor in a tight embrace and just waited for Wren to talk.

Tears coming to Wren's eyes, she had laughed through the pain choking out, "How do you always do that, how do you know?"

Fae had stayed quiet then. Wren looked up from her place within her arms and knew that she would not let go until she had told her and so rested her head on Fae's shoulder and began to speak.

"It's my birthday, it's silly really, and it should be cause for celebration. But it's the first birthday after she passed, my mother. And I just — I just miss her." She looked up at Fae's face from her place on her shoulder and watched the emotions run through her eyes as she decided how to respond to what Wren had just told her. Wren noticed the way her eyes would twitch upwards at the corners and her forehead would wrinkle slightly as she ran through things in her mind and she found herself feeling less sad and a slither of happiness shone through as she smiled at the girl who in reality had changed her life. She felt safe in her arms, and let her guard come down even more as she felt the warmth of Fae's body against her as she was squeezed closer as Fae lowered and twisted her head to meet Wren eye to eye without losing any body contact.

"Ya know you could 'a told me that it was your birthday today? I know you don't like talking about our family but you need to know I'm always here and willing to listen? We are best friends after all," Fae had said with a sincere amusement to her voice that Wren had come to know was the most serious she ever really got.

Wren looked into Fae's eyes at this and looked to see if she could see in her eyes what she could hear in her voice and she found Fae doing the same examining her every movement and taking her in as if she never wanted to forget this moment. They were so close and Wren could feel her breath catch as she began to realise just how close their bodies had become, heat tingling through every part of her body that touched with Fae's own. Not knowing whether to lean in further to Fae or to put distance between them, her choice was taken away as Fae lifted them both abruptly from the ground sending her a smirk and a wink her way before bouncing off into the forest with a shouted "Come on slow poke" as Wren shook herself out of her daze and with a smile ran carefreely after her, thoughts of heat and a new sense of longing forgotten.

In the months following, Wren let down some of her walls and knowing that she was safe to let them all down and talk with Fae about the darker pats of her life, she felt freer. But the need and want to see Fae had become stronger; she had begun to dream about her and the all too familiar sense of pulling in her chest had grown stronger, drawing her back to the forest for longer periods of time staring out of the clearing and to the girl's window, sometimes catching her looking at her and giving her the strength to train harder. Their friendship had given her a sense of joy that she had not known before and allowed her to act her age rather than the little adult she had been forced to be by her circumstances since she was old enough to hold a basket.

She thought back to a few weeks after her birthday, they had explored deep into the forest and had found a tree whose trunk was wider than both of them put together, its branches hanging low to the ground and in Fae's usual brazen way she had bet that she could climb higher than Wren could. Not one to take a challenge lightly, Wren's competitiveness had kicked into overdrive and before Fae could even set terms she ran at the tree jumping into its branches and swinging up to the ones higher. Looking back she had laughed and exclaimed, "Put your money where your mouth is, Princess!" She had only used Fae's title to get a rise out of her and from the look on Fae's face it had worked a treat as she took a running starting to jump and swing onto the branches next to Wren. Wide eyed, Wren had made to scramble to the next branch a level higher than they were and Fae went to make a grab for her to slow her down. This resulted in them both losing their balance, loud swear words were shouted as they fell in a fit of giggles from the tree. Fae had hit the floor first, still laughing and slightly winded, Wren soon to follow landing with a thud onto Fae, nose and mouth mushed against Fae's cheek, arms splayed out above her. Winded and in shock Wren realised that she was still pressed against Fae and went to push herself up from the floor to look at Fae.

"You cheated, I won!" Wren said indignantly.

As she rested on her elbows either side of Fae's head she felt colour rise in her cheeks as she realised that Fae wasn't looking at her face but down towards her body. Following Fae's gaze downwards Wren saw that their bodies were pressed tightly against each other and she currently had her thigh pushed up against Fae in the most private of places. Unable to speak as she felt the tingling heat rise in her body she looked to Fae who once again looked to her red face with a smirk and brought her hands to Wren's hips, pushing her further into a daze before flipping them smoothly over, pinning Wren underneath her.

"Actually I think you'll find, I won," Fae breathed out before pushing off of Wren's hips to stand back up, putting some much-needed distance between their bodies. Wren lay on the floor red faced and in shock at what had just happened before brushing the tingling off, pushing herself up to follow Fae, laughing and complaining all the way about Fae's cheating ways and demanding a rematch.

Over time it became harder for Wren to push aside the way that their dynamic was beginning to change. With each visit their training sessions became less intense, they began to play more and find excuses to sit and talk and just be together. Physical contact became less about showing movement and more about finding comfort within one another's arms. They would talk about the way they wanted he world to be, Wren's wish to become the first female guard and the way that Faeryn wanted to travel the realm to truly know her people and bring everyone together rather than have this fragmented land that barely knew about each other and their needs. She wanted change, just like Wren. As they became closer, Wren would find herself losing herself in her thoughts as she looked at Fae, caught looking at the way that the moonlight would reflect from Faeryn's light skin, and her frown would cause the moonlight to bend and cast shadow over her face strands of her auburn hair moving with the breeze to dance across her face. And Wren would think that she had never had a friend quite like this, she had never felt so safe and content with anyone else. She was lucky.

15

Wren

It had almost been a year since Wren had told Fae of her mother's passing and with the change in their dynamic she was feeling more hopeful about her upcoming seventeenth birthday. Seventeen was the age where you were considered an adult in Wren's culture, when you became eligible for marriage and could complete marriage arrangements that had been pre-arranged by parents. This had been the age that her mother had been introduced to her father and it was clear to see around the market place that more girls had begun to talk with the men of the village, dressing in finer dresses and doing what they could to secure themselves good husbands. This was the farthest thing from Wren's own mind and she had never factored into the life plans a husband and children, with the way her own family went she did not think she could submit herself to a man, and she knew none that were kind enough and of age to even consider an arrangement anyway.

No, she would resolve to stay true to her plan and continue training to become a guard, only another year before she would be able to pass the age restriction on the application day. As she set up her market stall for another day of selling, she was alone for the first time in a while. She had sent her boys off to gather information from around the different villages and ensure that she and Letta were kept up to date with all of the goings on to better protect the Street Children. She thought about her training and how she needed to focus more on her sparring, she would need to convince Fae that they needed to spar more often rather than go on their adventures. She needed this; it was a matter of life or death for her in the end not just a game as it sometimes seemed to be for Fae. She was brought out of her stream of consciousness by a man clearing his throat in front of her.

"Ex — excuse me, Wren?" he stuttered, looking worriedly up to her.

"Yes, who's asking?" she replied stiffly, not recognising the man in front of her. Body taut and now on alert, she focused on the man and her surroundings.

"My name is Jahed, I am the spice seller's son and I am here to ask if you would care to take a walk with me this evening," Jahed spoke out more confidently now, his little speech clearly rehearsed many times.

Wren looked at the six-foot man sternly as she considered his request; she had never met Jahed before and had only dealt with his father on the market since he had taken over from his own father when she was fifteen turns. Like both of his older counterparts Jahed was brown skinned, darkened by the days drying and grinding down spices to sell at their family's market stall. His hair was thick and long, tied into a plait at the base of his neck to keep it from falling into their products. His eyes were friendly enough but his nervous demeanour did nothing for Wren, unlike Faeryn this man was quiet where she was loud, and quiet where she was brash. He would not be able to work as effortlessly beside her as her best friend. Let alone a lover and husband. She could see the attraction, he was clearly well built and his jaw line was strong and angular, the girls across the market were clearly looking him up and down and whispering between themselves, waiting with bated breath for Wren's answer to his nervous request to court.

She better stop their agony, she thought to herself as she looked back to Jahed. She gave him a slightly pitying smile as she said, "Sorry, Jahed but I am busy this evening."

"...Well what about tomorrow evening then? We could walk around the village and talk? Maybe grab a bite to eat at the Tavern?" Jahed went on, somehow finding confidence from her answer.

Bewildered at the new found confidence Jahed had scrapped up from somewhere, Wren steeled herself to be quite blunt in her next answer. "Jahed, you seem like a nice guy, but I am not free any evening... Why don't you try Iris at the meat stall? She's been looking over at you since you started talking to me."

At this Jahed seemed to perk up and whispered out in shock, "Really?" With wide eyes he quickly glanced over to Iris, a younger blonde girl who quickly looked away as he caught her eye and blushed. He looked back to Wren and let out a quick "Thanks, Wren!" before marching straight across the market and to the girl he would most likely end up marrying.

Wren looked around and similar conversations with acceptances and denials were happening all across the market, in quiet corners and to the sides of stands, people were whispering and like a wave she realised that maybe this is what has been happening all these years, boys and girls courting and talking and getting to know one another before they eventually get to their seventeenth turn. How had she never seen it before today? Looking back on the last few years she realised that she had been rather busy, hell bent on her plans to become a guard and change the city for the better and that alongside helping Letta to look after the children and the market and training and meeting with

Fae as well, she never had time to really see this side of the village and the people around her.

As she watched Jahed talk to Iris she began to wonder why she hadn't considered him for even a second. She had just compared him to Faeryn, found him lacking, and dismissed him without regret. She saw the way that Iris was looking up at Jahed, seeing the way her cheeks coloured and his smile pulled into a half smirk, and she was taken back to Faeryn and the time they had fallen out of the tree, how she had flipped them over and that exact same half smirk had covered her face and the red blush had crept up Wren's skin like fire. Confusion filled her head as she thought back to all of the other times across the last year where the same thing had happened. The moments where they got lost in each other's eyes and silence took over for just a moment longer than felt usual, the extended touches, holding each other, the smirks and winks from Fae and the red flush that took over her body when Fae would run her fingers along her arms as they talked about the world. She had always thought that was just what friends did, never having had proper friends her own age before. She needed advice, and despite not wanting to go to her, Wren knew she would need to speak to Letta about this.

The rest of market time felt like an eternity as she kept seeing over and over again different couples, the soft touches between loved ones and the lingering looks given by the girls to boys across the market and she kept thinking back to how she and Faeryn were together. She couldn't possibly have feelings for Faeryn, she was a girl. She was her best friend. Oh god, what if she lost her? Had she been making her feel awkward this whole time? She really needed to speak to Letta. Letta was always calm, quiet and blunt to a point; she would give it to her straight and not sugar coat what she thought. She would know what to do.

As the market closed for the day, Wren's nervous energy was spilling out and showing in clumsiness, completely opposite to her normally composed self. She dropped the baskets of flowers, and tripped and stumbled as she went to rush to put away her things before dashing back out of the house to avoid her father and make her way quickly to the hideout to find Letta. Two falls and a near death experience with a roof ledge later, Wren had made It to the edge of the hideout. Skidding to a stop she looked around to find the rooftops of the territory deserted, this was not unusual but slightly odd for the time of the day as she made her way across the roof to the entrance into the building.

Descending the dark steps into the main room of the house, she could hear the chattering of the young children as they helped some of their slightly older counterparts to prepare and cook meals for the group.

Rounding the corner she saw them all hard at work but immediately noticed that none of the older children were there, Aab and Ber were absent, along with Letta and some of the older girls who usually patrolled the city as she had sent Aab and Ber to do today. Waving hello to the young ones she journeyed on down to the bottom levels of the house and out onto the street. She knew that the building they usually used to train held a smaller back room that Letta usually held her meetings in and she went straight through to there to see if she could find them, thoughts of Faeryn clouded by her worry for her people.

Whispering could be heard from behind the meeting room door and Wren knew whatever was going on must be serious. As she opened the door the whispers stopped abruptly as Aab, Ber, Letta and two girls whose names Wren could not remember looked up with frowns across their faces at Wren who had disturbed their meeting. Noticing the awkwardness in the silence as Aab and Ber looked at one another, Wren quickly made her way further into the room and closed the door firmly behind her before leaning against it and as casually as she could said, "Who wants to fill me in?"

With a scoff and an eye roll, Letta looked to Wren and motioned to a chair in next to her. "Just sit down and be quiet."

Not one to ignore clear instructions from Letta since becoming a part of the family, Wren rushed to move across the room to sit next to Letta as the meeting continued and she caught a glimpse of a crudely drawn map on the table that the Children surrounded. It soon became clear that the meeting was about a stronger guard presence near the edges of their territory that had previously been left alone. Letta believed that the Guard wanted to take back some of the previously abandoned buildings to expand the villages and make room for renovated nicer guard houses. She could just be being paranoid but for now they would need to be extra vigilant and that would mean that Aab and Ber would be needed here more often and not looking out for Wren's father and working the markets. Letta mentioned briefly the possibility of taking some of the younger ones that had started training and using those for Wren's jobs but Wren knew she would prefer to do it alone without the boys so the idea was dismissed quickly.

After the meeting Wren murmured to Letta that she'd like to speak to her after their evening meal and with an incline of the head in acceptance Wren's nerves began to start building all over again now that immediate danger was not a possibility. The evening meal went by quickly: a stew made from spices from the market, goat's meat and dhal. She was still getting used to the way that the Street Children cooked, it had been one of the contributing factors to her not moving in with them. She would help and provide those spices and materials as part of the family and they would help her in return but she still liked to cook her own mother's meals and sleep In her own bed locked away from her father's room.

Soon it came time for her to talk to Letta, the girl had gotten up and looked across the room to Wren silently, telling her to follow as she left the room to descend once again out of the building. Wren got up and followed her out in to the dark cobbled streets, waiting silently, thinking of how to broach the subject that she wanted to ask about without sounding like a blithering idiot of a girl. Her thoughts were interrupted by Letta.

"Is this about the girl you've been seeing outside the wall?" came Letta's bored tone.

Wren stared at her in shock, how had Letta known that she had been going out of the city wall? Only Aab and Ber knew of the exit and no one knew about Faeryn. Her mind began to reel as Letta opened her mouth to speak again.

"What, you didn't think I would find out or notice you sneaking out somewhere every night? It didn't take long for one of my girls to find out where you were going off to. From what I've heard your girl is rather pretty."

"She's beautiful, Letta," came out as Wren thought over the implications of Letta having known for the last three years that she had been sneaking out. "Why didn't you say anything sooner?"

"I was waiting for you to come to me. I knew you were safe and you're old enough and wise enough to make decisions like this on your own. You did not endanger any of the children, you've been loyal," explained Letta blank faced.

"I just wanted to train with the sword my mother gave me, but it became so much more and then I met Fae. Oh, Letta, I am so confused," whined out Wren, finally giving in to the need to spill everything and get the advice of the only person she had left in her life that held some level of authority over her.

"Talk to me Wren, what are you confused about?" Letta said.

"We are so close, Fae and I, and there's been these moments where it's felt like time's stopped and I feel hot and flushed, not like myself but they pass and I've always brushed them off before. But today I've noticed the girls in the market are all flaunting for the young men, and I'm coming of age soon and I don't feel that way towards any of them. Oh, Letta, Jahed the spice seller's son asked me to court today and all I could do was compare him with Fae. Why am I comparing him to my best friend? I am so confused. I don't know what's wrong with me," Wren cried out as she hid her head in her hands.

Letta chuckled as she leant into Wren. "Do you think perhaps you may just have those feelings for Fae rather than the foolish boys down at the market?" asked Letta.

"Bu — but Fae's a girl, I can't have feelings for a girl, I — I — I, oh god I do don't I?" cried out Wren.

"You know, Wren, it's not as strange as you seem to think it is, I know of lots of relationships between boys and boys and girls and other girls across all of the villages in the city. It just has to be kept more hidden," Letta calmly explained as she brought Wren's hands away from her face.

Wren considered this for a moment as she looked up into Letta's eyes trying to ascertain if Letta was just taking pity on her and resolved that she would need to watch out for these, she couldn't be sure if Letta wasn't just telling her this to make her feel better. Looking away from Letta's face her thoughts went back to Fae and the predicament she now found herself in and in a small voice she whispered out, "What if she doesn't feel the same way?" Not knowing if she wanted to hear the answer to that question, she rushed to speak again before Letta could answer. "I'm going to need to tell her how I feel, there's no way I can just carry on like we have been, not now."

"Do what you need to do, Wren, I don't know who your girl is but she makes you happy, that's all I need to know really. Just make sure you're ready to tell her and do it when it feels natural. You don't want to risk losing her," were Letta's final words on the matter before she patted Wren on the shoulder and moved back inside to ensure the children were behaving and had finished cleaning up after the evening meal.

Letta's parting words left Wren to go into a spin thinking of how if she shared her feelings with Fae that she might lose her and how would she feel if she didn't see her again? Would it be easier than living seeing her every week and not following the possibility of them being together?

Letta's advice had been fantastic but she didn't know that Faeryn was actually the Princess, how would that work? They would be left to always have to be hidden, Faeryn would certainly have to get married at some point and what would happen to Wren then? There were so many things to consider. But Wren knew it wasn't just her decision to make. It could be that she had read this completely wrong and the lingering looks, smirks and winks had not been Fae flirting with her but actually just who she was as a person, Wren had never seen her interact with anyone other than herself. So many questions, and no answers. The next time she was due to see Fae was on her birthday, seventeen turns, she had to talk to Fae then or she never would.

Why did it always have to be her birthday?

16

Faeryn

For weeks Faeryn had been planning and worrying over Wren's upcoming seventeenth birthday. Seventeen turns was a big deal within the city of Ekoni and marked the moment a girl would officially be a woman. Availability for marriage was only a small part of it and Faeryn wanted to get Wren something amazing. The trouble was acquiring that amazing present without anyone noticing or asking questions. It was now only a few days away and despite Faeryn's thoughts being dedicated to planning a way to get this present she had come up with nothing. She knew that she wanted to get Wren a wooden bow and arrow set to go with her wooden sword and it would also give them an excuse to continue training and a new type of training to do together because they had gotten to the point where they were able to spar without too much thought. In fact they had in the last few months spent most of their time, playing and talking, and there had been minimal training, it worried Faeryn as she thought that maybe Wren would see the lack of usefulness and would want to stop coming to the forest to meet her. This would mean she didn't lose her and would show her how much she valued her friendship.

  They had been meeting once a week for a few years now and the passageways had become very easy to navigate for Faeryn. She knew her way around so well that it didn't take much thought and she could concentrate on other things while walking to her destinations. She used these to get around a lot of the time now, not wanting to be bumped into by Tutor Tobin and her mother, and the guards that tried to follow her around every day to no avail. This would only take a few moments for her to get to and from her destinations but going out to the forest time seemed to move too quickly and she would be gone for hours before she knew it, spending most of her next day sleeping or in a tired daze. She knew that despite her wanting to go and see Wren more often there was no real way for her to excuse her tiredness for more than the one day as she didn't have tutoring on the rest day. The pulling in her chest had only gotten stronger and she found that she would stare out to the forest and day dream most days.

Walking through the passageways, Faeryn had almost resigned herself to the idea that should would have to think of a new birthday gift for Wren when she came across the guards' viewing window. Looking out, an idea came into her head and as her idea grew so did the mischievous smile on her face that could only mean trouble. Feeling to the left of the window, she had discovered last year during her adventures that there was a small hole in the wall just big enough to crawl through for someone her size. She knew that what she wanted to do was extremely risky and someone would most likely get in trouble but it was definitely worth it in her mind. As her fingers found the crease in the wall and gently peeled back the cloth that covered the wooden flap into the guards' courtyard she quickly peeked through the window again to make sure the coast was clear before pushing her way through the hole to hide behind a waggon set in the corner of the yard. Heart pounding, she looked across the court yard and at her target, the training armoury, from her observations she knew that it was full of wooden equipment and there were two bows with matching quivers and arrow sets. And she was going to steal one.

Steely eyes looked out and set her course across the courtyard, she could see that there was the stairway up through to the walkways on the walls, there were also storage boxes lined slightly further away; from there it would be a clear sprint to the training armoury door and she would be there. Crouching to make for the back of the stairway's hiding spot she counted to three in her head before whispering to herself "Fuck it" and going for a full sprint. Barely stopping at the stairs, she made straight for the storage boxes as soon as she realised there was no one in the room or on the above walk way. Heaving slightly from the adrenaline she looked around once more, thinking that this was her lucky day, she went to make the final sprint to the training room door. Just as she readied herself for the run she stuttered to a stop and pushed herself flat up against the storage boxes, peeking around the corner she saw one of the young guards rounding the doorway to the training armoury room itself; he had been inside this whole time. Trying to stop the panic from rising in her chest, she put a hand to her chest and began to count her breaths like Wren had shown her during her training. Her breaths coming more evenly now, she peeked around the corner and began to listen. She could no longer see the guard and she could hear the clipped rhythm of his shoes against the cobbled stones begin to get fainter. Letting out a sigh she could feel that she was once again alone. Making a run for it before she hesitated again and talked herself out of the whole ordeal she moved quickly to run through the door. Back now firmly against the back of the door she took a minute to look around her, having never been in this room in her entire life stuck in the castle, experiencing something new in her own home was an oddly exhilarating feeling for her.

The training armoury was bigger than she had expected, which in retrospect was silly of her because she knew they had A LOT of guards around the castle, let alone in the city's villages within the wall. That's not even taking into consideration the armed force that would be outside of the wall and across the realm that would consistently come back into the walls to train and report their finding etc. from their missions. They would always bring news and gossip from other lands and, from what Faeryn could tell from the snippets of conversations she had managed to overhear, things outside of the wall and in the far-off lands were magical. The walls of the room were lined with hard oak shelving units, holding sword after sword made from various woods and different lengths with different hilts. Faeryn pondered over these for a second before thinking better than to present something to Wren that her mother had given her before her death and moved away and looked to the padded training armour that hung in lines across the back of the room. Wren would benefit from this but she didn't think she would be able to lug one of these across the yard back into her hiding hole and back to her room without being caught.

Part of her doubted she would even be able to lift it without great struggle despite all the muscle she had gained from training with Wren. Shaking her head she moved across to the other wall and looked at the bows, she had known there were two in here as the guards only ever had two out at once despite needing more. It had never crossed her mind that there would be a third in here. It was clearly the least used, and its design was slightly different, smaller and much more detailed with the engraved wood along its arch, vine leaves wrapping around the edgings with small birds at the very ends of the wood. Faeryn knew this was Wren's bow. The quiver underneath was made from the best brown leather and had been polished into a stunning shine, embossed with its own vines and birds along its strap and full of arrows with fletching made from glimmering blue feathers that reminded her of Wren's eyes.

Grabbing the bow and quiver from the wall she slung them across her back before creaking open the door of the training armoury and saw that the yard was once again bare. Rather than waste time trying to be stealthy, confidence brimming from her pores as she felt the weight of her accomplishment in finding Wren the perfect present, she ran full pelt towards the waggon in the corner of the yard, dropping into a slide to push through the small hole she knew to be there but could not be seen. Effortless, was the only way she could describe the feeling when she stood back up now, safe within her passage, prize in hand.

Stashing the present in the end of the passage nearest the exit to their forest, she made her way back to her room. Getting into bed that night she knew she would sleep soundly knowing how happy Wren would be with her birthday present. She fell asleep that night with a contented smile on her face, dreaming of her best friend.

Waking the next day, Faeryn couldn't keep the grin from her face, today was Wren's birthday and tonight she would be able to see her and finally give her a happy birthday. After the last two years she knew she needed it. Rushing through her lessons and listening to Tobin drone on about her own upcoming birthday and what it would mean for the realm, she completely zoned him out as she planned in her head what she would steal from the kitchens today to take for a birthday picnic for Wren. She knew there was no way she would be able to get a cake but she could definitely pull off grabbing some pork pies, maybe an apple or two and some bread and jam maybe.

Her meetings with Wren had quickly become her favourite part of the week and now she could not imagine her life without the stoic and hardened girl. It didn't matter to her that she clearly didn't know the whole story about her life, what mattered was that, no matter what, she always knew that Wren would be there when she came to the forest. She could count on her to listen while she ranted about her mother and her tutors and she would let her figure out things on her own rather than just telling her. Faeryn had even managed to get her to open up a bit more over the last year, getting her to act more like a child of her age rather than this little adult with the weight of the world on her shoulders, making her laugh and making her flustered which was personally Faeryn's favourite reaction to bring out in her because it was so far removed from her usual self.

It wasn't long before Faeryn found herself running through the passages, cloth food bundle in hand and rushing to pick up the present she had gotten for Wren in her arms. She had decided she would hide the present in the bushes next to the clearing on the hill so that she could surprise Wren after training and the picnic she had made. She ran forward, moving through the entrance to her forest and, as the moonlight hit her skin, she felt the easing of the pull in her chest and she lifted her head and smiled at the moon taking in the feeling of the moment.

"Wren, I'm coming," she whispered to the wind with a soft smile on her face.

17

Faeryn

The Journey up the hill and to stash the present felt like it lasted a life time, for once she was the first in the clearing and her heart hammered as she waited in anticipation for Wren.

It didn't take long for Wren to come out from the thick brush on the opposite side of the clearing. In a moment Faeryn knew that there was something different about Wren that day, she seemed nervous, almost jittery, in the way that she was acting as she walked up to Faeryn. Instead of the usual hug that she would receive and smile, Wren stopped two paces early and gave a half-hearted wave before saying "So shall we train?" Looking anywhere but at her.

"Hello to you too, Wren, how're you? Oh I'm fine, ya know just doing Princess things every day," Faeryn smirked out as she cocked her head to the side. Usually this would get something from Wren but today not even a smile crossed her face, instead she just looked to her feet and shifted her weight from foot to foot.

"Right okay then, sure, let's spar," sighed Faeryn.

Moving into the familiarity that came with their training sessions, Wren seemed to relax more and her shoulders dropped their tension as she focused in on her movements.

Wren's hand jabbed out to hit against her shoulder with force and speed. Faeryn was able to bring her forearm up to block the punch and swing around to produce a kick to Wren's back. On her toes tipping forward, Faeryn was able to move from her forward position to dodge a lower kick by Wren to bring up her fist forcefully into Wren's stomach surely winding the other girl. At some point their sparring had become much more forceful than usual and Wren was actually trying to land punches. Faeryn did not take this personally, knowing that Wren's distraction and tunnel vision was from the emotions that she supressed from her birthday and the memories that were brimming under the surface. Faeryn knew she would need to stop this before it became too much, Wren was much faster and stronger than she was due to the daily training she put her body through and her friend was not fully here right now.

Backing away quickly, she made for a run and jump to bring her legs around Wren's waist and used her body weight to swing them round and down to the flower, landing fully on top of Wren's stomach. Breath heaving with exertion she looked down at Wren and waited for her eyes to slowly uncloud and bring her back to the present moment.

"You're safe, Wren, you're safe, come back to me now… please come back," Faeryn whispered to her pleadingly as she stroked her fingertips along her cheek.

Under her, Wren was clearly distressed as she came back to herself, her face scrunched up into a ball, body squirming to be set free from Faeryn's thighs and she looked into her eyes with sadness as she stilled and gave into the safety that was Faeryn. Words were not spoken as Faeryn adjusted herself to lay on top of Wren using her body weight to leave a weighted pressure to her body hoping that she was right and that it relaxed Wren.

Breathing her in, Fae rested her forehead to Wren's neck and murmured, "I've got you." No longer sure if she was reassuring

Wren or herself, she let herself relax into the warmth of Wren's body. They lay like this for a long moment before Wren finally spoke.

"I'm sorry, Fae, did I hurt you?" Voice breaking as she asked.

"No you're all right, I was taught by the best after all." Fae smiled as she replied.

"I don't know why I can't seem to ever get this day right." Wren shook her head as she said this — a nervous habit Fae had noticed Wren always did when she was out of sorts. "We could just go home and try again another day I guess?" Wren manically let out as she pushed away from Fae and began to get up and pace.

"Wha — Wh — what no! Don't be so stupid, woman, sit the fuck back down. I did not do all this work for you to freak out and storm off home upset because you have emotions! Jesus Christ, Wren!" Fae's voice got progressively louder as she said this and grabbed onto Wren's shoulders, spinning her to face her and shake the sense back into her.

Exasperated, Fae pushed Wren to the floor before disappearing into the bushes to grab the picnic bundle that she had hidden for their midnight birthday snack. She left the present where it was for the moment knowing that she needed to give Wren some time to settle back down into her stoic comfort zone before she sprang that on her.

Peaking back to make sure Wren hadn't run off while her back was turned, she smiled to herself as she saw Wren sitting exactly where she had left her, feet crossed and head rested grumpily on her hand as she was clearly grumbling to herself. Laughing under her breath, Fae turned back and brought the treasure to her grumpy companion.

"How did you manage to sneak this out?" a shocked Wren exclaimed.

"Simple really, I snuck into the kitchens when cook was having her afternoon nap, the twins nearly caught me though mind. It was kind of a fuck it moment," mused Faeryn as she remembered back to her lunch time escapades.

"You seem to have a lot of so called 'fuck it' moments Faeryn, you may even be beginning to make me believe that you're a little bit crazy," Wren joked as she nudged Fae's side.

"You like my crazy," came the automatic reply from Fae as she lay the feast out on to the cloth it had been wrapped up in. "Plus you seem to benefit from it more often than not!" she said with raised eyebrows and a knowing smile.

Rolling her eyes, Wren looked at the food and then back to Faeryn with a small smile that Fae couldn't quite read. "Thank you Fae," Wren whispered as she touched her hand lightly to Faeryn's arm. Faeryn noticed the way Wren lingered slightly longer than usual as she touched her and the slight blush to her cheeks and couldn't help but be curious as to what was going on with Wren. She had never acted like this before. As they ate their dinner in comfortable silence, Fae thought back over the times they had spent together over the years in this clearing and the surrounding forest, nothing but good times, sometimes hard but always good; the pulling in her chest was always eased here, feeling relieved and content and for once free and happy for the time they spent together before she had to go back into the castle and bring her mask back up.

They had gotten closer over the last year, and before, Fae had never really chalked it up to anything other than unlocking the next part to this beautiful friendship, and the warm fuzzy feeling she would get when being with Wren was just an indication of just how happy she was to be here with room to breathe for the first time in her life. This was her safe place.

With Wren.

Faeryn knew how important to her Wren was but she was almost certain that Wren didn't understand that she valued her just as much as Wren valued their friendship. Her present to her and all of this food for the birthday and being here like this was how she planned to show Wren that she needed Wren just as much Wren needed her. As they finished their meal Wren looked to her and, before she could speak, Faeryn cut her off knowing that she needed to get this out of the way.

"So I got you something, I know you don't like your birthday but please just bear with me for a minute. Okay?" Faeryn rushed out. Running back to the place she had hidden their food she searched in the thick bushes for the bow and quiver she had stolen from the training armoury. Spotting the wooden vines of the bow, she grabbed onto it and shouted behind her for Wren to close her eyes., Trusting that she had done this, she picked up the bow and slung the quiver full of arrows behind her back and started to walk back through the thick bushes to Wren, heart speeding up slightly with anxiety hoping that Wren liked this, that she had picked right and it wasn't too close to home for her.

Coming back to the clearing she saw that Wren had actually listened to her and closed her eyes, stood in the middle of the clearing with her eyes shut and clearly slightly on edge with one of her senses obscured. Faeryn couldn't believe how lucky she had been to meet her free girl. Taking the steps from the bushes up to Wren, she flipped the bow and quiver into her hands and grasped them sideways together ready to place into Wren's hands.

"Keep your eyes closed," she asked and as Wren gave a

small nod she continued, "Hold both of your hands out with palms flat facing the moon." As Wren did what she said Faeryn braced herself for her friend's reaction placing the present slowly into her hands.

"Okay open them." Faeryn smiled.

Faeryn watched as Wren slowly opened her eyes and looked into her own before she looked down to the present in her hands. Almost in slow motion, shock passed over her face, eyebrows rising impossibly high and face reddening. As she looked up a single tear left her eye and for a moment she thought she had gotten it wrong and that she had made a mistake getting this for Wren but before this thought could take hold her body was assaulted with Wren's own slamming into her and holding her tightly, face buried into the hair around her neck and her warm breath skimming across her skin making goose bumps rise as a deep warmth settled over her. Taking Wren in while she could, she breathed in deeply, senses overwhelmed by the familiar spice and pine scent of Wren that she wished she could bottle. She wished she could be wrapped in this moment forever, the pulling in her chest mellowed and a calm and safeness anchoring deep within.

As Wren began to pull away, Faeryn couldn't help but whimper at the thought of losing the feeling that she was currently bathed in. Eyes closed trying to hold onto the warmth for a moment longer she did not see the way as Wren leaned backwards her body faltered, hope flickering across her eyes and a surging forward brought her back to reality. Faeryn could feel the softness of lips touch her own, sending warmth and tingling shooting back through her body as her brain stuttered to a stop and she got lost in the moment. As those lips began to move against her own, she began to step forward into the kiss to fall into those lips, wanting only to deepen what was being shared when a fierce cold hit her as Wren fell backwards creating distance between them once again.

Caught up in the loss of warm lips upon on her own and the renewed ache in her chest she was frozen to her spot as the panic screamed from Wren's face, no longer red but draining to white in fright as she continued to back away from her. Faeryn raised an arm the word "stay" lost in her throat as Wren turned and ran through the thick bushes ahead.

Cold.

Lost.

Scared.

Pain.

Faeryn couldn't think straight as she tried to process what had just happened. Her chest was sending painful shocks through her body, constantly aching, and she had never felt the pulling in her do this before, cause her so much pain. Crumbling down into a ball on the ground she couldn't move past the fact that Wren had left, she had left her here alone. The trees of the forest for the first time seemed imposing and dark, not like their usually welcoming feel. Each shadow seemed to be moving and she felt unsafe for the first time since passing the city's wall. She closed her eyes and let the feeling overtake her slowly drifting out of consciousness.

18

Wren

What had she done? Panic had taken over Wren as she had pushed her way through the thick bushes at the edge of the clearing, trying to get away from the situation she had put herself in. How could she have done that? Faeryn would never forgive her. How stupid could she be? She didn't even say anything, she had just kissed her! This was not how she wanted to tell Fae about her feelings. But god she had been so sweet and she had stood so close to her and that present, it was so well thought out, she had just rushed at her; she couldn't keep herself from expressing her love through a kiss when she had seen the vines running along the bow and the small birds, just like on her sword. Her chest screamed at her to go back and make things right, it ached so badly that her tears were running like rivers down her face and snot was building in her nose ready to start running as she choked back a sob running and stumbling her way back to the stream to get back to the mundane safety of her tunnel and the small family of Street Children that had gotten her through the darkest times.

    As Wren looked across the stream and to the vine-covered tunnel entrance, she tried desperately to calm her thoughts. Beginning to jump from rock to rock, she skidded and hit her knee against the last foothold sinking her leg into the freezing water. The shock from the cold worked to sober her thoughts as she picked herself up and focused on getting into the wall. Legs aching, she forced them to move as fast as she could bear to get past the vines and into the safety of the tunnel entrance. Crashing into the tunnel wall she let herself slide down to the floor, tears again running freely down her face, body wracked with the silent sobs mourning the loss of a friendship she knew would never be the same.

After what felt like hours, Wren was finally able to lift herself from the cold tunnel floor. All she wanted to do was sleep, emotionally and physically exhausted, she was sure things would be clearer in the morning. Staggering down the tunnels she tiredly reset the entrance to the tunnel; she made sure that it was hidden again properly.

Moving through the territory, she knew it was likely that she would end up bumping into one of her boys or Letta or god forbid one of her girls. Isla and Sofia had always been very loyal to Letta and for some reason just did not like Wren at all and had only just begun showing her some begrudged respect. Her face she was sure was puffy and red, eyes rimmed with pink, sore from crying and clothes dishevelled. It would be silly to think that the children would be asleep at this time of night when it was the best time to sneak around the city, it would be her lucky day if everyone other than the littles were out at this point. Lost in her thoughts she did not feel the eyes on her from the roofs of the buildings and as she journeyed through the seemingly abandoned streets, two sets of feet scampered across the roofs above her going to let Letta know of Wren's return.

Coming to her house, Wren knew she would need to be as quiet as possible sneaking in and to her room, there was no way that her father was still out at the tavern. She knew that if she didn't go to bed then she would be up pacing all night long pondering over what she had done and the implications of what she now considered to be one of the most important parts of her life. All she needed right now was to go to sleep and forget for a few hours.

Creaking open the door she looked around solely to see if her father was anywhere to be seen. The fire had died out, the room was cold and seemed empty, and sneaking further into her home she let the door whine closed behind her, wincing at the sharp click of the door shutting completely. The room was bathed in darkness as she held her breath to move slowly across the room heading towards her door. The silence was only broken by the eventual growl of a snore from her father's unconscious form spread across his bed, door swaying open with the slight breeze from his bedroom window.

Letting out her breath, Wren moved quickly now and flung herself inside her room, pausing only to gently close the door behind her; the last thing she needed tonight was to wake her slumbering father. Finally alone and in the abject safety of her own room, Wren flung herself onto her bed and let out a silent scream into her pillow, finally letting the full extent of her tears flow from her eyes, broken sobs rising from her throat as the horror of what she had done finally sank in.

Unable to help the thoughts that snuck into her head as she lay crying in the dark, Wren despaired over the ruined state of her life, the thoughts that had been trying to barge their way into her and make her lose courage now struck like knives in her chest as her sorrow poured from her eyes. Her thoughts flitted from one topic to another, this was no longer just about the devastatingly stupid way she had run from Faeryn without a word and just a rushed kiss, but had turned into so much more. Convinced that there was no positive outlook she thought to her father and mother. He had cared so little for her that turning to drink did not seem to bother him, it did not even seem to bother him that he had left his teenaged daughter to fend for herself. But why should he care when it had been his actions that had led to her having to fend for herself now with no mother to care for her? Wren had begun to doubt whether he even remembered beating her mother to death, it would make sense with how the guards had just let him go after questioning. She would never forgive him or the guards for that.

Her anger and despair extended out from there, to her mother who had left her, who hadn't fought back and had for years just taken the beatings that her father handed out, never once thinking to go to the guard with her bruises. Instead she taught Wren to fear, to spy, to creep and to be hidden. But she was so much more than a meek little mouse: she needed to be free, to laugh, and skip and have a childhood that was so mercilessly stolen from her. She was strong. She just wanted to be able to fight. She had never told anyone of this but, for taking the choice to fight away from her, Wren hated her mother and she knew that was wrong, to blame a dead person for their own death and her own misfortune but a hidden part of her believed that if she had only been able to fight then maybe, just maybe, she would have been able to save her. Then how different might their lives have been. She did not dare wonder truly.

Her anger, she had taken out on her training sessions. She had hit those trees over and over again hoping that somehow the world would change what had happened; that as if by her doing this she would be able to grow, to make change, to have her life back. To at least help others. She knew she wasn't the only one, the only hidden child, the only beaten down spirit. She had been so close to breaking when she had heard that snap. So close to giving in when a nest of auburn hair had risen from the opening in her clearing. She had never met someone so loud mouthed, so uniquely blunt and honest, so irrevocably beautiful. And she had wanted to meet her, she had called Wren her freedom and had made her feel safe for the first time.

And she had ruined it.

But when she had seen that bow and quiver, the vines engraved across them with little wrens worked into the vines, so life-like in the craftsmanship, she had felt the pull the strongest she had ever felt it and so had not felt her feet move forward or noticed the way that Faeryn had looked at her. She was clueless until warm, soft lips touched her own and the world had been set ablaze.

Eyes wide and tears staining her cheeks, Wren's hand came to her face and small fingertips came to her lips as she thought back to the kiss. Her first. She had never thought that it could feel like that, like she had never seen in colour before. Even as she remembered now it felt as if the world had been unmuted, that everything she saw was sharper now, so much more distinct. Was this the way that Iris felt when Jahed had gone to speak to her, was the heat and the tingles coursing through her skin the same feeling they all felt?

The kiss had lasted. Wren was sure that she had felt the move of Faeryn's lips on her own, kissing her back. She could see that now. But her fear had caused her to back away and run. Why could her courage have not shown its face then? When she had pulled away so abruptly she had seen Fae's eyes closed and she could not bring herself to wait to see the disgust in her green eyes when they opened. So just like that she had turned and left. Walking away from the first person she had ever really loved.

That night Wren did not remember letting sleep take over as she tortured herself with the memory of that kiss and her cowardice.

Morning broke with the sun streaming in shining directly onto Wren's sleeping eyes. Stirring, Wren's senses began to come back to her, and for a moment longer she was able to forget the previous night's events. Nose stuffy and eyes sore she lifted her body from the bed.

As her mind caught up with her body Wren let numbness wash over her. And like that a light went out in her eyes.

19

Wren

As time passed, Wren did not go back to the forest. She went about her days completing her routine, going to market, eating with the Street Children and going home to sleep. She refused invitations from her friends, even avoiding Letta's call as she left after evening meal on more than one occasion. She could not understand how she had let herself get in this deep, how she had not seen the signs that she was feeling; this was after years of being there for each other. Wren did not want other's pity, she did not want to face up to their kindness and soft words. She knew Letta would come out with some soft and seemingly nonsensical advice that always left her more confused than before. It was coming up to the next day that she was supposed to meet Faeryn at their clearing and she didn't know if she could do it. Everything had changed and she didn't know if she was strong enough to hear her Princess tell her that she could not see her again. So as she sat looking out across the market she let her eyes turn downward to mourn what she thought she had lost.

Having lost concentration for just one second she had given room for Aab and Ber to sidle up to her unnoticed. Feeling the weight of their shoulders she startled and pushed out at them on instinct. Pulling an almighty laugh from Aab as Ber tripped backwards from the force of her dominant hand.

"So what's up, Wren? We haven't seen hide nor tail of you

outside of evening meal for four days. Don't tell us you're getting bored of us!" said Aab as Ber righted himself.

"I could never get bored of you two, I've just been working through some things and I needed a bit of space. I promise I'll do better," Wren said with a sad smile. She really hadn't meant to make them feel like she was leaving them, they had all had enough of that for a lifetime.

"Ay, Ay, Ay, don't think you're getting away with it that lightly. That girl of yours giving you some trouble? Point us to the village and we will go have a word with her," Aab said with underlying seriousness as Ber nodded along.

"Too right, Aab. Wren, we'll sort it for you. Just tell us what's happening," Ber agreed.

Neither boy had noticed the slack jaw look take over Wren's face at the mention of "her girl" otherwise they would have known to shut up.

"IS THERE NO SUCH THING AS PRIVACY IN THIS GOD DAMN PLACE?" Wren shouted as she smacked both boys upside the head. "And just for your information, she is not my girl," Wren said with a much lower tone.

"Ahh so that's the problem, you haven't got the girl!" Aab said as he rubbed the back of his head, not fazed by her antics.

Wren put her head in her hands as she shrivelled up from Aab and Ber's scrutiny, mind racing. How could Letta have told them about Faeryn? Wren had thought it blindingly clear that it was a private matter with the way things had been left. Clearly not.

"Who told you? I swear to all that is holy I will kill Letta before the day is through," Wren ranted, feeling bolstered by her irritation.

"Wooooohh slow down theere, Ma, Letta didn't tell us

anything. Isla and Sofia seem to have a bit of a soft spot for us boys and it didn't take long for Ber to get it out of them after you and Letta disappeared the other week," Aab rushed out.

"Look I really don't want to talk about this, guys, I made a huge mistake and I just need to put this all behind me," Wren sighed, she just wanted to go back to not having to think about it. About her.

"Wren, you know you can talk to us right? I know we are only young but you've taught us everything we know and we're supposed to be family," Ber said quietly, looking at her with such intensity she could feel it in her chest, guilt taking its hold.

"I kissed her okay, I kissed her and I ran. Now can we leave it? I love you guys and we are family, yes, but some things I need to figure out on my own," Wren said, frustration straining her voice. She did not want to talk about this.

"You ran? Wow, okay, Wren. I mean, did she kiss you back? Why did you run? That's so unlike you. We'll leave you to it but look around you, Wren, you're not the only one who has same love," Aab said in disbelief not having expected that from his older friend. Patting her shoulder he signalled to Ber and they left her at her market stall, alone again with her thoughts.

Sitting herself back down, Wren let go of some of the tension that had collected between her shoulders during her conversation with the boys. She loved them but god they could be stressful sometimes. Packing herself up she knew she just wanted to sleep, she could think about what they had said another day. Skipping evening meal, she settled into her room, barricading the door with her bed and lay herself down to escape into her dreams.

Waking up with a start, Wren heard her father kicking out at what was sure to be the furniture in the living room; she hadn't prepared any food last night and had left him to fend for himself.

She knew he would be angry and that had been why she had barricaded the door before falling asleep and giving in to her depression. As she wiped the sleep from her eyes she pushed herself up and against the door, placing an ear against its wood to see if she could figure out exactly what was happening. She could hear the loud scuffling of her father pulling on his boots, the heavy footsteps as they passed her door and the scrape of the chair nearest the fire moving. For a moment she worried that he was going to sit down and she would be trapped here for the day. But as she took in her surroundings she noticed that sunlight was coming in from underneath the door and the window to her room. She had slept through his coming home last night and through till morning. He must be going out and back to the taverns, there's no way that he would stay here all day.

As she thought this the slam of the front door came and she sank back into her bed. It must be just gone dawn, she had time to make breakfast and get down to the market easily. Taking a moment to stretch out her tight muscles, she yawned and realised that she hadn't trained at all this week. Faeryn shouldn't be a reason for her to stop her training, like an imbecile she had stopped training completely despite knowing Fae only came to the forest to see her once a week. Shaking her head at her own stupidity she pulled on her clothes for the day and went to make herself some well-deserved food. She had always found it was easy to get lost in her thoughts when she was cooking, it wasn't something she would openly admit to others but chopping vegetables and browning off meat always soothed her and the repetitiveness of it all would lull her into a sense of contentment. It was here that morning, chopping up some greens to add to her eggs, that she thought over what Aab had said the previous day. "You're not the only one." It had seemed trivial at the time and she had barely even registered that he had said it in her agitated state. He couldn't have meant that there were others in the market village that were into the same sex, surely she would know, would have seen it at some point. She couldn't have been that oblivious, surely.

Going about her day at the market, Wren began to look out for what Aab and Ber had been talking about; she wanted to see for herself that she was not the only one. It didn't take long for her to begin to notice the steps, the glances and the slight touches that identified the same love across the market place: things she would never have even considered before came jumping out of her like a candle lit sign that she had been missing up until now. The girls across the way that she had always thought were fawning over the boys loading on and off the sacks of rice from carts and selling at the various stalls were actually a mix, some of them were looking at the other girls, one was looking on with sadness in her eyes as Iris and Jahed grew closer. Another one was looking on giggling and smiling with her friends towards the boys but her body was leant into her friend, her fingers brushing along the inside of her wrist lovingly. The boys they were looking at, some were looking back and admiring them, as clueless as Wren had been before but others ignored it completely preferring to lean in closer than necessary to each other to talk, side glancing together at the other boys with their shirts off and sweat dripping from their muscular figures. How had she not seen this before?

Light laughter bubbled up through her chest as she laughed full heartedly at how stupid she had been, of course Aab had been right, the little git. She quietened herself down when she noticed the odd looks from some of her fellow market stall sellers. Sitting squarely on her stall, she thought across her life, how blind she had been to this love, how hidden it seemed to be here in the market village and she wondered was it this way across the entire city of Ekoni? Why did they need to hide their love? It was wrong, just like how her father had gotten away with killing her mother because of who he was. The city was corrupt and she wanted to change it. She needed to get back to training, she couldn't let what happened between her and the Princess distract her from her end goal: the first female guard for the City. She needed to tell Faeryn about this. Wren knew she would never let this continue when she was the Queen, if she knew of what was happening that was.

It was time to return to the forest.

20

Wren

The emotional build up for Wren had been grand, she had gained an absurd amount of confidence as she charged to the forest that night, riled up by the thought that people like her had to hide their love within the city and Faeryn could change that. She had quite forgotten that seeing Fae, she would also get to give her a piece of her mind about their kiss and running away. As she sat in their clearing she began to worry about Faeryn's reaction, it hit her all at once that she had come here and she hadn't planned anything to say; she had just followed her emotions, letting her indignation carry her to this point. Hours passed and Wren thought of excuses as to why Faeryn was late. It took waiting until the sun was rising in the East casting bright light through the trees for realisation to hit her.

Faeryn wasn't coming.

Shock set in as Wren made her way back to the village, she had never thought that Fae wouldn't show up. There was no way that she just wouldn't come, not after the years they had been meeting up. This had happened once or twice before, but not when something so important was happening with them. She must have gotten in trouble and it was too dangerous to come down. Yes that's it, it must be. If she had been caught she would have been met with guards, but then again Faeryn was strong, she would never have given her up, she wouldn't risk it.

She would keep training and she would wait for Fae to come back and then they could talk.

About everything.

Determined to get herself back in shape after an entire week away from any form of training, Wren pushed herself harder and harder in an attempt to get stronger. She cut her sleep and rest time down, and trained twice a day, waking before her father to get out across to the forest some days in the morning before dawn or going and waking her boys to train in hand-to-hand combat with her as her usual sparring partner was missing. She had done a complete one-eighty turn on her behaviour from after her kiss with Faeryn and her friends didn't know whether to be more concerned now than they were before. She was barely sleeping, she looked bruised and tired but the market stall was selling more than usual, she was still eating and she wasn't isolating herself any more. They would just need to watch her carefully.

Wren knew what her friends were doing but she needed to do this. Days went by with her increased training levels and the day for her to see Faeryn came again. She got to the forest having practiced what she was going to say. She was just going to tell her she was sorry, explain how she was feeling and let her talk and she was going to listen. Pacing, she rehearsed her side of the imagined conversation and tried to keep her heartbeat steady. The moon rose in the sky and the darkness of the forest was creeping into the forest clearing and Wren began to think that Faeryn would be a no show again. She began to train, she needed to get some of her frustration out. She wouldn't bring her negativity back into the village again to her people. She needed to be understanding, think how she would feel if she was Fae. This would be just as hard for her as it was for Wren. She picked the bow and quiver set up that had been left here by Faeryn after

Wren's tantrum and began to nock an arrow to the bow. Picking a sturdy tree on the forest side she began her target practice. Her breaths had to be steady and even as she took aim and released her bow otherwise they could not hope to hit home. Losing herself to the practice she did not notice that the night had been left behind until the warmth of sunlight hit the back of her neck and glinted off her arrow tip. Sighing to herself as she lowered her bow and arrow, she began to pack away her things.

She didn't come. Again.

Pushing down Wren's disappointment had been difficult as she went about the next few days training just as hard, she could feel the strain on her body now but her determination just grew stronger the longer she watched the hidden touches and worried glances as hands were held for no longer than a second going on around her in the village. She wanted to include Faeryn in this, she wanted to share with her the injustices she had discovered, she thought it was time she told her the whole story of her family: her mother's death,. how the village was, how the guard dealt with everything. She wanted to make her understand what was happening. But if she didn't come back soon Wren was going to have to make a decision.

Time passed for Wren as if she was in a bubble and as her body grew tired so did her patience. Anger started to build up from within, resentment for the way Faeryn could just leave her like this, no nothing, not a candle in the window to say she wasn't coming. After everything she deserved at least a sign. She was not some dog waiting for a bone. And she would no longer act like one, waiting for a girl, no matter her title. If Fae didn't turn up this time she would make plans of her own. She needed to speak to Letta.

Storming to the Street Children's territory, Wren went in

search of Letta. She needed to talk to her about all the thoughts swirling around her head, the anger and the agitation about the state of the village and the restriction made upon people like her who were not able to show their love openly. This mixed in with her own internalised worry about Faeryn's reaction to her kiss. She was spinning out of control and she needed to be grounded. Faeryn and her time in the forest usually worked to do this but with Faeryn's absence, Letta would have to do. Rushing through the doors, ignoring the little ones and even Aab and Ber as they shouted a hello from across the room, she went straight into Letta's room without even a knock. On reflection this was a bad thing to do and she deserved what happened next.

Within a blink of an eye Wren was floored. Winded by the sudden fall and the hit of her back to the bare stone floor a strong hand wrapped around her throat and the breath of someone else hot on her face.

"Down, girl, it's only me. Let me go!" choked out Wren as she gripped the squeezing hand around her throat, trying to pull it off of her.

"Did no one ever teach you to knock, Wren?" came Letta's voice in reply. Averting her eyes from Isla still gripping at her throat, she looked to Letta sat idly at her makeshift desk.

"Jesus, fine, I'm sorry okay, just call off your handmaiden. I need to talk to you," Wren rasped out, still rolling her eyes.

"That's enough, Isla, you can let Wren go now," Letta said.

With a huff Isla loosened her grip before baring her teeth at Wren in a mocking way and pushing back down on her to gain momentum to jolt herself into a standing position sending a smirk at Wren when she grimaced at her movement.

"Now what was so important, Wren, that you felt you needed to rush in here and cause such a scene?" Letta said with a raised eyebrow.

Casting a glance at Isla, Wren wondered where her counterpart was, they were usually attached at the hip.

With that creeping thought she focused back on Letta and said meaningfully. "I need to speak with you in PRIVATE." Making sure to put as much emphasis on the word private as was appropriate.

"Oh for goodness' sake this better be good, Wren, Isla go and find Charlotte," Letta muttered in exasperation. Isla hesitated only briefly before making for the door.

Waiting for the door to close fully and giving enough time for Isla to have made it away from the room, Letta looked back to Wren. "Now what's going on?" she said lowly.

"This cannot, I repeat cannot, under any circumstances leave this room. Okay?" Wren whispered.

"Right, it's like that then. I swear it will not leave my lips after you leave here today," Letta said curiously.

"The girl, the one from the forest. She's not a village girl," Wren let out.

"What do you mean? Is she from the castle, a live-in servant or something?" Letta asked confused.

"No. Oh god, I don't know how to say this," Wren said, more to herself, looking to the ceiling. "Her name is Faeryn."

"You don't mean? No, that's ridiculous," Letta said as she began to put together the pieces, there were only a few people she knew of with that name and only one who did not live in one of the villages. "Please tell me this is some sort of elaborate joke, Wren."

Wren let out a bark of a laugh. "I wish, Letta, I wish. No, the girl I've been seeing for the last two years, she's the Princess. Except she's not with me, she's just Fae."

"She's the reason you've been so out of focus lately. Wren this is beyond dangerous, not just for you but for us. You cannot be fighting with the Princess. What would happen if she decided to turn against you? She could expose us all? What would we do then?" Letta ranted.

"Look she's not like that, Letta, no matter what, she would never do that to anyone let alone me. The main issue I'm having at the moment is that I kissed her and she hasn't turned up for the last two weeks to our meeting point. I know that it might just be too dangerous to come down or she could have gotten in trouble and can't get here but she hasn't exposed me and she won't," Wren let out, instantly defending Faeryn, despite the lack of presence over the last two weeks, her loyalty wouldn't just fade.

"Right okay, so besides you making an utter fool out of yourself because I presume you ran out on her because of your attitude lately. What's the actual issue here?" Letta said sceptically.

"The issue, Letta, is that I have been blind, lulled into a sense of security! We have all been surviving for so long that we forgot that we deserve to live. The way the guards treat us, the way they treat anyone who hasn't raised a sword for the last war. The way that love, like mine, has to be hidden and no one is truly free. Letta, look at the city, we are surrounded by a wall. Only those authorised are allowed in and out of the front gate. We are prisoners. It isn't right and it needs to change," Wren said confidently, voice becoming steelier with every word.

"Well effectively yes we are. It's been like this for as long as I can remember. What do you propose we do about it? And what does your Princess have to do with it? Other than the obvious fact that her mother is the reason we live like this," Letta replied.

"If I can get Faeryn onside we could have her make change in the castle. We could rise up with the support of the next in line for the throne. We could make change for the future," Wren said excitedly.

"If she shows up. You just said the last time you saw her you kissed her and then haven't seen her for two weeks?" Letta remarked thoughtfully.

"Right, but even if she doesn't come back, we need to do this, we need to find a way. We can't live like this forever," Wren reassured Letta. "Look, tomorrow night Faeryn and I are supposed to meet again. I will make it the last time. If she doesn't show up this time we can start planning for the future and how we are going to do this. All right?"

"Are you sure you're not just obsessing over this because you're frightened that she's rejected you after your kiss? Wren, you kind of did the same thing when Maggie died. I understand the need and where you're coming from but I think we need to think this through before you involve the Princess," Letta said worriedly.

"Don't be ridiculous, Letta, this is for the good of the city, nothing to do with my feelings for her. Like I said, one last time and then we plan without her okay?" Wren retorted defensively.

"Okay, all right," Letta sighed.

As Wren walked away that night, Letta's opinions swirling in her mind, she ran over in her head what she was going to say to the Princess. She wouldn't let her talk, she didn't want to hear the rejection that was already so keenly felt through her absence. She didn't need Faeryn for the uprising, to enact change, but it would make it a lot easier than it would be without her. She told herself this wasn't about her feelings for the girl; Letta was wrong.

The next day went by like a blur, Wren's focus clearly on the trip to the forest that she would make that night. It wasn't until she was at the end of the tunnel staring at the vines covering her exit out into the open that she began to feel the nerves set in. The fear and anguish rushing to fill her senses as she was assaulted with the memories of their last meeting. Frozen to the spot she carefully collected herself. When she left the safety of her tunnel she would be alone and she needed to keep her wits about her while making her way to the clearing. She mustn't act in haste as she had done before. Despite everything, and how well she knew the forest, it could always be a dangerous place, wild animals usually left her alone if she was careful and they never seemed to come near the clearing itself. Taking a last breath she broke out into the field, making for a natural sprint across the field to the stream, she glided across its rocks before bolting to the forest edge surrounding herself in the leaves of the thick bushes and trees around her. Filling her nose with the scent of pine and nature, she felt her body come to a natural poise. She was home. Smiling, she began the journey through the forest to the clearing, fingers brushing along leaves and feet walking carefully over the forest bed. There was a rightness about today as she picked up her wooden practice sword, bow and quiver from their hiding place in a tall hollowed-out tree and made the last move across the thick bushes and into the clearing to wait for her Princess.

21

Faeryn

When Faeryn came around she was met with the blinding brightness of the sun shining through the opening in the clearing. Her eyes hurt to open, red raw from crying. Her chest still sending jolting pains through her body and the pulling was still there underneath with the grief she was feeling. She knew nothing would be the same again. Not after last night. But the first overwhelming need she had was to get back to her castle. She would need to figure out a way to get back in and situate herself within the castle walls in a way that would excuse her absence, someone was sure to have found her bed and chambers empty this morning. Sighing and muttering out expletives, Faeryn cursed the way Wren had reacted to a simple kiss. It would have been fine if she had just stayed and we could have talked about it, what it meant. What did it really mean to her though? Did she like Wren that way? Or had it been a heat of the moment thing? If she had just stayed she wouldn't have been forced to come up with this elaborate plan that would inevitably end up in her being caught out somehow and punished. She pushed herself up and looked around her. The forest was still tarnished, not feeling completely like home without Wren here to be with. Wren had left her sword and birthday present out in the open as well, in her rush, so Fae went about tidying up, putting everything back in its rightful hiding place before sliding her way down the hill to the wall and back into her passageways.

Taking a moment to rest as she entered through the hidden opening of the wall she ran over in her mind what she would need to do in order to get back into the castle unnoticed. She would need to figure out exactly where to enter from as her own chambers were now out of the question due to the late timing of the day. There would be servants going in and out at this point freely, probably wondering where she was. Faeryn hoped to the high heavens that no one had reported to her mother that she was missing from her chambers this morning. Tobin would be the real problem, the brown-nosing earwig literally hung on every word her mother said. Faeryn began to make her way back through the passages, taking her time, in no rush to get caught and face punishment.

Again. She found her way to the guards' viewing window, her point of reference for the maze-like passage ways that she was sure she had not yet fully explored. Looking out she could see that the young guards were being shouted at, full training now in steady progress. She noted how they moved and thought back to her training with Wren. The guards seemed so unimpressive now that she knew more of swordsmanship and hand to hand combat. Wren moved so much more elegantly than these men; she always seemed to effortlessly glide across the clearing in their sparring and with every training session. Her muscles, straining, were defined in the shadows cast by moonlight whereas these men seemed stuttered, bulging beer bellies on half of them, and violent juddering hits to training dummies lacked the finesse she was used to from Wren's training. She thought then to the kiss and her hand came up unknowingly to touch her lips, they still felt warm from Wren's touch. Her musings were interrupted by her own irritation as it lashed out and through her as she brought her finger tips away from her mouth, Wren had left, she had left her in that clearing, confused, without a word. Shaking her head, Faeryn carried on, feet taking her to the fork in the passageways; she could either go to Tutor Tobin's rooms first or her mother's chambers. Either could be a legitimate option for entrance into the castle unseen.

Deciding upon her mother's chambers she knew that it would be best to see if her mother was tucked away in her rooms before she half blindly entered into another area of the castle. At least if she was here she wouldn't be at one of the other passage doors. Striding down the passageways, Faeryn tried diligently to keep thoughts of Wren from her mind. She was angry at her, and she wasn't sure how to feel about that kiss, her head was a pile of confusion at the moment and as she came to the door in her mother's room, she wondered if a kiss like that with Wren, a girl, was even able to go further than just a kiss.

Would her mother ever accept that? She had never even seen or heard really of liking someone of the same gender before. Was it allowed?

"I've never followed the rules before, why should this be any different?" she mumbled to herself as she put her eyes to the peeping hole in the wall.

Queen Koni was indeed sat in her parlour perched on the edge of a gold-lined chaise longue talking hurriedly and worriedly to a figure Faeryn couldn't make out sat in the arm chair facing away from her hiding hole but directly opposite her mother. Straining to hear, Faeryn put her ear to the hole, opting for blindness to gain insight into the conversation at hand that had her mother seemingly so disquieted.

"I don't know what to do, it seems like her mind is always somewhere else. She doesn't focus on her classes, she moves around the castle like a ghost. How can I put the weight of looking after the realm on her?" her mother said, voice hoarse.

Faeryn couldn't hear the low reply of the person in the chair that her mother was confiding in but she could imagine her mother's face as she took in the person's mumbled words.

"No, no she's not seventeen for months yet. I couldn't just marry her off. I need to give her time to come around. Maybe if I just spoke to her directly about it, made her understand?" her mother whispered.

Again came the mumbling indecipherable words of her mother's guest. Faeryn was beginning to get frustrated at the one-sided conversation and cursed the person for being so lowly spoken.

"No you're right, we don't have the best relationship, and she probably wouldn't take well to my being so direct with her about this. Maybe you could speak with her? Make it seem like a lesson?" her mother queried.

"A lesson? Hold the fuck up," Faeryn thought to herself. Taking her ear away from the peep hole she could see clearly now as the person leant forward to take her mother's hand.

"Of course, my Queen," came a male voice.

"Tobin, that fucking rat!" She could clearly see her tutor's face now. That grovelling imbecile was clearly sidling up to her mother for a reason. Why was her mother taking solace from her tutor? Why would she take advice from him? This didn't make sense. Too caught up in her thoughts, she missed the lingering eyes and touch of her tutor on her mother.

"Where is my daughter this morning?" her mother cleared her throat and asked.

Straightening up in his chair, Tobin too cleared his throat before responding, "I'm unsure, she's been unusually quiet today, I have lessons with her soon."

Faeryn didn't stay to hear the rest of what Tobin was saying. She had completely forgotten that she had extra lessons this week, she would need to get to Tobin's room and make out as if she was there waiting for him. No one would question that and Tobin was in her mother's rooms so definitely wouldn't be in his library. Running now, adrenaline coursing through her veins, she let go of the pain from the previous night and focused on the task at hand. It would be close and she knew that, Tobin was sure to be on his way there soon and she needed to get all the way back to the guard viewing window before redirecting her sprint towards his room.

Coming up to the door she knew led into his room, her very first entrance into the magic that was the passageways, she calmed herself before making to push the door open.

THUNK.

The door wouldn't move. It was stuck. "Shit," Faeryn whispered out.

Pushing harder, Faeryn began to panic. This could not be happening, not after the night she had had. A strangled wail escaped her lips and she ran at the door slamming her shoulder into the door.

BANG.

A thunderous bang came accompanied by a whispered scream as Faeryn came tumbling out of the door landing on top of a small bookcase. Quickly getting herself together and climbing off of the bookcase underneath her, she inspected the damage. What had possessed Tobin to move the damn bookcase there of all places? It was a mess. Quickly slamming her doorway closed she set to work trying to lift the heavy oak bookcase back in place, even without all of the books on it was still awkwardly heavy and Faeryn thanked the gods Wren had insisted on doing strength training every single god damn week since they had met. With a huff and a grunt the bookcase slammed back into place in front of her door. Rolling her shoulder and looking at the rest of the mess of books scattered across the floor, she sat herself down in the middle of them and began trying to put them back in a Tobin logical order.

The hairs on the back of Faeryn's neck stood on end and a slow creak announced the presence of another in the room and Faeryn scrunched her eyes tightly wishing that it wasn't Tobin walking in on her surrounded by scattered books, obviously up to no good. Hearing the sound of footsteps fading away, she smiled to herself and began to put the books back on their shelves, thinking that luck had been on her side today. Taking her time now, it wasn't until the clipped step of a heeled shoe on the marble floors caught her ear that she realised she was wrong. So wrong. Luck was most definitely not on her side. Tightening her shoulders to her ears, she prepared herself for the impact of the high-pitched screeching that would surely come out of either Tobin or her mother as soon as they caught sight of her and the mess she had made.

It never came. Instead as she slowly opened her eyes and relaxed her shoulders what she saw made her heartache deepen. Her mother stood in the doorway shadowed by Tobin, a single tear escaping her eye, leaving a trail of chalked make up behind weaving a pattern down her cheek. Tobin stood back, a small smirk of satisfaction on his face, feeling as if he had finally convinced the Queen of her daughter's clear inability to rule alone. Her mother opened her mouth slightly and whispered out, "Go to your room." Voice wavering only slightly giving away the destroyed emotions coming from within.

In shock Faeryn stood, head hanging low, and silently made her way across the castle back to her chambers. Contemplating on her way the way her mother had looked so disappointed, defeated. Faeryn had never seen her like that before. She had always been this powerful, untouchable, emotionless figurehead. She had never let her in past the mask, at least not while she knew she was awake and it felt like a knife to the heart. Fae never thought she could feel so much heartbreak in the span of twenty-four hours. It had been one hell of a time. And now she was once again confined to her room. Or at least she thought she was. Her mother hadn't been very clear on that. At least this meant she would have some time. She had too much to think about, she needed to figure out this thing with Wren before she saw her again and she definitely needed to figure out a way to have a full conversation with her mother that didn't include her mask. Or Tobin.

Coming into her room and lying down on the bed to stare at the ceiling, Faeryn let her own tears fall as the adrenaline finally drained from her system and the events of the last twenty-four hours finally began to sink in. A deep sadness settled itself in her heart and all she wanted to do was sleep. For the next week all she did was sleep, refusing to get out from her bed and barely eating she lost herself in herself to the void.

Laying there staring at her window she knew that today was the day she was due to go and see Wren. But she was still so mad at her for abandoning her in the forest.

She didn't want to have to face her. She knew that as soon as she looked into those ocean eyes she would give in and forgive her once more and she knew she wasn't ready for that yet. So she would lie here and she would stare at her window and she wouldn't put out her light, she would let Wren wonder and hope and be disappointed just as she had been. That kiss, the kiss had been good. It had been her first kiss. The first time someone else's warmth had filled her up and made her feel whole. Her lips had been so soft and they had made her melt into them, she had not wanted it to stop. That's all she knew, she didn't want it to stop. She didn't know if this meant that she felt more than attraction towards Wren but that was enough for now. She would figure out the rest on the way. There was no point in falling in love anyway, not with her mother talking about marrying her off to some nobleman.

Knowing that she would need to talk to Wren at some point and discuss the kiss, she settled on sneaking out to their spot when her punishment was over. She wanted her to understand the pain she had felt but she didn't want to lose her. Rolling her eyes at herself and letting out a frustrated "For fucks sake", Faeryn rolled out of her bed and slammed open her room door.

"Get my mother, now," she barked out to the guard who stood shocked at her appearance. "Please?" Faeryn urged. She knew she was going to have to play this right. She needed to get an end date for punishment, apologise to her mother and convince her mother that she could do better and that she would, but they needed to work together because things needed to change.

The guard scurried off, leaving a young man who was obviously shadowing the guard to watch over Fae.

Looking the boy up and down she realised that she recognised him, he was the same scrawny boy that had delivered her breakfast rather oddly a few years ago. She had scared him then and didn't think she would now.

"I've met you before haven't I?" she enquired of the boy.

Looking shocked to have been spoken directly to, the boy

gave a wide-eyed slight nod to confirm that they had indeed met and Faeryn was certain then and there it was the same lad.

"What's your name then? Might as well be on a first name basis if you're going to become one of my guards," Faeryn probed.

"Erm — right well, erm," the boy stammered.

"Oh come on spit it out," Fae laughed.

"Benji, my name is Benjamin, your highness," he finally came out with.

"Rule number one, Benji, when it's just us, I am just Faeryn," Fae replied, eyes shifting as the older guard came back followed by a rather agitated mother. Fae made her way back into her room knowing it wasn't wise to have this conversation with her mother in front of the men.

"Faeryn, what on earth is so important that you needed to have a guard collect me so abruptly? Couldn't you have just come to find me?" the Queen asked.

"Mother, if you remember rightly, you decided I needed to be confined to my room again. I was left with no choice but to send them to get you!" Fae retorted.

"Right, yes, yes I did," her mother sighed, clearly tired. "What is it you wanted?"

"I wanted to apologise," Faeryn spoke softly, her mother's eyes opening in shock. "I didn't mean to cause a mess in Tobin's rooms. I had every intention of going into the room and studying but when I went to pull out one of the volumes it tipped the whole bookcase and half the books came crashing to the floor! I was just starting to tidy it up when you came in. I am sorry it happened though, I know I'm a disappointment," Faeryn ranted, her improvised lie hitting too close to home.

Open mouthed, her mother studied her face in disbelief that

the girl sat in front of her was the same bad-mouthed daughter that had, since going into her teen years, been anything but interested in her studies and duties. Not wanting her mother to confirm her voiced thoughts, Faeryn continued on.

"Mum, I want to do better. I want to rule the realm as firmly and confidently as you have. I want to make changes and do my duty for our people. I just want to do it my way and I know I need to work with you on this not against you. I have just been feeling so trapped; I want to go out and meet the people. Our people." Faeryn's thoughts came tumbling from her mouth freely now.

Looking to her mother whose face now showed a mix of approval and concern she knew she was buying into what she was saying. "Maybe I could start working with you instead of resisting? Wouldn't it be better that instead of just sitting in Tobin's repetitive lessons that I could come and shadow you like the young men shadow the guards while training?" Faeryn raised an eyebrow and sat back against her desk chair now letting her mother have space to think.

The Queen looked on curiously at her, expressions conveying her emotions flitted across her face that Faeryn was unsure of what exactly her mother was feeling. Even more unsure of what emotion it would land on and how she would reply to Faeryn's first real expression to her mother. Fae knew this was about more than just getting out to see Wren now. She really did want to change the way things were and she needed to be honest with her mother and be persistent in reminding and talking to her in order to alter the way their lives were heading. She did not want to end up married off to some nobleman who would ruin the realm with insufficient rule. Caught up in her thoughts she startled when her mother spoke.

"I need to think about it, Faeryn; I need some time," her

mother spoke softly. "You are confined for one more week, and then I will come and discuss with you what I have decided on this topic." The Queen straightened now, mask coming back up, having decided on a course of action for the short term. With this, she stood and silently left the room leaving Fae smiling to herself.

Her mother had never listened to her before, not really. This was a massive step and Faeryn felt a sense of calm wash over as she thought of the way her life may be about to change. Her mind drifted to Wren then and she knew that no matter what, she would never want to be without her. They needed to talk. Soon.

22

Faeryn

The Queen's mandatory week of further confinement was nearly up and Faeryn was certain that the guards were not checking on her at all during the night. Tonight was also the day she was due to go and meet with Wren again. She had missed two of their last meetings: first, because of her own confused feelings and the second because of her mother's punishment. She wouldn't be missing this week's meet. The shadows had started jumping again every night after their absence for a few days after her and Wren's kiss. It seemed Wren had not been going out into the forest after what had happened. But their return had been quick enough and Faeryn was certain when she ventured out to the clearing tonight that she would find Wren there waiting for her.

As Fae made the journey to the clearing that night her heart seemed to be jumping out of her chest, excitement and longing mixed in with the ever present pulling in her chest and her emotions seemed to be overwhelming her. She barely even registered the passageways as she made her way into the crisp air of the night, taking her first steps outside of the wall in weeks.

Looking up she could see shadows moving against the moonlit trees, and her heart came to a standstill in her throat. Wren was back. Rushing to climb up the steep hill to their clearing, Faeryn grabbed onto the grass above and crawled on all fours to quicken the process. With some effort she made it to the top of the hill slightly out of breath, peering over the ridge, she looked in to see Wren thrashing away at a tree like the day they first met.

Climbing over soundlessly, Faeryn seated herself crossed legged on the floor watching Wren as she worked.

Fascinated as always by her strength and elegance as she moved, she waited silently for Wren to notice her presence. Watching as Wren made to spin around in a slashing sword movement, Faeryn smiled as Wren's face came into view and let out a slight chuckle as Wren's eyes widened as she finally noticed her there and she proceeded to trip over her own feet and stumble to the floor in front of Faeryn.

"Took you long enough, Wren. Anyone could have snuck up on you then," Faeryn laughed out, excitement now bubbling out of her. The pulling so strong in her chest that she felt she needed to step forward into Wren's personal space. Unable to resist, she quickly moved forward, holding her hand out to help Wren to her feet.

Grabbing hold of Fae's hand, Wren pulled herself upright and pulled Faeryn into her with the pull, so close that their bodies were flush against one another.

"Look who's talking, Princess," Wren quietly mumbled out, eyes shifting between Faeryn's own and her lips before softly clearing her throat and moving to take a step backwards.

Faeryn felt her body against Wren's and was unable to quieten the roaring heat within her own, skin prickling from the proximity, there was no denying that she found Wren attractive, no denying that at this moment the warmth spreading across her body wasn't for Wren. She was still unsure if there was more to this feeling other than attraction and lust but she would need to talk about it with Wren herself. As she felt more than heard Wren clear her throat and begin to step backwards, she was panicking. She was not ready to lose the heat of her touch or the feel of Wren's breath on her skin and so she stepped forward as Wren stepped backwards and as she looked up her eyes locked onto Wren's lips and without further thought she captured her lips with her own. Wren's lips were as soft as she remembered, leaning further into the warmth that the lips gave her she gripped onto Wren's shirt and began to deepen the kiss. She wanted to feel the taste of her tongue with her mouth, and to her surprise she found little resistance, taking the taste of spice and pine in as her tongue twirled around Wren's, a small moan breaking out from her lips as she moved them against Wren's. Her moan broke the silence between them and like déjà vu her body became instantly cold, her eyes closed, she didn't see but felt it as Wren pushed back again and away from her. It took moments before she could bring herself to open her eyes again to what she knew would be an empty clearing, not wanting to let the pain in her chest release itself and end with her on the forest bed crying out again.

Slowly she felt her chest relax, the pulling had been quietened by the kiss, and had not returned with a vengeance and in confusion she began to open her eyes.

As her eyelids fluttered open she was met with the tilted head of confusion from her best friend, stood not but two steps away.

"I thought you left me again," Faeryn stated.

"I'd never leave you, Fae, maybe the forest, but not you, not really." Wren's voice reached her in hushed tones as if her words were a secret she was only just about willing to share. "I thought perhaps it best that we talk first, there's been a lot left unsaid," Wren continued while playing with her fingers, a nervous habit Faeryn had noticed appear a lot more often over the last year.

"Christ, of course, yes talk. That's what I came here to do and then you distracted me with all of your youness. Yes, entirely your fault. Talk," Faeryn replied rather manically as she realised she had just done exactly what Wren had done last time they had seen each other, spontaneous kiss and all; it was a miracle that no one had gone and run off again.

Wren stood amusedly looking at Faeryn, clearly taking in her flustered demeanour before opening her mouth to speak. "I have two different things to talk to you about. First of all I think it's clear anyway but I will say it regardless, I like you in more than an 'I just want to be friends' kind of way. I'm hoping that kiss, amazing by the way, means that you are feeling the same way and I've been an idiot to worry," Wren spoke seriously looking to Faeryn to reassure her of her assumption.

"Well, erm, you see, shit this is hard. I am definitely attracted to you. Yep, definitely attracted. But the thing is, you're my first real friend and I haven't quite figured the 'I like you more than friends' bit out in general yet. I will need some time, I think," Faeryn replied confusedly, she didn't want to lose her friend and even though she knew she liked Wren she didn't want to share that until she was a hundred percent in case something happened and it broke them apart.

Wren seemed to weigh this up as she paused to think over what Faeryn was saying. "Okay, I understand that, I don't mind waiting for you to figure that out, we could go about our meetings as we have been doing and just see where things go? Maybe having the door open will help you figure this out?" Wren compromised with her.

"Soooo, I can kiss you?" Faeryn said as she stepped forward back into Wren's personal space, testing her limits and waiting for Wren to talk.

"Yes…" Wren said, taking a slight step back to keep focus. "But, Faeryn, this is important. Listen to me, okay? I need to discuss something with you," Wren whined out, self-control clearly being tested.

Narrowing her eyes, Faeryn looked into Wren's own and, seeing the seriousness taking over her expression, sat herself down once more to the floor and motioned for Wren to join her.

"Now tell me what's got you so rattled. It must be important if it's taken over from this which had you running out of here so quickly before," Faeryn asked once Wren had settled beside her.

"Right, this is long and I want you to just listen before you say anything, once I've finished you can ask anything you want, and talk to your heart's content, okay?" Wren looked to Faeryn and waited for her to nod to confirm she would do as asked. Upon receiving a slight tilt to her head she continued, "Nothing is right in the city of Ekoni. Things need to change, they have to change. The wall doesn't just keep you in or our enemies out, your own people are trapped in the walls, a select few guard will be let in and out to deal with trade before bringing it in the gates themselves and helping themselves to a portion of the produce. The people in the villages are not happy. The orphans of those who died in the Pirate Wars were left to fend for themselves; they have to look after each other, it's never safe for them and I am certain if I hadn't have been helping them out these last few years they would have had to resort to thieving just to live. The guards do not care for us, or their duty, not in the villages. And same love — when two girls or boys like each other — is having to be hidden away from others and people are forced to hide who they are because of this. There is no clear law against it, just words and implications from other laws that make it impossible to live out in the open with your love. The people are getting restless, the Street Children are growing up and they want change. We want change," Wren spoke passionately breathing heavy as she tried to read Faeryn's shocked face. "We want your help, Fae, help us make change for a better future... Please," Wren continued quietly.

Faeryn considered what had just been thrown at her. She had had no idea that things had been getting on so badly in the villages. If she thought about it she didn't really know anything of the goings on down there and outside of the castle other than the odd talk she had overheard while out in her passageways. She felt shame take up space in the bottom of her stomach as she realised that she should have been working to ensure she was fit for the throne when the time came, it should not have taken her this long to get serious. How could she help Wren and the others now? She wasn't in a position to enact change, not yet, and she likely never would be if her mother decided against the proposal Faeryn had given her last week. Realising Wren was waiting for an answer and noticing the slowly increasing look of worry on Wren's face, she let out a slight cough to give herself a minute and organise her thoughts.

"I had no idea how bad it was. I want to help you but how? It's my mother who oversees the goings on around the realm. I don't really have much to do with it yet." Faeryn worried her lip. Not wanting to tell her of the proposed changes in her royal tutelage and raise Wren's hopes if her mother said no.

A smile of relief and joy spread across Wren's face as she spoke, "Okay, good, this doesn't have to be now this is just the beginning but the fact that you want to help and make change possible is enough. You're the next leader, you are the next Queen, Faeryn. Just knowing that you want things to change will make everyone happy. There is so much we can do and we will be able to make a plan now, a realistic one. Thank you, Princess," let out Wren gratefully.

Faeryn studied Wren's face, seeing that this was something that Wren was truly serious about, and how truly important it was to her, she brought a hand to Wren's face and traced the side of her cheek with her fingertip.

"I told you not to call me Princess," Faeryn whispered as she leant forward and placed a light kiss to the end of Wren's nose.

23

Faeryn

Leaning back on her hands, Faeryn inspected Wren's face; she seemed more relaxed now than she had ever really seen her in the last 2twoyears. The silence between them comfortable, Faeryn began to think about how much she actually knew about Wren. Today had been the first time she had spoken about any specifics of her life down in the village; before this, all Faeryn really knew about her was the fact that her mother had died and she wanted to become a guard. The guard thing made a bit more sense now that she had shared the fact things weren't great, she'd be able to help people if she got into the guard. But until today she hadn't known nearly anything, and thinking about it now, she hadn't really shared anything with Wren either. They had both been so desperate to get away from their everyday lives that they had left each other out of their own realities. Wren had taken the first step unknowingly to including Faeryn in her reality and now Faeryn needed to give that trust back.

"My father was a great man, if there's anything that I've learnt during my lessons it is that he was a great man. My tutor Tobin, his family has been with ours from the beginning of the realm, or so it has been written, he taught me of the plans my father had, the things he put in place when he was a young man. Things would have been so different. And then the Pirate King arrived." Faeryn started looking off into the night's sky, feeling

Wren tense slightly at the mention of the Pirate King and her father.

Sighing, Faeryn continued on, knowing that Wren needed to hear this; she needed to understand. "I was nearly three turns when we won the war. My mother likes to remind me that my father gave his last dying breath to ensure that the Pirate King died with him so that we would be free. My earliest memory is of her telling me that story and as I got older and more adventurous, the look on her face got darker, the walls came up and eventually I wasn't allowed to leave the castle any longer." Fae looked to Wren now, trying to read her eyes, did she understand?

"I am a lot like my father I am told — by my mother more than anyone. Too much for my own good. She's not changed a thing since his death, she's stuck in time, only changing things to make sure they stay the same, and to keep me safe. She's terrified that someone will rise up in the name of the old Pirate King and come from the Unknown to start war again. And so I am kept inside the castle; the wall has stayed up and its gates closed and the realm has been left to stay unmoving while its people grow frustrated." Faeryn's head dropped at this last part unable to hide the conflict of emotions settling within her, she could understand her mother's actions to a degree but she didn't know why her mother couldn't see that things needed to change before it was too late.

"But you couldn't help that, Fae," Wren insisted, clearly taking issue with her mother's treatment of her, regardless of its reasoning.

"I do know that, it's just hard to remember sometimes," Faeryn murmured.

"Tell me more about your lessons, Tobin sounds like an

interesting man," Wren asked to distract Faeryn from her dour mood.

"Ha, is he fuck. Tutor Tobin is one of the most traditionalistic monotone boring men I have ever had the displeasure to know in my life," Faeryn barked out in laughter. Wren could tell she had hit a sore spot and kept quiet waiting for Fae to continue on. "The man has been teaching me since my tenth turn and he refuses to teach me anything other than my own family history, or at least how he has written it. He won't teach me anything of the world outside, the Pirate Wars that my own father died in, the man is controlling and limiting and what's worse is I am now convinced that he holds some sort of influence over my mother," Faeryn ranted, face reddening in her anger.

"…What do you mean, Fae? Why would your tutor be influencing the Queen of the Realm?" Wren asked, concerned.

"Well, you know the passages I used to get outside of the wall? They run all over the castle itself. It seems my ancestors were either a little paranoid or we already had servants' passages when we built new ones? I'm unsure, anyway, they're how I get around unseen and there are hidden windows and doorways into some of the different rooms across the castle. One of which looks into my mother's rooms. Anyway, I've seen them talking in there, far too close for comfort, and the way she was with him, I've never seen her so submissive before." Faeryn trailed off.

"It could be nothing, Fae. I mean if his family's been with yours for so many generations there is bound to be some level of familiarity isn't there?" Wren stated.

"I suppose. He just treats me like I'm so stupid and I am sure he is the reason my mother thinks I don't know our history or my duty. I'll show her though." Faeryn smiled half-heartedly. "It's issues with him that I keep getting in trouble for, and trouble means confinement in my room and the times I haven't been here on our day has been down to those punishments and not being able to sneak out. I felt so alone before I found you," Faeryn finished.

"Maybe one day when we've changed things we could go and see the realm together," Wren said softly.

"I'd like that." Faeryn smiled at Wren's sincere expression.

"Right, now that's done with, why don't I show you what I've learnt with this bow set a very pretty young lady got me?" Wren asked, standing up with a smooth wink and smirk. Fae watched as she held out her hand to help her stand up.

Faeryn watched as Wren went to go and pick up her bow and quiver from across the clearing, forgotten as soon as she had gained Wren's attention after arriving in the clearing that evening. She went to go and join Wren as she saw her swinging the quiver over her shoulder and testing the string on the bow with the right hand.

"Right, now look, see that tree on the other side of the clearing, the one with the small berry bush at the base of its trunk?" Wren asked. Faeryn nodded her affirmation quickly and focused in on what Wren was trying to show her. "Okay, so watch this." Wren moved her to the side slightly, nocking back an arrow and drew back the bow string. Eyes narrowed and focused in on the tree, with two steady breaths she released the string sending the arrow hurtling forward, slicing through the air before hitting the tall oak dead centre with a thud.

"Well shit, I've only been gone a few weeks, how did you do that?" Faeryn asked in disbelief.

"Practise I guess." Wren shrugged with a bright smile plastered across her face, grinning at her with pride. "Here let me show you how to do it," Wren continued.

Before Faeryn could get a handle on what was happening Wren had grabbed onto her hips and spun her around placing the bow into her hands and settling against her back, breath tickling her neck as she tried to concentrate on keeping the weight of the bow upright in her hand.

"Fantastic, Fae, and then look here is the arrow, put the tip against the little notch in the wood and put the end against the bow string here. Look how I hold it," Wren said, reaching her arm further around Faeryn to demonstrate the correct way to hold the arrow against the bow string. "See, index finger, this one near your thumb, on the string above the arrow and then the bottom two underneath. Keep the little one curled into your hand, mind. Pull it back," she said. Wren pushed her body closer against Fae, lifting the body to eye level and pulled the bow back before whispering "and release" before letting go of the bow string and sending the arrow hurling once again into the wood of the tree.

Wren moved away and went to collect the arrow. Letting out a breath Faeryn didn't know she was holding, she hadn't realised when she admitted her attraction towards Wren that her body would give into the heat and jittery excitement that tended to rise up when they were in close proximity. Clearing her head of the fog that had clouded her mind, she watched as Wren came back to her.

"Now you give that a try on your own," Wren said amusement covering her tone.

Faeryn repeated what Wren had shown her and with only a small amount of effort hit the tree dead centre with a loud thud. Looking around proudly to Wren she was delighted to see her staring at her in open-mouthed shock.

"But how? It took me a week to get it to hit the tree!" Wren whined.

"Natural talent?" Fae answered with a slight chuckle to her voice and a tilt of the head. "I have something to show you too by the way," she said as an afterthought. "I told you about the passageways, well there is one of the viewing windows in the wall of the guards' training courtyard, so I can see in and watch them train. I've wanted to try this for a while, I saw this young guard called Benji doing it and I wanted to give it a go," Fae explained to Wren going to exchange the bow and arrow for the wooden practice sword.

"Okay…?" Wren responded.

Faeryn moved to the middle of the clearing and leant back on her right foot bringing her left foot forward thinking back to how she had seen Benji make this movement. Following her thoughts, she allowed her body to move of its own free will. Crouching low on her right foot she swung her left around and out to the side of her body before jumping slightly and twisting her body around as her left foot moved underneath her right. Bringing her sword arm to follow slashing diagonally through the air, she spun to a stand, chest heaving from the unfamiliar movement. She had no idea if she had done that right but she had at least gotten it close to what she had seen. Walking steadily over to Wren she waited for her feedback.

"Well, it looked amazing. I have no idea though if it would work in an actual fight with someone. I've never seen anything like that before," Wren said animatedly.

"I'm glad you liked it, Miss know it all," Faeryn joked back. "But seriously, I want to see if we can work it into our sparring, it felt amazing!" Fae replied.

"Okay, yeah, I'll have a think about what we can do and we can try it out next week," Wren said looking out across the clearing and to the sky. "Ah, Fae we should probably get back now though, the night's almost over," Wren observed sadly.

Faeryn looked out and with a frown realised Wren was right, the nights seemed to be getting shorter and Fae found the thought of saying goodbye hurt. Awkwardly she looked up to Wren, the spell they had been under all evening cracking and she didn't know how to say goodbye: should she hug her or maybe this new thing meant she should kiss her now? The confusion must have been clear on her face because for the first time tonight Wren leant forward and placed a kiss on her lips. The kiss was soft, it felt as if Wren was pouring all of her feelings into the kiss and Fae was left unable to catch her breath from the intensity of it. Pulling away flushed she let out a high-pitched, "Bye, Wren." Before awkwardly waving and moving away to go back to the castle.

24

Wren

Grinning, Wren watched as Faeryn disappeared over the ridge and down the hill to the wall, she could not believe how well tonight had gone. Letting out a loud laugh and spinning around, raising her chin and looking at the tree tops and stars, she let her joy bubble up and come out easily. Never had she thought that this would have happened. Faeryn had agreed that change needed to happened and even more surprisingly she had kissed her. Wren had half convinced herself that Faeryn wouldn't feel the same way and that they would both need to agree to just forget what had happened. Her entire body felt like it was tingling and unable to let go of the happiness she had gained from that night she stowed away her sword and bow and quiver before beginning to make her way down to her own area of the wall.

With a spring in her step Wren made it easily to her tunnels, almost skipping through them as she made her way to the exit. Pushing the burlap sack to the side and shoving the bookcase across, she quickly righted everything before making her way through the Street Children's houses, smiling and stopping to help the younger ones where needed. She saw Letta watching her with a curious face, but not wanting her to put a damper on her good mood she decided she would wait until the following day to tell her that Faeryn had decided to help them and of her own personal success with their conversation. Right now all she really wanted to do was go home and get some rest before having to get up again for the market. Aab and Ber would be setting up for her like every day after her meetings but she would still need to go down for the actual day and help to sell and order in new stock etc.

Jumping across the rooftops of the village she mused over the night she had had and what was to come. She knew that everything was about to change. There was no way things would be the same. She would be able to work with Letta and the boys and maybe even Isla and Sophie too to come up with a long-term plan to improve the lives of everyone in the realm and Faeryn was the key. Maybe she would be able to sneak Faeryn into the Street Children's territory one night and introduce her to them.

That might be a bit too dangerous, but perhaps she could convince the others to come out to the forest to meet Faeryn one night. It would have to be somewhere other than the clearing, that was her and Faeryn's special place, but she was sure she would be able to find somewhere.

This was the start of something incredible. Her thoughts turned to Faeryn and the conversation she had shared with her; she knew things about her now that she never really thought she would find out, maybe it was time she told Faeryn how her mother died. It would be something she would need to think about, it's not the same as just talking about the way her life had been and has been. It was darker, much darker than she thought Fae would ever be used to. What would the future hold for them if Faeryn did indeed say that she had real feeling behind her attraction? Despite that being what Wren wanted to hear, she couldn't help but feel that they would be doomed from the start. They would be able to see each other once a week like they have been doing but what then? What when Fae turned seventeen?

When she'd be expected to marry and continue the Ekoni bloodline, the realm has to have a ruler after all. Wren wouldn't be able to just sit there and watch would she? The changes they wanted to make wouldn't come in time to stop any of that from taking place, she knew that. But she was getting ahead of herself, she thought, as she climbed down to the street from a roof top near her home. She didn't even know if Faeryn would develop feelings here, hell she didn't even know if this was anything more than an infatuation for her. Fae had always been this escape for her, the one time she was able to act truly herself and forget about the responsibility she had inside the walls. It was no wonder she had developed this attraction towards her. Wasn't it?

Mind spinning, she pushed open the door to her home rather roughly not thinking to be more careful and check for her father as she walked into the main room of the house. Still looking down and going over the night's events and how things would be able to move forward, she didn't see her father swaying next to the fireplace with an empty bottle in hand before he was charging at her growling out incomprehensibly.

Wren on instinct was able to step out of her father's path as he hurtled towards her, he went to swing his arms around to grab at her shirt but was met with thin air moving through his fingertips as she once again moved out of his grasp. This is one of the many things she had been training for since the death of her mother. The day he decided to do the same to her as he had done to Maggie that night. Wren wanted to blame herself, this was the first time in years that she hadn't been careful entering her home. She had just assumed that he would be at the tavern like always, she still had another hour or so before they closed. She didn't even consider that he might be here already. Why was he here already? she thought as she stood staring at his panting form trying to awkwardly push himself up from the floor where he had landed when he staggered to grasp onto her.

"You ungrateful child, you're disgusting, no child of mine. Need to be taught," he slurred out, unable to string a sentence together. He was looking rather green around the edges, Wren decided.

"Ryn, you need to go to bed, we don't need to do this tonight." Wren tried to defuse the situation, keeping in her anger the best she could as she balled her hands into fists, nails digging into her palms to keep her focused.

"I'll give you bed, it was your whore of a mother who taught you to be this belligerent towards your betters. Fucking disgusting," Ryn ranted out at Wren, seeming to have gained some semblance of sobriety in reaction to her words.

At the mention of her mother the small hold on her temper that she had burst open and Wren stepped confidently forward grabbing onto her father's wrist stopping the unbuckling of his belt.

"What did you just call my mother?" Wren gritted out between her teeth, face tense, gripping tightly to the wrist she had hold of.

Unperturbed, her father narrowed his drunk eyes at her and slurred out, "She was a fucking whore." Before shaking off her wrist and going to push her down. At this, Wren thought of the movement she had seen Faeryn do that very same night and quickly ducked down to avoid the blow her father was trying to deal. Swiping her leg around as quickly as she could, she was able to build enough momentum to swipe his legs from underneath him. Unable to stop her movements now as she heard the bang of his body hitting the floor, she twisted her body as she remembered Fae doing and flew through the air, arm coming down as if with her sword, fist hitting her father squarely in the chest as her feet landed comfortably to the side of his downed body knocking the wind straight from his lungs. As her father spluttered for breath underneath her, a wave of confidence overtook her and she chuckled lightly as she realised Faeryn's movement did indeed work in sparring and she would be able to tell her so next time she saw her. Wren's smile slowly fell from her face and was replaced by a stern frown as she focused back on her father.

"My mother was not a whore. She was a saint and you were lucky to have had her love," Wren whispered down at him vehemently. Still in shock, Ryn lay in silence staring wide-eyed up at his daughter, vomit rising up in her throat as she continued, "You are nothing but a failure. You murdered her, your own wife, you came back from the war and you failed. You drank so much that any piece of the man you once were disappeared in the booze. You treated us so badly that we did not want to come home yet she still looked after you, night after night. She taught me to be strong, she taught me to fight for what I believe in and she taught me to walk in silence, to be quiet, when I need to and to be as loud as a beast when required. I am your daughter but I am here in spite of you," Wren said voice raising with every word, passion behind each syllable, a hardness to her tone that even she was surprised by.

Looking down at her father she could see that he would not be able to get up of his own accord, his moment of sobriety clearly knocked from him as he sunk into his pit of self-despair.

"Goodnight, Ryn," she hissed out firmly before turning and walking away to her room. Wren did not even stop to turn around when she heard the quiet splutter gurgled out from her father's place on the floor. She would not give him the benefit of her help, not now, not ever.

She had not planned what she had said to him. In fact, she had quite hoped that she would never have to have an actual conversation with him again. But she felt good about what she had actually said. Maybe now would be the time to get out on her own, leave behind the house with all of the reminders of what he had done to her mother. She would talk to Letta in the morning about it along with her discussion with Faeryn. It would help their cause, and give them more time for planning everything, that was for sure. Falling asleep that night, Wren felt real hope taking over as she drifted into her dreams.

25

Wren

Sun streamed in from the bedroom window, casting a strip of yellow across Wren's eyes. She squinted in response, eyes fluttering open, feeling well rested for the first time in months. Moving to sit up and feeling confused she looked up to the window. Sun light. Listening more carefully she could hear the hustle and bustle of the streets and the slight murmur from the market down the road. Confusion made way to clarity, she had slept in. In shock Wren rushed to get up quickly, she was meant to meet Aab and Ber at the market to sort out the order for the following week and ensure that sales were on target for the day and help look after the day so they could grab some food.

    Pulling on her shirt and britches in haste she stumbled out of her room; noting the closed door of her father's room, she hesitated and slowed her movements. Usually he just left the door open after stumbling out in his haze to get to the taverns for opening. Moving to push the door open, unable to keep a hold of her curiosity, looking through the open doorway she wasn't surprised to see the bed an empty mess. Shaking her head and laughing at her own paranoia she moved back out of the doorway and walked down the small hallway to the living area. As she looked around the room she felt off, everything was in the same places as she had left them the previous night, normally things would be moved as her father came through to grab some food and make his way out again to the taverns.

Moving further into the room she looked around towards the dining area and her breath caught in her throat.

Lying in the same spot as she had left him last night was her father. Skin deathly pale and lips tinged blue, his chest wasn't moving and the soft drunken snore she usually heard from his room not present. On closer inspection there was a small pile of sick right next to his head. Wren felt that maybe she should have checked on him once more before going to sleep last night. As she realised the situation she was in, anger began to boil inside of her; this was not the way that she wanted things to end, she was supposed to become a guard, expose him for the man he truly was and he was supposed to be punished, death was just too easy for him.

Sitting down in one of the dining chairs, Wren put her head into her hands; she had no love left for the dead man on the floor but she couldn't help but feel some ambivalent force was messing with her. She needed to figure out what to do. First thing she knew she would need to do is report his death to the guard, it was pretty clear what had happened here and she didn't think she would have much problem with them. Then she would need to figure out what to do next, the house she was certain would be hers, her mother had ensured they owned the property when she was still very young.

With one last look at her father's body laid out on the floor Wren stood and took her leave from the house, taking the long, cobbled road up to the guard house, mind blank, unable to process exactly what was happening. Coming to a stop outside the door to the Guard house she puffed out a heavy breath before putting up her mask and entering the building. There were two guards on duty at the front of the house, neither she recognised and as she walked up to them they both looked up at her with irritated faces, clearly not wanting to deal with anything other than the card game they had going on in between them.

"Hello, my name is Wren Lao, I have found my father dead this morning. I am here to report his death," Wren spoke out strongly, unwilling to show how uneasy it made her being back in here after the way they treated the investigation of her mother's death. Her words had clearly gotten their attention and they looked to one another recognising her last name before one stood and made his way into the back of the house and the other stood to address her.

"Wait right there, he has just gone to get the Sergeant; he will want to hear about this," the guard stated in clipped tones. Just as he finished what he was saying the other guard came back through the door followed hotly on his heels by the Sergeant. The exact same Sergeant that had come storming through that door when she had reported her mother's murder years earlier. She had later found out his name was Sergeant Rakoff, he had served with her father during the Pirate Wars, he had come back a hero having seen very little fighting and her father had come back a drunkard scared with the memories of defending this pompous man. The Sergeant owed her father, and Wren wondered more often than not if that is why her father was never jailed for her mother's murder. As she looked at him come through in his shining uniform she realised this might actually be a longer process than she intended.

"Right, what's going on here then?" Sergeant Rakoff asked with a smirk.

"My name is Wren Lao and I am here to report my father's death," Wren repeated, trying desperately to keep her anger inside. She hated this man for what he had done and his attitude made her want to knock some sense into him.

"How did Ryn die? We only saw the man in the Tavern last night," I Sergeant enquired.

"It looks like he choked on his own vomit, I found him on the floor of our dining space next to his own vomit this morning," Wren reported, voice monotone.

"Take us there at once, Miss Lao," Sergeant Rakoff commanded her, anger seeping out into his voice.

Wren led them down the cobbled pathway to her home in silence, wanting this all to just be over with before her anger and frustration became too obvious to the guard. Arriving at her front door, she shoved the door open and then stepped to the side to let the guards do their work. Sergeant Rakoff led three of his guard through the door she had opened and shut it behind them. Wren huffed out a disapproving sigh before leaning herself up against the front wall of her home. A stark difference to how she had acted when they had come to look at her mother. It didn't take long for them to cart off his body and for the Sergeant to follow them out of her home.

"Miss Lao, we would like to bring you in for questioning," he told more than asked. This had been the last thing Wren had expected to hear from his mouth, she should have known he would pull something like this. She knew of course that they would not be able to charge her with anything: they had no evidence and it would be too obvious if they tried to jail her without any.

"Lead the way, Sergeant," Wren spoke clearly with nothing more than a shake of her head.

It didn't take long for them to get back up the hill to the guard house and for the first time she was led through the front of the building into the back and into a little room with a table and two chairs. This was clearly supposed to be imposing, but came across similarly to the back room of a tavern that was being used for some dodgy dealings. Taking a seat without waiting to be asked, Wren crossed her legs one over the other and waited for the Sergeant to arrive to get on with his questions. It quickly became apparent that she was being held for much longer than just a few quick questions. She could feel boredom setting in after she was sure the light from under the door vanishing meant that the day was coming to a close. Hours went by and her stomach began to rumble loudly at her and she just sat and waited. There was no way that Wren was going to let them break her, she would be able to wait them out, they had no idea what real guts looked like. She was a survivor.

It wasn't until she could make out the whisper of drunken men across the village that the Sergeant came shuffling in through the door and raised an eyebrow at her apparent calm demeanour. Sitting down heavily he looked her in the eye and began his questioning.

"Tell me again how you found your father?" Rakoff asked.

"When I woke up I went into the main area of the house, I found him near the dining area, he was laying still, I could tell he wasn't breathing, I moved closer, his lips were blue and there was vomit next to him. From there I came to the guard house and reported his death," Wren repeated what she had told him earlier that day.

"And when was the last time you saw him before his death?" Rakoff enquired, not put off by Wren's confidence.

"I saw him in the middle of the night. I came in after having been out to see friends just after he had arrived home from the taverns. Words were exchanged and then I went to bed," Wren said curious as to where exactly Rakoff was leading.

"And do words often lead to bruises, Miss Lao?" Rakoff grinned slyly now.

Wren looked at the man with a head tilt in the slightly unnerving way that Faeryn would sometimes look at her when she wanted something. Sergeant Rakoff clearly thought he had caught her off guard with this question.

But she knew she had left a bruise on her father's wrist and she also knew that with her previous statement on how her mother had died and some of the training bruises she had that she could show them and pass them off as being from her father, they would have no case.

"When the conversation is with my father then yes, Sergeant, you know more than anyone that he often used his fists to get the point across," Wren stated raising her own eyebrow at him, hinting heavily at the state Sergeant Rakoff had seen her mother in when he went in to take her body away after her murder.

Ears turning pink and neck slowly flushing, Sergeant Rakoff went to stand.

"Why you," was all he was able to get out before he was interrupted by the slamming of the door opening. A young guard in training came through rushing to hand over a note to the Sergeant. Rakoff took the note with a snatch and proceeded to read the report that had been given to him. Face going pale he looked back to Wren and begrudgingly grunted out "You're free to go."

"What? You've kept me in here for hours and now you just want to let me go after two questions. What changed huh?" Wren shouted out, pushing her luck.

"Liver failure" the Sergeant murmured before chucking the piece of paper at her and charging from the room.

In utter disbelief at the turn of events and still in shock for the day's events, Wren moved slowly from the room feeling oddly triumphant in her small victory against the Sergeant. As she left the guard house and the night air hit her face, for the first time in many, many, years she smiled as she thought to herself,

'Time to go home.'

26

Wren

There was no funeral held for her father. She had not wanted to give him one, he was being buried in the veterans' plot near the church and that was the most she could bear to give to him. Walking away from the graveyard had been painful as much as it had been a relief. Wren thought that maybe she felt that way because although she knew that he wouldn't be able to, a part of her had always sparked hope that her father would one day realise the mistakes he had made and try to atone for his discretions and regret what he had done to her mother.

But that day had never come and although it was a relief to know that she would no longer have to hide in her own home, sneaking about as if she did not belong, the man she buried today was still her father, even if he was a bad one. As she got back to her house that night and had to stop herself from slowly creeping in, remembering the absence of the threat of her father, she took a breath and forced herself to push the door open loudly and, against her instincts that now were irrational, she strolled into her living room and looked around, closing the door behind her just as loudly as she had entered, and let out a breath as she realised that this was all hers now. She could really make it a home, if Faeryn were to come down to the village she could show her her home. It would seem like such a small thing to anyone else but the feeling of home and the warmth and safety of that word she could now actually feel towards where she lived: It was a feeling she hadn't felt since her mother's passing and even then it was attached to Maggie as a person embodying the sense of home rather than a place in and of itself.

Going through the motions that evening she felt as if she was in a bubble, nothing felt quite real and she found she didn't really know how to tackle this new sense of freedom. She didn't need to hide away in the streets until after her father was home and she didn't need to keep everything the same way as it had always been around the house. But breaking out of routine was difficult and so she found herself making dinner at the same time as she always did and nearly leaving it on the side for her father as she went to leave the house. Only blinking out of her dazed state as the fresh air of outside hit her face when she opened her front door. Frowning and shaking her head, she stepped back and closed the door once more. She didn't need to leave. Deciding she would have the food she had made, rather than eating with the Street Children, she went to sit down and shovelled the food into her mouth realising she hadn't eaten all day.

Rest. All she needed was rest. She hadn't had a chance to process how her life had changed, the implications that her father being gone would have on her day to day, the small things she wouldn't usually notice that she wouldn't need to do now. Moving swiftly towards her room she faltered slightly as she looked into her parents' room. They were gone. They were both gone. She was an orphan. Tearing her eyes away from the blanket-covered bed she closed her eyes, unwanted tears prickling her eyes for reasons she could not understand, and she moved to her bedroom. Their room was a problem for another day; Wren's only goal now was to sleep.

Wren was woken the next morning by a sharp knock on her

front door. Agitated, eyes still crumbed with sleep and dressed in the crumpled clothes she had worn the day before, she rolled out of bed shouting, "Coming." Another impatient knock came as she changed into a clean shirt on her way through the house. Who could possibly be knocking at her door, no one ever knocked on her family's door. As she neared the front of her house she could just hear the sound of whispered squabbling coming from the other side. With a small smirk and a raise of the eyebrow she had an inclination as to who it could be. Straightening her face, Wren ripped the door open. "WHAT DO YOU WANT?" she bellowed at Aab and Ber who both jumped out of their skins at how abruptly the door was yanked open alongside her loud bellow. Laughing at her two boys, she leant against the door frame trying to catch her breath from laughing so hard. "But seriously, what's up, boys?" Wren asked, breath finally caught.

"What do we want? Are you kidding me, Wren?" Ber asked exasperatedly pushing past her and into the house.

"You were supposed to meet us at the market yesterday!" Aab added as he too moved into the house.

Looking at the boys, shocked at their irritation, she shut the door and looked at them trying to understand what was happening. Looking at the two boys both rubbing their arms which were crossed over their chests it dawned on her. It wasn't a dream, her father was dead.

Barking out a laugh she could see the boys looking at her like she had lost her mind but unable to stop herself she just stared at them.

"Wren, you were supposed to meet us and then you just didn't show up and a few hours later we hear that the guard were at your house carrying out a body," Ber let out slowly, trying to get her to comprehend what he was saying.

At the blank look on her face Aab blurted out, "We thought you were dead, Wren, we thought he got you like he got Maggie!"

Head in hands she realised she was going to have to tell them everything that had happened, she owed it to them really for everything they had done for her since her mother died. Hell without them she would never have met Fae, never have been to the forest. She probably wouldn't even be here any more if it wasn't for them. Looking up seriously at them, she saw how they waited patiently for her to speak, they had always been like that ever since she had met them as little ones. With a final breath in she let out her story, from the very beginning. Aab and Ber listened intently; she could tell from the way they sat slightly leant forward in the chairs they had pulled up from the dining table that they were hanging on every syllable that she spoke. Always believing, never for one second doubting. They were her boys, through and through. And as she came to yesterday morning and finding her father dead on the floor, Ber brought his hand to rest on hers and Aab his atop Ber's. They were family. She only left out one detail in her story and that was that Faeryn was the Princess.

"We do actually need to go and sort out the market now, though, unless you guys don't want money for meat with your dinner tonight. Somehow I can't see Letta being too happy with everyone having to go without?" Wren laughed out, breaking the tension her story had created, not wanting to carry on and answer questions right now.

Popping up from her chair she flitted out of the door not waiting for them to catch up, only slowing down to grab the stall baskets from next to the front door. The boys knew where everything else was and would meet her at the marketplace, she was sure of it.

Sure enough, within five minutes of her arriving at the market place and taking up residence in their usual spot, the boys clambered into her peripheral vision, everything needed for the day in hand. Smirking she set the baskets down on the floor by her feet moving only slightly as they placed the stall in front of her. Setting everything up she sent the boys off to see the spice man and to go and arrange a meeting with Letta for that evening for her. Really she could have gone and done these things herself, she knew the boys had a good enough handle on the stall to run it themselves for a few hours but she just really wanted some time to herself before the madness that she knew would unfold after her meeting with Letta, and the familiarity of her stall felt right.

Looking around her, Wren took in her surroundings, feeling content as she let herself fall into the routine of her market stall day. She could see the other same love couples around the market clear as day. Now that she knew they were there it didn't seem so covert, she couldn't honestly believe that she had never noticed them before. How had she been so blind to her own feelings, to everything around her? She had always prided herself on her observation skills, but here they had obviously been severely lacking. She wanted to shout out to them that they wouldn't have to hide forever, that the future was bright and that change was coming. It hurt her to keep her mouth shut, they seemed content to their hidden touches but she knew the real pain of hiding as strongly as they must.

Wren's thoughts then turned to Faeryn. Would she like to see all of this, would she ever really be able to?

Wren knew that she would need to bring her down here, to share this with her, her life. She understood why she would not be able to go and see first-hand the way Faeryn lived, but she could bring her here, if they were careful.

Wren wanted to share her life with her the way that Faeryn had, she was not as good with words when it came to these things but if she could show her then it might be easier. Maybe her life wouldn't seem so bleak that way? It was safer now that her father was gone. She could even show her the home she grew up in. The longer she thought about this, the stronger the pull to bring Fae here became and as she looked across the market she knew that she would ask Fae to come here next time they saw each other.

It wasn't long after this decision was made that Aab and Ber came waltzing through the market, bags of spices over each shoulder and a swagger to their steps that was so uniquely them. Wren could not help but chuckle as some of the girls blushed at being caught staring at the boys and having them both send winks their way. Wren knew it was all games, the two could not be more smitten over Isla and Sofia if someone drugged them with a love potion. Come to think of it, she wouldn't put it past those two girls to do that. Shaking that disturbing thought from her head, Wren returned her focus on the approaching boys and moved to greet them.

"How'd it go, boys? Looks like you scored with the spice man?" Wren asked as they came behind the stall.

"You know us, Wren, always working the angle. Taught by the best," Aab said winking at her.

"Shush, you, that winking malarkey won't work on me. Now report in," Wren said more firmly, knowing that Aab was too cocky for his own good sometimes and it would lead him into trouble one day.

"All right, all right. The meeting with the spice man went well, we got four bags of spices, Paprika, Turmeric, Garmin and Chilli. Enough to last a month at least with the number of mouths we currently have. Ber also haggled a bag of pepper and a bag of Salt free of charge," Aab reeled off.

Wren raised her eyebrow at Aab, it was an impressive taking for the trade they had made but he had left out the details about their meeting with Letta. She noted he was now looking at anywhere but her eyes as she inspected him. Turning to Ber she asked, "I said report, don't miss out details. Ber, what have you got to say?" she asked in her more authoritative voice that she knew neither of them could ignore.

"Letta wants to see you now..." Ber trailed off, giving her the bit of information that Aab had not included in his report for their tasks.

"Did you tell her I requested this afternoon or after evening meal? What is honestly the point in suggesting a time if you two are too scared of her to actually push when she tries to go against what I've asked?" Wren let out, marginally irritated at the situation. She had wanted to have some time to herself before talking with Letta. To make her house more of her home than her parents. But things never really went the way she planned these days. So with a sigh she looked back at her boys, both clearly embarrassed if their slightly pink-coloured necks were anything to go by. "It's fine, look, you guys will have to look after the market this afternoon." Looking at Aab she added, "Properly, no flirting with the girls, we are behind with the money for new clothes and shoes for the little ones let alone us. I'll go and meet with Letta, I will be with her until evening meal at least with everything we need to go over." Looking at the market stall she looked to Ber. "Ber, can you make sure all this gets packed away and taken back to the house and put in the cupboard?" Wren asked, waiting only for Ber's nod before she turned and began to walk away to go and meet with Letta. It only took three steps before she turned herself back around. "Boys, my house is your house if you want to use my parents' old room?" Wren stated more than asked. She knew they would say yes, they had been a family for longer than any of this and their place was with her, they had never liked leaving her with Ryn to live when she could have joined them in the relative safety of the Street Children's territory. Both boys nodded at her and letting out a breath she hadn't realised she was holding, she turned back around and marched off to find Letta.

It didn't take that long to find her. As soon as she crossed the threshold into the territory she was joined soundlessly by Isla and Sofia who walked by each of her sides, guiding her to a small room to speak with Letta without prying ears. The room was slightly suffocating, the walls and floor bare, the only light coming from a candle sat in the middle of the room where Letta sat crossed legged patiently waiting for Wren to join her. Walking cautiously to join Letta in the centre of the room, Wren felt cold with the room's bareness, there was no spark of warmth here that was usually felt across the Children's territory and she wondered why Letta had really taken her here. Coming to sit on the other side of the candles she looked into Letta's eyes and instantly felt warmth build up from within; it was strange how she could go from feeling completely isolated and cold to safe and warm in the span of a second and with one look. But that was why Letta was the leader here, why she looked after everyone.

Wren's thoughts were interrupted as Letta spoke. "Report," rang out in the room, Letta seeming so much bigger than she actually was with one word.

"Oh come on, Letta, skip the intimidation tactics already," Wren stated firmly, not liking the discomfort Letta was clearly trying to bestow upon her.

"Why is nothing ever easy with you, Wren? Just report, for god's sake!" Letta half shouted, as always struggling with Wren's lack of respect for her authority.

"What no how was your day? Are you okay? I heard your father died, how was that? It's always just business." Wren matched Letta's half shout. This was how they worked best.

"Ugh fine, you're right, yes I should have asked if you were okay. Now can you just report? You can include how you are in that if you want. Just tell me what's happened," Letta grumbled out.

"Much better," Wren laughed. "Right, well, Faeryn is in, she had no idea what it was like down here for us and by the sounds of it she's been extremely isolated and isn't being given a realistic education of the realm and her people so I was thinking of asking her to come down here incognito for the day," Wren rambled, beginning to get lost in thoughts of what she would do with Fae when she came down when a sharp slap on the knee brought her back to the present moment. "Sorry yes, so, what else? My father died, liver failure, my family home is now a base for me and my boys, I hope that's okay with you, I already told them they could move in," Wren stated not wanting to see the agitation she knew would be growing on Letta's face.

"Go on. I know that's not all of it," Letta gritted out.

"Well, she kissed me, a few times actually. That's it really," said Wren with a bright grin spread across her teeth.

"You are literally the most infuriating person I know, Wren. Seriously, you just reported to me that the Princess of the Realm is joining up with our uprising that hasn't even been formed yet and that your father died all in one sentence and all you seem to be concerned with is getting in the Princess's pants. So much for the scared and worried Wren who didn't even know if she liked girls, or even knew about same love for that matter! Absolutely infuriating!" Letta ranted at her, voice pitching in places as she moved through her emotions from anger, to worry and eventually settling on exhaustion.

Wren didn't really know what to say to that, still on a high from sharing with someone else that Fae had wanted her back. Looking to Letta, she was unsure if she wanted her to go or not.

"Just go, Wren. I need to think about the implications of everything you've told me. Be back here with the boys tomorrow at day break," Letta said.

Wren looked at Letta, confused for a second. As she moved to stand, Letta grabbed her wrist one last time and looked straight into her eyes. "It's time to plan an uprising." Letting go of Wren's arm, Wren felt the excitement of hope bubble in her chest as she left.

27

Wren

The Forest of Kasia had somehow become her home, and walking away from Letta knowing that she now had a house that was safe with four walls she knew that it still would not be her home, not until Fae was there. The forest that kept them safe and let her get to know Faeryn over the last years, hid them until they were old enough to face the troubles of the world and say no that's not right, was their home. Maybe one day when the wall was ripped down and the expectations of the world weren't on their shoulders they could build a little cottage in their clearing overlooking the castle and her village and just be.

The day to go back to the forest and see Faeryn came around quickly after the chaos that was the week's events. Chopping up the vegetables for dinner, she was making a broth, she thought about how already things had changed for the better. Aab and Ber had moved into her parents' old room and the house seemed warmer. The only thing that was really missing now was Faeryn. Her absence made Wren's heart ache. The pulling in her chest had remained at the constant low tug since Wren and Faeryn had met again and agreed to see where things would go. The pull always led back to Fae; Wren knew it would not lead her wrong. Wren had come to believe that the pull was the magic of the Fae, pulling her back to the magical forest and their Fae-kissed child, Faeryn. It was fantasy but one Wren would happily indulge if it gave her hope when she was feeling down. The fate of the Fae was on her side. She had decided that she would tell Fae that night about what had happened to her this week and ask her to come to the village. It would take some planning but Wren knew that with Letta, Aab and Ber to help as well as the rest of the Street Children she would be fine. The boys clamouring in from their room, sniffing the air and smiling, wrapped in their blankets, brought her out of her musings and she smiled at them, her boys.

"It's nearly ready, give it ten minutes and you'll be eating," Wren told the boys.

Acknowledging what Wren had said, Ber sat down on the counter top and asked, "Are you going to the forest tonight?"

"Yes, I'll be heading there as soon as the sun begins to set. You know I go every night," Wren answered.

"Are you meeting her?" Aab pried.

"She has a name, Faeryn, but yes I am, not that it's any of your business. What's got into you both?" Wren let out, beginning to show the signs of irritation.

"The way we see it, now that we live with you and you feed us and have always looked after us., Ber began.

"We're kind of officially family now aren't we?" Aab continued.

"So we need to look out for each other, starting with the girl," Ber finished.

Rolling her eyes at them, Wren huffed, "We have always been family, we have always looked out for each other. You don't need to worry about Fae, you'll meet her soon enough," Wren reassured, letting slip her intentions for Faeryn to visit.

"You're bringing her to the village!" Aab clapped excitedly.

"Only if she says yes," Wren said smiling widely at her boys.

Ber kept quiet at this and Wren was sure he knew more than he was letting on. He had an awfully good way of getting information out of Sofia and she and her sister never missed a trick. It wouldn't surprise Wren if they had someone listen to her and Letta's meeting the other day. But what was more surprising was that clearly whatever Ber knew he hadn't told Aab, his younger counterpart, it was unlike them to keep anything from each other. Wren noted to herself that she would need to keep an eye on that as she dished up their broth.

Rushing to finish her evening meal she quickly swallowed down her broth, knowing she was running behind schedule and that at this rate Fae would beat her to the forest. Telling the boys that it was their night to clean the dishes as she had cooked, she grabbed another layer and left their house heading to her hidden entrance to the tunnel. She was so used to the journey now that she had to put little thought into getting out and across the stream, only minding to make sure she wasn't being followed.

Arriving at the clearing she pushed through the thick bushes to the clearing and smiled. As she suspected, Fae had beat her to the forest tonight, she was lying on the floor bed staring up through the leaves; she had always been able to make out shapes in them in the moonlight. Wren had always thought she was a making it up, just a little, when she said she could see a cat or some other intricate shape in the leaves. Yet here she was leaf watching on her own, waiting for Wren to arrive. A cold breeze blew her into the clearing and as she stumbled closer to Fae she realised that it really was taking a cold turn to the year now and Faeryn was just sitting there in her sleeping clothes as if she couldn't feel the cold ground beneath her. Hastily she grabbed her second layer off of her shoulders and held it out.

"Will you sit up and take this? You are going to freeze to

death. How can you not feel that chill?" Wren said.

Taking the second layer from her and putting it on her shoulders, Faeryn looked at Wren with a dreamy smile in return, choosing not to speak. Wren couldn't help but smile back openly at Fae's antics, deciding to sit down next to her on the cold forest floor. Looking at Fae now, she could see the beauty that she held illuminated here in the moonlight, tinted with the greens of the forest leaves.

Wren could understand why they said she was Fae touched, you could get lost just staring at her.

"Come to the village," Wren blurted out. Another reason she was sure Faeryn was actually fae touched, the pulling and the tendency to lose her cool and blurt out her thoughts bluntly only happened around her.

The look on Faeryn's face screamed startled and Wren scrambled to think of something to say to reassure her that it was okay if she didn't want to but before she could think of something, mind now blank in her panic, Fae's startled expression turned to a wicked grin.

"There is no way in hell I am letting you take that back so don't even think about it! Fuck yeah! Trip to the village!" Fae exclaimed, jumping up from her space on the ground, excitedly pulling Wren up with her and into a quick forceful kiss.

Ears red, Wren worked to keep control of her thoughts as they raced, she needed to talk to Faeryn properly and share things with her, let her in. If she didn't do it now then she never would, she couldn't let her distract her.

"Fae, calm down!" Wren said firmly, grabbing onto Fae's arms and stopping her from her jumping celebration. Watching as Fae slowed down, she looked at her with her usual head tilt of slight concern that she pulled out whenever Wren went into serious mode.

Knowing Fae would keep quiet now and wait for her to speak, Wren weighed up in her head how to start what she needed to say.

"You've told me so much about yourself and your life in the castle and I know I can't come into your world and see everything first hand but maybe you could come and see mine? I know we would need to be careful and put you in a disguise and oh god we would need to find a way for you to come out maybe during the day or would you prefer night? Ahhh I need to slow down." Wren stopped her own verbal vomit from escaping her lips, she had no idea how Fae did this to her. "Look all I'm saying is we can figure out the logistics, but I want to share my life with you, Fae, I want you to see how I live, where I live, I want you to meet my friends, the Street Children. Letta. There is so much I want to show you." Wren came to a stop there, not knowing what else to say to convince Faeryn it was a good idea, she hoped that she would see it her way because she wasn't sure how she would be able to explain everything that had happened properly. There are some things you just have to see or smell or feel to understand. Turning her attention back to Fae she watched as she processed all that Wren had said.

"Let's do it! I will have a think but I am sure we can figure something out, I would love to come during the day but I'm not sure it would be a good idea. I would have to figure out how to get away for a whole day without being missed and with there being so many people in the village, how would we be sure someone wouldn't notice someone new about. It's not like people are coming and going all the time from the city or villages, that would kind of defeat the purpose of that big old wall now wouldn't it?" Fae laughed as Wren let out a sigh.

"Right that's settled then, one trip to the village coming up," Wren joked. "I do have something to tell you though, I, erm, didn't want to bring it up without knowing that you'd said yes to coming down," Wren continued nervously.

"Go on, you know I can tell when you're not right," Fae said.

"Well, you see, my father, he died the day after I last was here," Wren said waiting for the pitying are you all right? to come from Fae but was startled by a barked laugh she had not been expecting.

"The bastard who killed your mother? Come on. What? You think I didn't notice you coming here with all those bruises all this time and then when you told me about your mother dying and couldn't talk about him for weeks. I knew something was up, I am smart you know. I put two and two together. Fuck him," Faeryn ranted out, dark mirth in her voice.

Mouth hanging open, Wren could not believe that she had been so transparent, Faeryn had not just been listening to her, she had been watching, taking in everything about her. "You knew. And you didn't tell me?" Wren whispered.

"Of course, Wren, what was I supposed to say? I knew you would tell me when you were ready. I could wait," Faeryn explained. "Are you okay?" she asked quietly, realising she may have been too harsh vocalising her ill opinion of Wren's father.

"Yeah, I'm fine, the house is mine now. My mother paid it off when I was small. Aab and Ber moved in with me. You'll have to meet them when you come to the village," Wren rambled. Looking down slightly at her hands, she went on, "You'll probably need to meet Letta properly too. She runs things, she'll be helping us with the resistance, heading it up with me really. She's a bit odd, intense, but I think you'll like her," Wren finished, looking up to Faeryn and waiting patiently for her reply, hoping that she would move past the matter of her father. Wren was unsure how to feel about Fae having known that he beat her and had done the unforgivable to her mother and not having said anything.

"Yes, I would like to meet your family. Letta sounds interesting to say the least and I'm interested to find out more about this uprising you're planning. Especially if I am going to be involved." Fae smiled at her. "Now shouldn't we be training? I want to see if that move will work," Fae exclaimed, moving away from their serious conversation. Wren looked on at her and considered for a moment if they could possibly just do this forever. This really was home. Casting her eyes around, she could almost see the little cottage; a vegetable patch, children and animals running around ghosted over the current landscape. Broken from her thoughts she brought her attention back to her girl coming back into the clearing, her own wooden sword in hand and bow and quiver slung over her shoulder. She was a vision.

"C'mon then," Faeryn called out and Wren could do nothing but answer her call, running across the clearing to meet her.

28

Wren

The rest of Wren's night with Faeryn had been fun, sparring and training together as they had been doing since they first met. It was a tradition and they probably didn't need to do it as much as they did but Wren felt as if it was their routine, it created a way to take their minds off of everything, the seriousness and intensity that was their everyday lives. Wren would be able to let her thoughts wander, her body relax and she was able for a while at least to feel like she was free and there were no expectations on her shoulders. She liked to think this provided the same sort of feeling for Faeryn too. It must be hard to be the Princess of the Realm, especially with her personality, she never really had a choice about what or who she wanted to be. Wren knew that must be difficult.

They had agreed that they would make the trip to the village the following week and try to make it for early evening and through the night so that Fae would be able to see the market but she wouldn't be around massive crowds and would have less chance of getting noticed. The evening would be for her meeting with Letta. That was going to be interesting, she thought, subconsciously rolling her eyes. Wren hoped beyond hope that they got along. It would be vital to the uprising that they could all work cohesively together to make this happen, despite it being a long-term plan. Wren knew as well that her life would become significantly more difficult if Letta decided that Faeryn wasn't right for her, regardless of them being of similar ages. Letta's leadership of the Street Children and influence over her boys and her life in general had the potential to cause difficulties if she actively sought out to stop her seeing Fae.

Despite Fae not having left the castle since she had been a little girl, her description was the stuff of tales told by mothers to children and of consistent gossip through the ladies of the villages whose cousin's friend's cousins and the like had sent word from the castle of her beauty and other gossiping topics. Due to this it had also been decided that Wren needed to find Fae some form of disguise to hide her appearance for her visit to go unnoticed. During market days it would not be unusual for Wren to buy cloth as she would on occasion make her own clothes, like her mother had for her, and she then would also make clothes for the boys and the other Street Children as they grew fast out of the clothes they did have. More often than not they would get ripped and the hand me downs would become damaged beyond repair. She was due to make some new shirts for some of the smaller children and it would be hardly noticed if she bought some cloth that she could make into a woman's hooded cape or something similar. Just something simple that many of the other women in the market would wear day to day during this time of year to add an extra layer of protection during the colder months.

Wren herself often wore an over coat made from thick hard-wearing wool that she had taken from her father's uniform from the war. He had never noticed the missing pieces she had stolen from the back of his cupboards to use as her own. Growing up she had always been more inclined to wear more masculine clothing, much preferring the free reign of movement britches gave her and the security of a long sleeve shirt, laced at the chest and wrapped tightly around her waist with a thick strip of leather. This style was an imitation of what she had seen many of the young men who helped their fathers around the villages across the city of Ekoni wearing and she found that she felt much more herself in this than the dresses she had worn as a young child. It was unusual and she did not know many girls who dressed the way she did, even Letta had opted for a dress: in a different style than the girls at market, but still a dress. Wren's mother had tried to make it more feminine with the colour choices, often veering to navy and burgundy rather than the plain white and browns the men wore. They had become Wren's favourite colours quickly and now she more often than not would replicate this with everything she made for herself. She had had stares for her choices when she had first begun to wear the style but over time the other villagers had gotten used to it and her, everyone except her father. She still could remember vividly the day he had beat her for dressing like a man. The sting of his slaps, the smell of iron as her nose had bled and the metallic taste in her mouth that made her cringe. It made her wonder if Faeryn had ever been given the choice to wear something other than a dress, she would ask her when she brought her here. She could even make her something, it would be easier to train in britches, Wren reasoned with herself, and she decided then and there that she would have to buy some extra material just in case.

Wren also realised that she would need to tell Letta and her boys that Faeryn was coming to the village. She would need to meet them. There was so much to do and it felt slightly overwhelming now that she was back at her house thinking of all the things that needed to be done in preparation. Letta would be happy that she could meet Fae and start planning but she would need to ask and make sure it was okay for her to tell Aab and Ber who Fae actually was. She had told them all about her but had just left out that one small — okay huge — detail. They had assumed that she was from one of the far-off villages and was travelling to the forest like she was, through a hole in the wall someone partially abandoned. She had just let them believe that and hadn't corrected them when they spoke of it. She didn't know how they would take it, she was sort of dating a Princess: the Princess. It was a big deal and pretty unbelievable. They would probably think she was joking or messing with them until they could see her for themselves. That was if Letta agreed that she couldn't tell them.

Bringing herself back to reality, Wren realised that a lot of her plans seemed to depend on the will of Letta. She understood that is what it means to have a leader, but she had never really been a Street Child. The lines between authority figure and friend were very blurred and she knew that many of the children now looked to her as well for guidance and she wasn't sure how okay with that she was. She had never meant to become a leader of anything she just wanted to do what's right for people. These thoughts flew by and she soon found herself outside Letta's room, hand raised poised to knock on her door. It was a wonder that she hadn't been stopped by Isla and Sofia, she had surely not been as stealthy as she usually would be coming here on autopilot.

Nodding to herself in reassurance she brought her knuckles to rap on the wood of the door in front of her, once, twice and three times before bringing her hand to her side and waiting in bated breath for Letta to answer. She didn't have to wait long before the door came swinging open, a tired-looking Letta standing on the other side.

"What do you want, Wren? It's not even daylight yet, why

are you even here? Shouldn't you be in the forest somewhere?" Letta grumbled, gesturing for Wren to enter the room. Stepping forward Wren felt the swish of air from the door being shut behind her and heard the click of the lock moving back into place.

"It's about Fae," Wren answered simply, noticing the slightly widened eyes that gave away Letta's interest.

"What about her? The Princess change her mind about joining us?" Letta said, voice pitched with sarcasm.

"Quite the contrary actually. I'm going to be bringing her into the village this time next week. I thought you might like a meeting?" Wren deadpanned. This seemed to fluster Letta as Wren failed to rise to the bait she had laid out with her sarcasm.

"You are bringing the Princess of the Realm into our village?" Letta asked in disbelief. "How the fuck do you think you're going to pull that off? She only just manages to meet you in the forest once a week. You've lost it, you're delusional, Wren!" she continued.

"Look, don't worry about that, we have a plan, no one will see her or know it's her. She wants to see what it's like down here, understand how we have to live. And it will give you an opportunity to meet her, plan for the uprising," Wren calmly replied.

"Right, you're right, okay. Just know that if you get caught, I don't exist. If we both get in trouble there will be no one to look after the children. No one can know about this, Wren," Letta said leaning forward in her chair and looking into Wren's eyes with seriousness creasing their edges.

"No one, except Aab and Ber," Wren whispered out her condition, feeling the anxiety from pushing her boundaries in her chest. Hearing this Letta leant back heavily in her chair and Wren watched as she got herself comfortable, spreading her mass widely across her seat and feigning relaxation as if Wren's hint of insubordination didn't bother her. The longer Letta sat in silence looking Wren up and down, the more the uncomfortable feeling in Wren's chest grew and she felt as if she needed to say something more.

"My boys are old enough and smart enough to be involved in this now, the uprising, and they need to understand who she is and how important she is to this cause. If anything were to happen to us, they and your girls would be leading this thing. They need to be prepared for that!" Wren stated, passion causing her voice to raise in volume and a closed fist to hit the table punctuating her last sentence. She had no idea where that had come from. She had just wanted them to meet her girl, the one who had saved her but the pulling in her chest that she so often felt pulling her to the forest had taken over and forced a new action and from there she had spoken without thinking. But from the look on Letta's face and the processing of emotions and her words that flitted across her eyes, Wren knew that the pull had pushed her in the right direction and Letta would give in.

Letta's posture had tensed, and she looked as if she were made from stone as she searched for the words to answer Wren. To win back the power in the conversation. "The boys may know. But we will also tell my girls. Your reasoning is sound and it is only right that they ALL know. We tell them together, with Faeryn at the meeting. No sooner, no later," Letta stated firmly, leaving no room for argument.

Wren narrowed her eyes at Letta then, she had wanted to tell the boys alone, in their home, show them the missing part of their family in private. Letta had given in though, she had made compromises and it was clear that this was a play to keep some semblance of power in the relationship. It was all about control.

But she had given in, and that give confirmed for Wren that yes, she was becoming an unintentional leader. Her voice meant something and if Letta would listen to her, then the rest of the children definitely would. The boys had been right.

Looking over Letta one more time she rose to her feet and held out her hand, puffing out her chest. With a strong handshake and a firm nod, Wren agreed to Letta's terms.

Without another word she left, closing Letta's door behind her. This had all become so much more than she had ever expected.

29

Wren

Getting the materials for Faeryn's disguise had been as easy as she had expected. And making up the clothes for Fae as well as the load of clothes she had needed to make for the children had been time consuming, occupying all of her free time in the week and eating into her training time significantly but she had managed to finish everything and even scraped together a fresh pair of britches and a more feminine shirt for Faeryn to train in using some of her own older clothes matched with some of the newer material.

They weren't the usual quality of clothes that Fae would be used to but Wren was sure she would appreciate them even still.

The time was creeping ever closer now that she had agreed that she would go and collect Faeryn for her trip to the village. She wasn't a hundred percent sure that Fae would show up, they had agreed that she would try to get to the clearing as early as possible so that she would have a chance to see the market, which even at early evening just before closing would be decently busy. She bundled up the womanly disguise and the training clothes into a leather bag along with some cheese and bread, in case Faeryn hadn't eaten at evening meal with her plan to get to the forest and disappear from the castle early on. Aab and Ber were in charge of the market stall today and at her insistence would be closing up and getting everything in the house before having evening meal with the Street Children and then, much to their chagrin, they would go to the meeting with Letta and her where they would finally meet Faeryn. It all seemed convoluted to Wren but this is what she would need to do to keep them distracted long enough not to see Faeryn and get the truth of her identity before the meeting, as Letta had insisted that must be when they discover the truth.

After packing up and sneaking through the village to the entrance to her tunnels, she made sure no one was following her, checking every corner and making sure to remember to check the roofs and as she disappeared into the building that held her tunnel entrance she stopped and sat two rooms in and waited. If someone was going to follow her they would only wait five or so minutes before making their way into the building after her, and with her sat in wait just far enough in not to be seen from the entrance to the building, she would be sure to hear and see them before they noticed her lingering presence. Isla and Sofia would not catch her out today. If her boys couldn't see Faeryn first, neither could they. Waiting, Wren thought of Letta and her intentions, she knew that she was tired and that she cared for her, and the rest of the children, she had been looking after them as best she could for years.

But it had hardened her, and Wren worried that she would not be able to see the bigger picture and the benefits of a long-term plan rather than rushing in fast and half-cocked to make change. Wren worried how this would affect Faeryn, the pressure would be immense and she would need to stand her ground.

No one had come through the open door of the building and Wren concluded to herself that Letta was sticking to her word and unwilling to ruin the progress they had made for the sake of control. Breathing calmly, she focused on her task and smoothly got up from her position and silently slung the leather bag onto her back strapping it to her body so that it would move with her and not impede her on the journey to the clearing. The bookcase was still firmly planted in front of her entrance and as she moved the large wooden piece of furniture, the creak rang around the room loudly. Wren noted that she would need to check it another day to make sure she didn't need to replace or fix it. Removing the burlap sack from the wall now in view with the bookcase having been moved, she entered the tunnel closing the way behind her. She had made this trip nearly a thousand times before but this time felt as if it were the first, her heart pounding and a sheen of light sweat misting her forehead. Unlike the first time, however, her muscles were strong, her movements sure of themselves despite the anxiousness building inside her, but the pulling was stronger, pulling her forward to her Princess.

Getting to the clearing had been easy once Wren had pushed down the worry and leaning against a tree, leather bag between her legs, she felt her mind begin to wander, questioning if what she was doing was the right thing. Faeryn would need to get there soon so that she didn't talk herself out of this. She didn't want to be the reason Fae got in any more trouble than she was already in with her mother and she knew that she was working to fix that bridge and bring her mother round to change slowly, aiding the uprising the only way she could for now.

Closing her eyes she tried to calm her warring mind, listening to the sounds of the forest that had come to feel like home. She could hear the birds chirping in the trees above her, the thrashing of the running water against the rocks of the stream. And she could hear the thrum of life that seemed to vibrate from the very ground of the forest. Revelling in the feeling of the thrum as it ran through her body, her ears twitched to the sound of footsteps coming towards her and the quiet labouring breaths that she could tell even here in her heart were Faeryn's; she had managed to get here before evening meal. As Wren opened her eyes her vision was filled with the face of a grinning Fae lighting up her world.

"Hey," Wren whispered, the feeling of contentment given to her by their forest seeping out of her every pore.

"Hey," Fae matched as she practically floated forwards to sit in front of Wren under one of the ancient trees that lined their clearing.

Wren looked at her. Faeryn was dressed differently today, her dress wasn't the usual plain night dresses that she usually wore but much finer, richer-coloured clothes, layered up and tied tightly to her body. Wren had never seen something quite so elaborate and completely impractical. She definitely wouldn't be able to wear this today, she thanked the heavens that she had made her training clothes as well as the hooded cape, if Fae didn't have anything appropriate under the first layer of dress she would at least be able to wear them.

"You're going to need to get changed, here, I made you some things so you can blend in," Wren said chucking the hooded cape at Fae playfully. Faeryn picked up the hooded cape and looked at it with a raised eyebrow.

"You made this? Why, Miss Wren, don't you have some hidden talents?" Fae teased, moving to try and put it over what she was currently wearing Wren moved to stop her, cheeks blushed pink from Fae's teasing remark.

"Look you won't be able to wear all of this down there, you'll be spotted straight away. How many layers is that? Can you take the top one off at least? It needs to be a plainer colour, browns, whites, anything beige?" Wren enquired, tugging awkwardly at the top dress Faeryn was wearing.

"You want me to strip? Wren, I didn't think we were there yet?" Fae exclaimed, feigning being scandalised, flinging her head back and putting her hand on her head barely holding in a laugh.

Wren had no idea how to respond to that and spluttered out an incomprehensible stream of sounds staring wide eyed at Fae.

"Oh for fuck's sake, Wren, I'm joking. You are amazing but you need to let loose a little, babe," Fae laughed out.

"Look, Fae, you know this isn't a joke, do you have any idea how much trouble we will get in if we are caught? I could go to jail. Hell I'm not even sure what they'd do to me. And you, your mum will marry you off and some greasy idiot of a man will take over the Realm and we will never have a chance for change and you might never be happy again!" Wren ranted out, seeing Faeryn become more sombre as her words fully impacted her.

"Right, we can't get caught. Is this any better?" Fae responded pulling off her top layer of dress to reveal a simpler dress slightly yellowed. Next to the deep brown hooded cape it would look like she was one of the wealthier villagers and although people may stare, it was entirely possible that she would be able to go unnoticed for what she really was.

"Much! Before we head off, I wanted to let you know that I've arranged a meeting with Letta for tonight, late on so we can see the market and everything else first. But it's important that you meet her. Her girls will be there too and Aab and Ber, my boys. But until then it's just us okay?" Wren reassured.

"Right. Get to know you better and then meeting with semi-scary Uprising Girl. Right. I've got this. Not like I've been locked up in a castle for my whole life with only you to give me a dose of reality," Faeryn sarcastically said.

Moving forward suddenly with a grin and stealing a kiss from Wrens pursed lips. "Can we go now? I don't want to waste any time, I want to see everything," Fae asked, swaying side to side with wide eyes and a pout, trying to get what she wanted from Wren.

Wren set the leather bag with the training clothes she had made for Fae down hidden with her wooden sword and bow and quiver set. She would show them to Fae another time, for now it was time to get her into the village. The journey to the edge of the forest was easy and with their frequent trips exploring further out of their clearing over the last year, she found that Fae had become light footed, barely making a noise as she moved across the undergrowth. The tricky part, Wren knew, would be getting her across the stream quickly and unseen. Just because the guards had never looked down before didn't mean that today they wouldn't. So before they made the run down to the water, Wren turned to Faeryn who was already looking at her expectantly.

"Right, the stream is fast, don't let your legs fall in, it'll try and pull you down stream and it's freezing cold. The rocks that we will use to jump across are slippery but you shouldn't have too much trouble with them," Wren warned.

"Its fine, Wren, relax. Plus if I fall, you'll just catch me. Right?" Faeryn said with confidence. Wren could see she didn't seem to have any doubt that if she fell Wren would be able to save her. It made her feel proud that Fae had such faith in her.

"Right," Wren responded hesitantly, doubting herself for a minute.

They ran together down the hill to the water's edge, Wren making the first leap and pausing for a second to see Fae make ready to copy her movements. As she jumped to the second rock she felt more than saw Fae join her over the river soundlessly.

Wren had two more rocks to get past before she would make it to the other side of the stream. The next she knew was slippery and she would need to quickly leap from one to the other without hesitation that she knew would lead to a slip. The breeze was cold on her cheeks and she could feel the tip of her nose was raw from it. The water would be freezing today and if someone fell in she knew that a deathly chill would chase them for weeks. As she leaped with a quick one two and a slight wobble, she let out a breath as she made it to the last rock, the sturdiest of them all. Her relief was quickly cut through by a quiet gasp as Fae attempted the same leap as she had just done As her foot hit the second to last rock her toes slipped out from underneath her and her entire body came hurtling forwards towards the water, other foot flailing in the air with the momentum of her fall. Wren quickly braced her body, bending at the knees and reaching out with both arms to catch Faeryn before her front hit the water. With cat like reflexes she managed to catch Fae a mere centimetre from the water's surface.

Using the bend in her knees she manoeuvred her grip on Fae's body to allow for her to push her upright with all her power getting her half way to upright, with just enough height that she was able to swing her leg that was still in the air round in front of her and onto the rock Wren herself was standing on, the toes of the foot that had betrayed her clawing through her shoes to the very edge of the rock she had slipped on. With one last sharp motion, Wren made to hop backwards while pulling against Fae's shoulders, allowing her legs to hit solid land and extending her arms as she pulled Faeryn, who was able to safely land her back foot onto the rock Wren had just left, bringing both her feet to safety. Letting out a shaky breath, Faeryn leapt into Wren's arms on dry land before leaning back and slapping her across the arms.

"Why didn't you tell me there was one rock that was more slippery than the rest? Do you want to kill me?" Fae whisper-shouted at Wren as Wren rubbed her now sore arms before shifting her eyes to the top of the wall and grabbing onto Fae's hand and dragging her across the empty field to the vine-covered wall. Once she pulled Fae safely behind her wall of vines and into the cave like tunnel entrance, she turned back to her and waited. Wren had thought Fae would come out with a string of curse words before realising that she was okay and getting back to the journey in hand. What she hadn't expected was for Faeryn to launch herself at her quite so abruptly planting kiss after kiss on her face and lips with both palms plastered to either side of her head with a firm grip so as to not let Wren escape the onslaught of manic affection.

Red faced and significantly flustered, Wren let Fae capture her lips in one last kiss before forcing herself to take a step back, remembering why they were there.

"We should get going if you want to see the market before it closes," Wren stated awkwardly after clearing her throat.

"Lead the way beautiful," Fae smirked at Wren, clearly having put her near death experience behind her as she moved her arm down to grab onto Wren's hand.

Wren stared for a moment at Fae's hand in hers.

Her pale skin was soft against her own calloused hands and she could feel warmth spreading up her fingertips the longer Fae's hand was in hers. Feeling an odd mix of giddiness and anticipation, Wren tugged on Fae's hand and began to pull her along the dark tunnels at a run, smiling as exhilaration filled her. As they reached the end of the tunnel, Wren pulled back the burlap sack covering the bookcase and moved the bookcase partially to the side before turning back to Fae in the half-lit tunnel.

Checking her over, Wren fiddled with the hood of the cape and tucked Faeryn's bright auburn hair back further into the hood not wanting it to give her away once they moved out onto the streets.

"Once we go out from here there can be no mention of who you really are. Not until our meeting tonight. Your hair will need to stay hidden under the hood unless we are at my house. This leads out into a building and then into the streets right in the heart of the Street Children's territory, so it'll seem pretty deserted but don't be tempted to feel safe as most of the kids know how to stay out of sight and mind so could be listening in or watching us regardless of if you can see them or not."

Wren rambled off, nerves rising to the top as she thought of all the ways this could go wrong. She was brought out of her own spiralling thoughts when she felt soft lips on her own firmly kissing her that pulled away as quickly as they came. Opening her eyes as they left her, she looked at Faeryn who was looking at her in light amusement.

"We will be fine, Wren. Calm down okay?" Fae said softly as she squeezed Wren's hand still in her palm.

Taking a deep breath, Wren tried to let the tension fall from her shoulders as she thought of one last warning that Fae would need to know before leaving the privacy of the tunnel. "Okay, I'm calm. But one last thing, I promise. We can't do this." Wren gestured at their joint hands raising them slightly. "Like I said, same love is a strictly don't ask don't tell down here at the moment and if the guards see, we will have problems and attract unwanted attention," Wren finished as she let go of Faeryn's hand with an apologetic half-smile. It felt horrible having to hide with Faeryn right there next to her but she knew it was a fight for another time.

With a final nod Wren turned away from Fae knowing her point had been made and began to shove the bookcase the rest of the way off into the room.

With a loud creak it shuddered away and she remembered that she really needed to investigate the cause of that sound. Stepping through the hole and into the room, she felt Fae closely follow her and move further into the room as Wren went about putting the hole's cover back into place.

It didn't take long for them to reach the street, it seemed deserted but Wren could feel eyes on them from the rooftops and knew that at least Isla and Sofia would be watching them already. Moving her attention to Fae as she led her down the street, she watched as she looked around, eyes wide, taking in the new world around her. Wren didn't want to hurry her on too quickly, but if they had any chance of seeing the market properly and showing her the house before their meeting with Letta they would need to get a move on. They had gotten distracted on the way and it had delayed them more than Wren had realised, looking at the darkening sky. With one last glance to the rooftops Wren pushed forward, quickening her pace and ensuring Fae matched her haste. A few minutes later they arrived at the edge of the territory and Wren breathed a sigh of relief that no one had intercepted them before they could move into the main area of the village.

Lining arms with Fae like the girls in the market would usually do, Wren began to relax. "This is the main area of the market village, we've just left the Street Children's territory," Wren began to explain, gesturing behind her with her head. "There are other villages across the City, broken down to skill and interest, but they all venture here to buy their goods from the market as this is the village of merchants and sellers. We border on the village that holds the guards. In fact the Street Children's territory is the housing that held the young single guards who didn't return from the Pirate Wars, it was left abandoned as it was so close to the wall bordering the Forest."

"I see the people down here are just as scared by the legends of magic that linger about our forest. Better for us I suppose though," Fae noted. "How far is the market?"

"Just down this road, and yes, they are still very superstitious," Wren answered as they continued on down the road, shortly coming to the opening up to the market square. Luckily they had gotten here while it was still open, the noise hit them like a symphony, blending into one continuous hum. The sellers were all shouting out their end of day offers and none of the stalls had closed yet.

Even her own flower stall was there, being run by Aab, Ber oddly missing from his side.

"Oh, Wren, this is amazing. It's so alive! There's so many people!" Fae exclaimed excitedly, grabbing onto Wren's arm in her excitement.

Smiling at Fae's reaction she knew she would like this. Wren started telling Faeryn of the different stalls, the people, giving even more life and meaning to this place for Faeryn. Naming the sellers she knew, how she would haggle with the spice man for Paprika to use for the Children's evening meals and of how his son had approached her once but she had redirected him to Iris, who she also pointed out. She started speaking of how she had noticed the same love even here in the market, telling Fae of the lingering looks between people, the skimming of fingers and how although hidden you could see it if you paid attention. And then her eyes hit Aab who had found them in their hidden nook overlooking the market. Urging him with her eyes to stay where he was.

"And that over there, is Aab, you'll meet him later at the meeting. Right now he is running my stall." Wren acknowledged the staring contest between them so that Fae didn't worry.

"Your mother's stall?" Fae whispered before recollecting herself. "I thought you told me Aab was one of your boys? He's fucking huge?" Faeryn exclaimed, seemingly back to her usual loud self.

Wren couldn't help but smile, shaking her head she chuckled in reply, "Wait till you meet Ber. They might not look it but they are my boys. I've known them since they were this big." Wren raised her hand and held it against her waist indicating how small they used to be. "Come on, we haven't got much more time left and I want to show you something."

It didn't take long for them to climb up the cobbled street to her front door, Wren paused momentarily before pushing open the door and pulling Fae inside. "Welcome to my humble abode."

Fae looked around, awe written across her face.

Wren knew she had never seen a house like this, especially not from the inside where she could explore and ask questions. She watched as Fae looked around the main living room and then went down the small corridor to the bedrooms and noticed that there were only two doors. Before Fae could even open her mouth Wren began to talk about the house.

"So the kitchen, eating area and living space are all in one room and then there is a bedroom for me and the other bedroom that used to be my parents, I've given to Aab and Ber to live in. It's small but it's home; I grew up here and now that both my parents are gone it's mine to make a home out of," Wren rambled off. "I wanted to show you how I lived."

"Tell me about them," Fae asked. Wren watched as she

settled herself down on one of the chairs by the fire.

Joining her Wren sat in thought of where to start.

"Well you know some of the basics. My father was injured in the Pirate War, when he came back he was a different person. I don't really remember him before he started drinking but Mother loved him, always. She taught me how to cope with him, how to be sneaky, she'd send me on missions that would teach me how to be stealthy, fast and strong and it would always involve reporting back in to her where my father was — well which tavern and in which village — that's how I learnt so much about the different areas. She loved me, taught me how to survive and how to be strong but would always tell me to: maintain humility, retain dignity and always show kindness," Wren recalled. "It's something I've drilled into Aab and Ber as well, after she was gone. She started making me these clothes when I was young and she realised that working on the stall and going on missions wasn't suited well to wearing a dress and they were one of the best presents she ever got me. My father hated them of course. But before she died we had gotten into a good routine so we could avoid him when he came in drunk at night. It was just after my fifteenth birthday when she died, we slipped up and didn't stick to routine and she took the punishment. I was too weak and afraid to step in. The guard did nothing, siding with their old war buddy," Wren gritted out, looking into the fire with anger in her eyes. "That's when I decided to start to train, to get stronger and work to change things. I wanted to become a guard, work my way to the top and change things from there."

Lost in her own memories of the past, Wren stayed transfixed on the flickering flames of the fire that the boys had left on for her, thinking of how things had changed since her mother's death. She felt the soft touch of Faeryn's hands on her cheeks wiping away errant tears that had somehow escaped her eyes. Feeling the weight of Fae's body rest itself in her lap she looked up from the fire to look into Faeryn's eyes searching for a flicker of understanding. It was there staring into each other's eyes that Faeryn said just the right thing. "Your mother would be proud of the woman you are today."

The fluttering in Wren's stomach bloomed and spread throughout her entire body. Wrapping her arms around Fae she brought their lips together in a passionate embrace. This kiss was unlike the others they had shared. It was slow, endearing. Filled with so much emotion it felt like the world was coming to a stop as they stayed there wrapped in each other's warmth. She wished it could last forever. But as she pulled away and leant her forehead to Fae's she sighed and with a smile she broke the silence. "You always know what to say don't you?"

"I'm always right too, remember that," Fae chuckled. "Now something tells me that we need to get to that meeting with your scary friend."

"What? No we've only been here…" Wren started and turned her eyes to the window, it was pitch black outside. They had been in here for at least a few hours.

How had time gotten away from her like that? If they didn't hurry now they would miss the meeting. Letta was going to kill her. "Oh dear." Wren stood up abruptly, nearly flinging Faeryn across the room from her place on her lap, just catching herself in time to stop her face-planting on the floor.

The quick run from Wren's house to the territory went by like a blur and it was all Wren could do to make sure that Fae was keeping up with her. She needed them to get there in time otherwise Letta would never let her hear the end of it and this would need to go smoothly. As they crossed the invisible border into the territory via the cobbled streets off the back of the market square, two figures moved out of the shadows and stood in front of them. As Wren approached she thought this would be the girls. But as they got close enough to make out details she saw that it was Isla and Ber. It was an odd mixture to see and with a slight frown she greeted them. "Evening, Ber. Isla. I see Letta sent you to take us to the meeting," Wren stated, stepping slightly in front of Fae as they came to a stand in front of them.

"This way," Isla returned in way of a greeting, turning and marching forwards, Ber turning with her soundlessly leading the way.

It didn't take long to get to the old training building that Wren had met Letta in the last time they had a private meeting. Ber's behaviour was bothering her, he had never acted like this with her before. The silent treatment and passive aggressive behaviour coming off him in waves was worrying her and she couldn't think of a reason for it, which was even more of a cause for concern. Coming into the room Wren could see that everyone was already there. Sofia closed the door after they all entered and Wren looked to Letta across the room to begin.

"I expect you are all wondering why Wren and I have called this meeting today," Letta began. "Why don't you all take a seat, we have a lot to go over." Wren let out a slight snicker at this as there were no actual seats in the room just seven haphazardly placed cushions in the centre of the room. Slowly everyone began to sit down and Wren nodded to the pillow next to hers for Faeryn to take a seat.

"Why is Wren's girlfriend here?" Aab blurted out, the other nodding along. "Not to be rude or anything but none of us know you," he directed at Fae, still hidden for the most part under her hood. Letta looked to Wren then, letting her take the chance to speak.

"Well. How do I put this? Fae is special, she can help us. I don't really know how to explain this bit." Wren was cut off by a hand on her thigh. Fae's hand.

"This might make things easier," Fae said as she slowly brought her hands to her hood and took it away from her face and hair, revealing her long mane of auburn hair. Isla and Sofia gasped as realisation hit them. Aab looked confused as he looked between everyone and Fae and Ber sat rigidly next to Aab.

"Right, thanks, Fae. Everyone, Princess Faeryn." Wren waved her hand at Fae letting out a nervous laugh. This was the bit she was worried about, their reactions to Fae's real identity.

"You've been banging the Princess?" Aab exclaimed, voice breaking as he used Fae's title.

"Don't be so crude, Aab!" Wren said firmly, looking to Fae, she smiled lopsidedly. "Sorry, Fae, he's usually not this rude."

"Its fine, and no, Aab, we have not been banging as you put it. By the way, my name is just Faeryn, or Fae as Wren calls me, please do not bloody call me Princess." Fae rolled her eyes.

"Oh, Princess has a potty mouth," smirked Isla, over the surprise of it all and now lounging back on her elbows.

"Isla," Wren warned.

"Oh come on, clearly she is here for a reason other than the fact you two have the hots for each other. How did this happen anyway? Thought Miss Royalty over there couldn't leave the castle?"

"Oh, the forest is our home," Fae giggled knowing her words would serve two purposes. Firstly to make Wren giddy at her use of the word home and secondly to freak out the others who she knew would be at least a little superstitious from Wren's lessons earlier that day. Just as she had expected, the two girls practically choked on their own tongues at the mention of the forest. Ber became even tenser if that was possible and Aab's jaw swung impossibly wide open.

"Fae stop teasing them," Wren admonished. "Letta, can we just get to the meeting, you're enjoying this far too much?" Wren urged.

"Fine. Listen up," Letta huffed, getting the attention of the room. "We are getting older and the world is not changing; we are left to hide, to fend for ourselves while the guards treat us like dirt under their shoes and for no crime other than to be orphaned by the last war. We are all trapped in the walls of the city, there is no freedom. We want to change things. To make them better. So that the youngest of our people do not have to face the same injustices that we have, that Wren has. There is an uprising coming and it will start with us," Letta passionately spoke out, eyeing each member of their little tribe before continuing. "And with Faeryn's help we can do this without bloodshed. We have a chance to win." Leaving that thought to sit there, Letta sat back down letting the truth of what was happening wash over each and every one of them. This would be their lives now. Leaders of a movement as mere teenagers.

Seeing that they would need time to process this, Wren realised that time would be running out. They would need to get Fae back to the castle. Making her excuses she led Faeryn from the room, Letta watching their every move as the others began to whisper between themselves. Leading Fae straight to the tunnels with no hesitation they made their way down to the cave in silence.

"She wasn't as scary as you made out. In fact I think you are more intimidating when you get serious about something." Fae broke the silence.

"You just wait until this whole thing gets going, you won't think I'm the scary one then," Wren laughed, breaking the tension. "Come on let's get you home before you're caught."

Their journey back to the clearing went without incident. As the sky began to lighten, she knew that they would not have much time to say goodbye. The trip had been a success and very emotional and Wren found herself feeling overwhelmed with her feelings for Faeryn.

"Thank you for coming with me tonight, I can't tell you how much it meant to me to be able to share my life with you like that. I've never been able to do that with someone like that before, not someone who meant as much as you do," Wren whispered, stepping closer to Fae, wrapping her arms around her back and bringing their bodies to lean against one another.

"You're an idiot." Fae smiled. She kissed Wren then, open mouthed and hot on her lips. Wren could feel as their bodies pushed closer, wishing she could feel the warmth of her skin on her and not the rough friction of Fae's dress against her clothes. She could feel the softness of Fae's fingertips leaving trails of fire down the back of her neck where they had come to rest, entwining into her hair and stroking the back of her neck. To Wren this felt as if she was no longer alone, like Fae was filling up her soul, as a tongue stroked across her bottom lip, begging entrance. Knowing she would not be able to stop if she allowed entrance, giving in to the lust building within her own stomach, she broke away from Fae she studied her face and the need to say something itched at her throat.

"I lo—" Wren croaked out, stopping herself and leaning her forehead to Faeryn's as she realised what she had been about to say. They were silent then, taking a moment to just be before they both knew they would need to go back to their everyday lives. Stepping back, Wren looked to Fae with a shy smile. She said, "Goodnight, my Fae." Before they both moved away turning to make their journeys back to reality.

30

Wren

Had she really nearly said she loved her? Wren had gotten home that night dumbfounded that she had come so close to saying that without any real thought behind it. Her feelings for Faeryn were strong, really strong. But did she love her? She didn't know. Wren wasn't even sure she really knew what love really was. She had been so distracted when she got back to the house that she didn't realise that both her boys were absent from the house before she went into her room to sleep on her thoughts.

Waking up early she went about getting ready for the day, pulling on a clean set of clothes and washing her face in the sink. She noted how quiet the house was.

Usually Aab and Ber would be still snoring away and she would need to wake them up ready to come and help her down in the market but as she went to their door she could see it was not shut all the way. Pushing it open she could see that the room was empty. The beds clearly not having been slept in. They had changed this room and it was hardly recognisable as the same room that her parents used to reside in. They had split the double bed and made it into two large singles pushed to either side of the room, a small woven rug had been placed in the centre of the room and they each had crudely made chests at the foot of their beds, something they had clearly scraped together from the remains of the buildings in the territory. The only thing that remained of her parents in this room was the small red curtain that covered the window casting a blush glow on the room as the sun shone through. She had known that Aab and Ber wouldn't be happy with finding out about Fae with everyone else but she hadn't thought they would stay away because of it. Ber had been acting out of character lately and despite having meant to talk to him, she had been so distracted that it had slipped her mind. She would need to go and find them. It looked like the market would have to wait for a day.

It hadn't taken her long to get back to territory where she knew they'd most likely be hiding out. As she had skidded to a halt on the first rooftop she found herself face to face with Letta. Not who she was looking for.

"They're not here you know," Letta said, watching Wren as she moved to walk past her. The nonchalant tone instantly rubbed Wren the wrong way and her irritation bubbled over as she turned back to Letta.

"What do you know about it?" Wren half accused as she got up close to Letta, anger showing.

"Look, Wren, you chose to listen to me, you choose every day to follow my lead. You're not bound to me. You chose this. You're not one of my kids. So don't blame me because it didn't end well for you. You knew those boys wouldn't be happy about finding out like that. It doesn't matter to me, but they are your boys. Step up." Letta pushed Wren back away from her. "They're in the cave. Go fix it," she threw over her shoulder as she left the roof.

Wren had no idea how Letta knew about the cave, she would know about the tunnels if she knew about the cave. She knew how Wren had been getting out this whole time. Pushing her concern to the back of her mind at her secret being out she rushed to go and see her boys.

Slowing as she came to the end of the tunnel, she carefully emerged into the cave so as to not startle them. Both boys were sat backs against the wall staring at the green hue of vines that covered the exit. Softly she moved to sit beside them, she knew they had noticed her but both were refusing adamantly to look to her as she rested her back against the wall and slid to the floor to join them.

"You know I wanted to tell you both about Fae, who she was. Letta asked me to wait, before you start. I know I should have told you anyway. I know that now. I was just so damn nervous. You know you guys are my family. I know that neither of you hold love for the crown. I didn't want you to freak out. But it looks like holding back has actually made that worse. This is a mess," she told them, resting the top of her head to the wall and pointing her chin to the ceiling, eyes closed in frustration at her current predicament.

The boys looked to one another and spoke in their silent way that was so normal to Wren now that she hardly noticed it. "We thought you trusted us more than that," Aab spoke softly.

"I do, I just — I don't even know — I guess I was scared."

"That's bull! You were a coward, for months you've been going off, not paying attention, it's like you're hardly here any more even when you're standing right in front of us! You were too scared to face up to us. That's all it was. You know full well, we've told you before you're a leader to us, people listen to you and you know Letta would have listened if you had argued. Give over, Wren." Beer exploded from his seat at the wall's base, jumping up in indignation at her poor excuses, going red in the face the longer he continued shouting at her.

Knowing Ber was right and finally getting an answer to why

he had been so out of character as of late, she looked down guiltily. She had preached her mother's sayings and teachings to them about humility, dignity and kindness and she had failed to apply them to herself in the last months, becoming wrapped up completely in everything that was Faeryn. Unable to pop the bubble of her new found feelings that surrounded her and overwhelmed her, taking over her every thought of the day. She didn't know what to say, everything he had said was true; how could they trust her to be there for them when she hadn't even realised how unavailable she had made herself?

Aab's voice broke through her thoughts then. "You love her don't you?" He had always been more in tune with the emotions of both himself and those around him than Ber had been; Ber was the more logical of the two. He had hit a sore spot, she didn't know if she did love Fae or not. It had been something she had been considering since the previous night and hadn't given thought to prior to that.

"I don't know. I think I might. But I don't know if I really know what love is," Wren replied letting herself be vulnerable in the truth of it. "I'm sorry, ya know. You're right, Ber. I'm sorry."

Ber groaned from where he stood watching her before flinging himself onto the floor next to her and leaning his head on her shoulder. "I hate that I can't stay mad at you. He can't even get really mad at you. It's hopeless," Ber exclaimed in irritation. "Anyway stop being an idiot, you know what love is. The way your mother treated you, the way you've always treated us. You know love."

"Ber's right. You know love. You're just scared of admitting you love the Princess, you know it'll be harder to love her than anyone else. Almost impossibly so," Aab continued.

"How did you guys get so smart?" Wren gently teased.

"Well it certainly wasn't from you or Letta, you two surrogate mothers both have the emotional intelligence of a tadpole," Ber dead-panned earning a playful shove from Wren.

"I am not your mother! I'm not even in my twenties yet!" Wren screeched.

"Except, you kind of are. We even live with you now," Aab shot back amusedly.

"Oh god, shut up both of you!" Wren groaned pulling herself up from the floor. "Can we go home now or are you two planning on spending more time staring at the vines?"

"Fine! This was getting boring anyway," the boys said together, getting up to join Wren.

Getting back to the house wasn't too difficult and on the way they stopped off at the market and haggled with some of the vendors to get some fresh meat for evening meal.

Wren decided that that night she would skip training and spend some time with her boys, cook a meal and play cards and start trying to be better. They had a simple meal of Potatoes and spiced meat, Aab offering to clean up while Wren ran to the nearest tavern and picked up some ale from their stores — the keep owed her a favour and the boys were old enough now to try some. Ber had gotten a warm fire going and lit the candles around the living space by the time she got back and Aab was coming out in sleep clothes and a house coat that looked like he had tried to sew it together himself from scraps of old clothes.

"You know I would have made you one of those if you had asked?" Wren enquired.

"I don't know what you think is funny," he replied, catching her mirth before chucking a bundle at her. "I made you one too! Ber there's one on the end of your bed as well."

Wren opened the bundle gobsmacked, when had he found time to make this? She really hadn't been present these last few months. She had never owned a house coat before, always out at night and usually sleeping in her day clothes as a by-product she had never seen the need for the luxury but she was glad of the thick and soft coat as she put it on to sit with her boys for the night, she realised the truth of Ber's earlier words. She did know love. They stayed up into the early hours of the morning playing cards and talking of the past and the possibilities the future could hold. Aab mentioned he wanted to expand the stall and open a second one for clothes, he had quite enjoyed making the house coats and he thought Wren's work would sell well if she wanted to. Ber spoke of the uprising and to Wren's utter surprise of how he and both Isla and Sofia seemed to all have feelings for one another and wanted to give it a go at being happy together in the future but they would need the uprising to be successful to do that. And Wren spoke of Faeryn, the wall, the forest and the realm, how she wanted to see everything, have freedom for all. It was a peaceful night full of hope and shared contentedness. As the boys began to yawn, Wren realised how late it had gotten and urged them to go to bed and rest. As they left, Ber came back to the doorway of their room to look back at Wren as she tidied up before bed.

"You should really tell her you know. That you love her. Before you don't have a chance. You never know what's going to happen," he said softly, sleep filling his voice as he wandered back into his room and to his bed.

Wren smiled at his back as he left. The pull in her heart had gotten stronger as he spoke and she knew that he was right. She did love her.

31

Wren

The next week went by quickly. Wren paid more attention to the boys and she was working to convince them to come to the forest with her. She wanted them to see it for themselves and she wanted them to train with her but they were both firmly against going there, clearly put off by the old wives' tales of its magic. The villagers had been quiet towards her since she had missed the day at market to look for Aab and Ber and although off-putting she tried to shove the uncomfortable gut feeling something was going on to the back of her mind as she continued on, they were probably just agitated that the stall had been closed down for the day.

Time for Wren to meet with Fae rolled around quickly and she went eagerly with a spring to her step to their clearing, wanting to tell her all about what had happened with the boys and how much better things had become from it. She wanted to hear what Fae thought of the village, what her thoughts on the meeting with Letta were and to just catch up. It had been difficult to not see her now that she knew that she loved her. Wren wasn't ready to tell Fae the extent of her feelings yet but she knew she would soon, she just wanted to find the perfect timing and the doubts that she held regarding Fae's own feelings for her stopped her from wanting to rush in with the information. It was, after all, Fae who had said that she just wanted to see where things went because she was unsure of her feelings, only knowing that she had a physical attraction to her and the emotional romantic feeling were unsure. It made sense considering her lack of interaction with others. It can be easy for anyone to misinterpret feelings of strong friendship for romantic ideations even without the isolation and social solitude. No, she would not be able to tell Faeryn yet; she would wait until she felt surer that Fae would feel the same way.

Looking around she realised that while she had been trapped in thought the night had carried on without her, the forest was alive with sound, but none of them were the tapping of Fae's footsteps as she scrambled up the hill to the clearing clumsily in her haste and excitement to see her. The night had taken on a chill and as Wren realised that she may be waiting her for a while she went to begin her training, Faeryn would understand. Making her runs around the clearing, varying her speeds, warming up and forcing her heart to begin pounding at an accelerated pace, Wren tried to pry the distraction of her love for Fae from her mind. She didn't want a repeat of last time she discovered her feelings and blurted out kisses and words with no capability of control. No, today she would stay measured. The zone she created for herself allowed her to get through her training routine with little thought for anything else, keeping alert to her surroundings but extremely focused on her task. It wasn't until she came to the space in her training that she would usually turn to Fae and begin to spar that she came around seeing the dark of the sky lightening and the dew beginning to form on the blades of grass and leaves on the edge of their clearing floor. Fae had not arrived. Wren felt confusion and moving to look out at the window of the castle she knew to be Fae's she wondered why she had been unable to show some sign that she would not be able to attend their meeting today. Acceptance and understanding were Wren's go to in this situation, it was not the first time that Fae had been unable to come and certainly not the first time she had been unable or unwilling to warn her; she knew that Wren trained here regardless of her presence. But that didn't stop Wren from feeling the pangs of hurt alongside the pulling already settled in her chest. Shrugging it off Wren reverted back to her solo training for some time to work off the annoyance at Fae's no-show and vowed to demand Fae send a sign in her window next time she was unable to come, so she knew she was safe.

Wren's annoyance quickly spread when the following week Faeryn again did not show up to their meeting and yet again there was no sign in the window. This continued on for another two weeks; each passing meeting time missed, the more intense Wren began to train. Thoughts and unanswered questions spiralling in her mind, surfacing in anger and irritability that she could only do so much in training to work it out of her system. The boys and even Letta got the ugly side of her frustration on more than one occasion. The villagers even were not taking much of a liking to Wren's new attitude, their glaring eyes, and curious and questioning whispers mocked her while she worked her market stall, gone was her chatty and loud influence on the market and the others suspicious gossiping ways were affecting Wren, pushing her bad mood further and further the longer that Faeryn stayed away.

A day after Faeryn's latest no show, Wren was grumbling to herself about Princesses and their fickle attitudes towards punctuality and ill tempered, troublesome manners when a young boy approached her stall. Wren barely thought to look up until she heard a slight clearing of a small throat.

"Are you Wren, Miss?" a young brunette boy asked her

nervously. The boy was clearly a servant, his clothes were slightly frayed but his skin was clean of the dirt that usually marked the villagers that came to the market.

"Yes?" Wren answered dryly, in no mood to be hospitable to anyone. Looking around, Wren could see that the other stall owners and workers, even the other people milling about the stalls, had also taken notice of the boy, noticing his cleaner appearance.

"I am looking for lilies, or tulips. Do you have them?" he asked with a hoarseness to his throat.

Wren, unable to pinpoint what exactly was wrong with the boy, gestured towards the yellow tulips and white lilies sat nearest her on the stall. "Of course, are you stupid? Anyone knows these are tulips and lilies. They'll cost you though. Not cheap flowers those."

"I will take one of each then… I've heard the Fae like them," the boy said, whispering the last part so quietly that Wren could barely make it out. Her ears and heart prickled simultaneous as she strained to hear the word Fae come from his mouth.

Curiously, Wren picked out one of each flower and asked the boy, "Come round to the side of the stall so that I can hand these to you more easily. That'll be two silver pieces."

The boy instantly moved across to the side of the stall where their transaction was further protected from view. "Here, take this pouch. It will have enough in it, no need to look." He thrust the bag into her hand and barely grabbed the flowers before turning and scurrying out of the market and to god knows where. Looking around the market slyly before placing the bag into her pocket, she could see that the majority of the marketplace were trying to watch and hear what was going on with frowns on their faces. Wren knew it would be best to stay and continue to work but she was certain that the boy had slipped her something in the bag and with the reference to Fae she was even more convinced that it would be something from her Princess. Unable to stop the jittering and the pull in her chest, she found herself shutting up shop and heading back to the house, despite it being early afternoon. The looks of annoyance she was getting could be felt burning her back but she could not stop her feet from moving as she approached her home. Finally she would have some answers for Faeryn's continued absence. Rushing into her home and plonking herself unceremoniously down onto her dining room chair, she began to read.

My Dearest Bird,
　Things have become worrisome within the walls.
　Mother is on a war path. Paranoid and suspicious. It is no longer safe to enter my secrets. We cannot meet. I am playing prisoner in my gilded cage, no comforts of my own space. Things will return to normalcy soon. They must. I miss you.
　Yours, Magic

Wren couldn't help but laugh as she read Faeryn's missive, she had clearly tried to keep the note incognito in case of interlopers getting hold of the note she had sent via servant boy. It was fairly easy for her to decipher the meaning behind Fae's written words, Wren was her bird, Fae her magic, the only secret would be the passageways she would need to enter to come to the clearing and she hadn't set out a candle to warn Wren because she was being confined elsewhere. That struck Wren as fairly odd, Fae had never been confined anywhere other than her room the entire time Wren had known her, it would have been helpful if she had managed to include something as to the reason she was moved these last few weeks. What really had caught Wren's eyes and had made them scrunch up and her head begin to ache with the arguing stream of consciousness that followed reading it was the one part of the message that had been crossed out. Two tiny, miniscule letters L & O. Had she meant to write these, clearly they were supposed to be the beginning of the word love, a common sign off between loved ones in letters. Had Faeryn been thinking along the same lines as Wren? Did she love her too? Wren reasoned that she could have just begun to write it out, out of habit. Or she had meant to write a complete sentence and the word wasn't love as Wren had assumed. But why had she crossed it out? Had she thought she was giving away too much information? These thoughts continued to swirl around like a hurricane in Wren's mind, blinding her with pressure behind her eyes as she could not move away from the two letters on the thick, clearly expensive paper that Fae had used. Clearly not having extended her thoughts of interlopers as to how the note would look being passed to a commoner, clearly too expensive to be a normal note from village to village or an order of new flowers to a high guard's house. Finally slamming down her head to table she groaned out her displeasure and frustration of only getting half answers to Faeryn's absence and date of return. Despite the early time exhaustion overtook her. Emotionally spent, Wren lugged herself to her room. She would start again tomorrow.

The next day as Wren got ready to leave for market her thoughts had turned to positivity, believing that it wouldn't be long now until Fae would return, two more weeks at the most. There was no way she would be gone for much longer. Grabbing on to her baskets and stall cover, she fixed a smile to her face and left her house. It didn't take long to see that people were taking notice of her; she hoped that it was simply because of her renewed sense of attitude, instead of the grumpy dispassionate woman she had been of late. Maybe her hair was particularly wild today, she hadn't done much different to it yet men and women were all sending her blank glances as she made her way down to market. Setting up her stall she waved to her neighbour seller and raised her voice to shout a greeting. In return she got a slight nod, and a tight and forced smile instead of her usual merry greeting.

    Frowning as Wren finished setting up her stall she went to take a seat when some of the young women who usually bought from her this time of the week entered the market. Sitting straighter again she went to wave at them with a smile before noticing them whisper and grimace with distaste at her presence. Narrowing her eyes Wren sat back on her stool, working through in her head what could have caused this reaction. Looking around to try and ascertain how far this new anger towards her had spread, she saw annoyed looks being tossed her way as quiet words were spoken from seller to seller, labour boys running stall to stall whispering to the next to pass on his words. Wren saw the looks of wariness and dislike taking over each new face that was whispered to before the sight shift of eyes to her way. She knew her attitude had not done this. There was only one thing that had taken place that could cause this storm of gossip.

    The note.

32

Wren

The marketplace was quiet, the villagers that worked there had yet to arrive to put out their wares for the day and Wren enjoyed the peace that this afforded, something she rarely was able to see due to her own schedule usually leaving her to arrive as the other sellers would be finishing setting up their stalls for the morning. The extra time to sleep benefited her greatly because of her night time escapades with Fae in the forest of Kasia and her flower stall took little preparation to become presentable for the buyers during the market day. However, her typical flow of clientele had begun to sputter out over the last few days. While Wren had originally put this down to her attitude after Fae's no shows, she was now realising that the problem was a bit more in-depth than she had anticipated. Which is how she landed here, first one to arrive, trying to set up in time to watch the reactions of people as they first saw her this morning and could not hide as she got ready, instead she would be able to analyse their faces and her situation with the advantage of no distractions.

 As Wren finished the presentation of her new flower selection she settled down onto her stool and began to watch as one by one the other sellers slowly trickled in from the side streets of the square, still doozy eyed and unaware of her presence, too caught up in their own merchandise and slow yawns. Wren smirked at this, even getting ready in the morning after little sleep she was much more alert than these people, she was used to the lack of sleep, albeit, but even still this was poor on their parts.

Plastering on a smile and making sure to give off a small wave as the first seller noticed her, she waited to see the chain reaction.

The spice seller had been first, the man whose son she had rejected and redirected to the meat seller's daughter. As his head rose and his eyes followed, Wren sat in his direct line of sight and she greeted him in her usual cheerful way. His face went blank as he froze in place. His son trying to get his attention soon followed his gaze and looked directly at Wren frowning harshly before placing a hand on his father's shoulder to knock him out of his stupor. It was with this action that the dominoes began to fall slowly, every seller and worker one by one noticed her. The quiet murmur of distasteful whispers welled up in her ears and Wren was able to catch some of what was being said as nasty looks of disapproval and annoyance were thrown at her.

"—Thinks she's too good for us."

"Did you see that girl she was with?"

"Suspicious if you ask me. She shouldn't be allowed here."

"Both parents dead before their time and she comes out tops up."

"Did you see that boy with that letter the other day? There's no way that was her stuff."

As Wren took in the snippets of hushed conversations a picture began to form in her head of why the other villagers had begun to block her out of the market. Why her buyers had begun to trickle out. And she understood. If she had seen someone go from two parents to none in a few short years, while they gained more from their deaths and then seeing them after associated with someone clearly of a higher class and beginning to receive notes, again clearly from a high-class person, she would be suspicious too. Wren clenched her jaw and realised that she had been wrong to let Fae come here, it had been more dangerous than she had thought and not for the reasons she had considered but because of the backlash this would and was having on her day-to-day life. If she had realised that the villagers would take such notice she would have at least insisted on Fae wearing full villagers' clothes, borrowed a dress from Letta, and she would have been more careful not to be seen, by anyone. She might have even decided against the visit for the time being. And Fae should have known better than to send a note through a servant into the village. The servants could be spotted by an observant person a mile away even if they tried to be incognito. The materials she had used for the note were even more blatant than the messenger and it most likely had been the nail in the coffin alongside her improved attitude since the note that caused the villagers distrust to be cemented.

 Letting the smile fall from her face and the blank look of disinterest cast itself across her features, Wren began to flip through the implied implications of this distrust from the village lingering, or even becoming permanent. The lack of money from her stall would affect not only herself and her boys but also the entirety of the Street Children as they had become significantly reliant on the money she provided them for meats, the cloth she would buy here and make into clothes for them, the spices she would haggle from the spice man in exchange for certain flowers. Without the access to the stall it would become much harder for them or her to gain access to much of these things, a problem for many of the number who were still in their growth phase. She could possibly look to let Aab and Ber take over the stall permanently as they had gained good rapport with many of the villagers here but she was unsure if they were going to be tainted with the same brush that had tarred her good name.

Perhaps she would need to switch product and train up two new Street Children to run the stall with Aab or Ber as watcher.

The possible solutions swirling and their pros and cons bouncing off of one another in her mind was giving her an awful headache and her blank mask had cracked into a small thoughtful frown as a bead of sweat threatened to fall from her brow into her slightly scrunched unfocused eyes. Wiping her face with a cloth she felt more than saw a shadow of a figure sidle up to her stall looming over her seated body, face blacked out by the shadow of the sun.

"No one wants you here, Wren, get gone," was hissed out before Wren could get her eyes to adjust to make out the person in front of her. She could make out from the intimidating gruffness of the voice that it belonged to a man but the gravelly baritone was not one she recognised clearly. The mystery man had kicked some of her flower baskets out from the bottom of her stall as he had left and as she got up and moved to collect the scattered baskets and attempt to salvage some of the flowers damaged or ruined by the man's act she felt eyes on her from all sides. Carefully casting her eyes up she could see the satisfied smirks of many of her former haggling partners; she could even hear the muffled laughter of Iris the meat seller's daughter. Cheeks reddening at her embarrassment but also a sentimental feeling of hurt washing over her she made sure to go about her intentions slowly and with purpose, trying desperately to not allow her feelings to show across her reddened face. These people had seen her grow, many had been in the market since before her birth, had known her mother, had played with her as young children before her path had veered for the worse inside the home and as she grew more independent. Some like the spice seller had even known her father before the drink, had seen the man he had turned into upon his return. And yet here she was, being treated as if she was an outsider, unknown to them all: with suspicion, hate and jealousy. To Wren it felt like the final step in her disembodiment from her childhood. All she had left now were her Street Children and Fae.

An overwhelming sense of clarity washed over Wren as this final break happened. She did not belong here. The world was not ready for revolution and their long-term plans would need to last over years if they were going to change things without a violent reckoning. It was likely that if things stayed the way they had planned, her and Fae would never be able to be anything more than they were now. A secret, dirty and hidden in the forest of Kasia, a perfectly ironic setting for their love as it currently stood in the minds of the people. It crossed Wren's mind whether her effectiveness for the cause would be better placed outside of the city of Ekoni's walls to amass greater change in a timelier manner. It would of course have an even worse effect on her and Fae's relationship, separation. But at this point she was speculating; she needed to talk to Faeryn and tell her of the way her feelings had developed, tell her of the changes within the village and find out once and for all if Fae felt the same way that she did. She prayed that for her own sanity her Princess would be able to come this time around. With this, Wren smiled and began to pack away her stall having had enough of the negativity for the day.

Later that evening Wren prepared to go to the clearing to train and see if Faeryn would turn up this time. Her mind kept going back to the forest and the realm beyond, there was so much she hadn't seen. Her thoughts turned further to her feeling of uselessness now that the village market had turned against her. Wren's thoughts raced, maybe she could get Fae to go with her, and she felt trapped as it was. Then the problem of leaving would only be down to the Street Children and her boys having to fend for themselves but they had Letta and she had taught the boys everything she knew; they may even be better off without her at this stage. A new idea began forming in her mind and she started to stuff more clothes into her satchel. If she could convince Faeryn to join her, they would run. The boys would be fine. They would understand.

A new steel to her eyes, Wren packed up her satchel to the brim, even stuffing in her kitchen utensils, her wooden sword would only do so well in the wilds. She had no belongings of more worth than sentimental value but she had enough that she would be able to get by as long as they were creative. Writing out a note for the boys explaining why she felt she must leave and a missive of revolutionary purpose for Letta, Wren took one last look around her childhood home and placing her key down on the dining table she left, refusing to let her second thoughts turn her back around.

33

Faeryn

Boredom.

The last few weeks had been the worst Fae had had in years and the darkness was lying in wait ready for her to let the shadows back in. The thought of Wren was the only thing keeping her sanity intact.

The fight had come the day after her visit to the village and she had been still very sensitive and irritated by the conditions that Wren and the villagers were forced to live in. They should not have to worry the way they do and the Street Children should be being looked after not ostracized. Her mother had come in to discuss Fae's proposal for new training to prepare her for the crown. And thinking back on the way things went Fae knew that she should have been more tempered.

Her mother had been docile, accommodating when she had entered and began the conversation, showing warmth and hope in the way that she spoke. "I want you to be by my side, I have taken in what you have said and I believe, as much as I hate to admit it, you are right, you need to see how it is to really rule, not just what you hear from Tobin," she had said soft and encouragingly. Fae had just smiled tightly, knowing and waiting for the "but" that would follow her mother's words. Not caring that her mother was being open and warm with her for the first time in what felt like forever, she focused in on the negative. "But, that being said. I still feel as if you need to be taking your lessons with Tutor Tobin, to drill in your heritage, and I can't think of a better way for you to learn patience and a sense of duty than by doing the lessons despite your distaste for them." Her mother had finished as if reading from a pre-rehearsed script in her mind, not even sounding like herself. Fae had known then that this must have been Tobin's idea.

The reaction to those words is what landed her here. Cooped up in the royal medical quarters on the other side of the castle. She had gone mad at her mother, unaccepting of the continued lessons by Tobin and the small compromise from her mother on being able to shadow her one day a week. Fae remembered that she had screamed, she had started spouting off nonsensical exclamations of poverty, a puppet queen, unsanitary conditions, prisoner princesses and how war came to the unchanging. None of what she had said would make sense to anyone but her and Wren; it all stemmed back to their experiences together, the unknown knowledge they had against the people of the castle and the way the realm was run, all the way through to how the villagers actually lived. The way she had screamed, shrill and words flowing out so fast, she wasn't even sure if half the words had come out in English or as a jumbled mess of syllables. Pushing forward into her mother and an infuriated Tutor Tobin entering her chamber with a flask of something that was forced down her throat by the guards was the last thing she had remembered before waking up here in the medical quarters. No company other than Tutor Tobin coming in twice a day with some physicians to check on her and talk as if she wasn't there.

It hadn't taken very long to find out that the overall belief was that she had a fever when the occurrence happened and she was being treated for hysteria induced psychosis. From what she could tell, they weren't blaming her for her actions and they were keeping her here until it could be determined that she was no longer a danger to herself or others and the fever had broken. This she was sure was part of some elaborate plan by Tobin to discredit her in front of her mother. The fever had clearly been induced by something snuck into her breakfast that morning and the attitude, regrettably, was predictable from her when things went as badly as they did. Tutor Tobin had known that she would react that way, her inability to keep calm had hit him on more than one occasion as she had grown and had only quietened as of late, where she had been able to keep from taking the bait he would lay with the thought of Wren.

    Fae knew that she should have been more careful, knew that she should have thought before she had acted and she had had plenty of time to beat herself up for it over the last few weeks. Her only reprieve had been when Benji had been guarding her and his mentor had left. He made for some good, if slightly awkward, conversation. He was young and scared, but he was fun to mess with. She had even managed to get him to take a note she had scraped together to send to Wren explaining her absence last week. If he actually took it to her, she did not know.

    But he still took it. It gave her hope.

    Today was the day though, she knew from her eavesdropping on the physicians that her supposed fever had broken and she was going to be getting to leave the medical quarters today. She had been careful over the last two weeks not to be rude and to even attempt to come across as submissive to Tutor Tobin and the physicians as they visited. The act had seemingly paid off and Fae was filled with quiet anticipation as she sat looking at the doors to the room. It didn't take long for Tobin to come in and falter slightly to find her already staring at the point he had entered, directly now into his face. Faking a meek tone in her voice, Faeryn asked, "Am I better now?"

With a quirk of his eyebrow Tobin lowered his clipboard and responded, "Your fever has broken, Princess, your psychosis seems to have righted itself... but you may need more time?" Smirking as he ended his sentence.

Clearly trying to get a rise out of her he waited for her to respond. When all he got was Fae's lowering eyes, a frown crossed his face at her ruining his fun. "But I don't think that will be necessary. You can go back to your rooms."

He finished dismissively and left without another word, done with his games for the time being.

Knowing this could be her only chance with how volatile things had been in the castle, Fae made her way to her chambers at a slow forced pace, determined not to give away her act of submissiveness and be put back under Tobin's complete control. Her mother hadn't even visited during her supposed recovery period. It didn't take long for her to get back to her room and as she closed the door she let out a heaving sigh at finally being alone. Looking around her she could see it was exactly how she had left it, the tapestry still firmly in place in front of her entrance to the passages. It was almost time for evening meal from the darkening sky outside of her window and she knew that tonight she would steal away into her forest. She needed to see Wren.

Solitary confinement, Fae had found, can be good for some things. Mainly thinking. After she had finished running through all the ways in which she would kill Tobin for the wrong he was committing against her, her thoughts had turned to her friend, her something more. Her Wren. She had told Wren that she felt the attraction towards her but didn't know how she felt. Faeryn had come to realise in her time in solitary confinement that this was a fucking lie. Of course she fucking loved Wren, how idiotic could she have been to try and deny it? If she didn't love Wren what was the pulling in her chest that had been there from the very beginning, what was the jumping beans in her stomach every time she got Wren to smile, the flutter of heat that simmered on her cheeks every time she brushed her lips along Wren's? No, she didn't like Wren. Fae knew that she loved her. She had nearly told her in her letter, it had felt so natural to sign off with love, but it hadn't felt like it was the right time. She wanted to tell her in person. See the way Wren reacted, get the off-guard facial expression of her emotions that Fae knew that Wren would guard if she found out before they were face to face.

What concerned Fae more was how this love would affect her duty to her mother and the realm? They had already discussed, and she had essentially joined, a revolution. But would she be able to be with a woman in the long run reigning over the realm? Would it not seem as if she was making all of the changes for her own gain rather than for the betterment of her subjects? Faeryn wanted to just say "fuck it" and be done with it, take what she wanted but no matter how hard she tried she couldn't help but think of the duty that her mother had had drummed into her since birth. Fae supposed that this was what her mother had wanted all along, her lessons to create a strong loyalty to the crown, her family and her duty, despite how hard she rebelled. Things usually seemed clearer when she spoke through things with Wren. She would need to just tell her and stop pussy footing around the issue, Wren had been patient enough.

Trapped in her own thoughts, she saw that the sky had darkened as a knock on the door indicating her evening meal had arrived knocked her out of her thoughts. Once the girl — Flora she was sure of it — had dropped off her meal and made her way out of the room she quickly scoffed down the bread and stew mixture that burnt her throat and lungs, making her face go red and her eyes water from the heat, rushing to finish so that the evening routine could be completed after the food and she could leave and make her way to her love. Licking the bowl clean and feeling slightly bloated from the speed at which she devoured her meal rather than waiting for it to be collected, she called out to the guards, she knew Benji to be out there shadowing her official guards, asking them to take away her empty bowls and call for the maids for her "bed clothes" — which she had now dubbed her training clothes — it was a wonder they hadn't noticed the dirt and sweat that spotted the layers every week. Rushing everyone about, exclaiming she was tired and being bossier and much more vocal with them than usual, she received odd looks from Benji as she went about her business and as she pushed out the last of the workers she sighed and blew out her candle. Faeryn looked to the tapestry above her bed and smiled.

Time to go back to the Forest of Kasia.

34

Faeryn

Waiting until the cover of darkness and the false assumption that she had fallen asleep, Fae crept out of her bed and placed her cloth shoes back onto her feet making sure to grab her wrap from her wooden desk chair.

Creeping across the floor back to her bed, she felt more than heard a loud creak come from the floor where her toes had just pushed upon. Freezing in place and straining to hear if the guards outside her bedroom door would move to enter her chambers, she could feel her heart pounding so loudly in her ears, the blood rushing through her as adrenaline spiked her system. Trying desperately to calm her beating heart, Fae began to count in her head as Wren had once taught her, timing her breaths in and out.

Thinking back, she remembered how Wren had stood behind her pressed to her body as she held up the bow and arrow aiming towards a tree they were using for target practice. Fae had been failing all day to hit the trunk, Wren had said she just needed to calm her mind and had moved behind her and held her still looking with her and counting in her ears. "In for seven, hold for three and out for seven. Now breathe." Fae had felt her whole body flush, and she had been hard pressed to keep herself under control long enough to follow Wren's instructions. It had worked then, as it was now, and centred her enough to get back across the bed soundlessly and re-focused in on what she was doing.

Fae's only hesitation was sitting in the entrance to her passageways holding the tapestry in her hand. She looked to the door and took pause to watch the shadows of the guard that could be seen from the gap at the bottom of the door. Slowly rocking from side to side it was unlike the stillness she was used to when staring at the shadows as she fell asleep. A nagging feeling of worry settled itself in her stomach as she let her arrogance and the pull in her chest overcome the worry she felt. Dropping the tapestry back down and falling gently into the passage, she tried to shake the worry from her completely, taking one last calming breath before setting her eyes forward, allowing them to adjust to the darkness and beginning her journey to see Wren.

Today felt different, as Fae moved through the passageways every soft noise or echoing knock on the stone walls of her passages caused her to jump, heart starting violently at the broken silence. The journey seemed to take much longer than her usual hurried pace and despite her breathing she was struggling to control the quick thumping of her heart against her rib cage. Faeryn knew that she needed to try to think clearly and move quickly; lingering only meant that she would be worried for longer and it would eat into the time she spent with Wren who she hadn't seen for weeks, they had lots of time to catch up on. She felt as if she had already wasted too much time having Wren not know that she loved her. This singular thought was what drove her on forwards into the dark.

It took Fae much longer to get to the outer edges of the passages than usual, she stopped at every peephole, hesitated at every door outlining. The guards were on high alert and so must she be. Something was not quite right within the castle walls. Faeryn's body sagged with relief as she skimmed her fingers along the last turning to her escape, her eyes squinting to adjust as the green glow of light emanated from the small exit in the wall. She was nearly there. Pushing her way through the thick brush that covered the hole from outside the wall, Fae emerged out into the base of the hill that led to her and Wren's clearing. She could see now that her caution had cost her, the moon was already high in the sky threatening to be cast away from view by ominous grey clouds surrounded by midnight blue sky speckled with lowly lit stars. Dismay at the thought that Wren might have already left, thinking her not to come like every other week in recent times, Fae crouched down low in the undergrowth, determined not to be spotted as she made the crawl at a near impossible speed up the hillside to her Wren. Sweat and dew drops clung to Fae's dress as she progressed towards her clearing, dirt staining the patches soaking into the ground as her knees pressed against them, sodden and sending a chill to her bones. She pulled through it all without a second thought, ignoring the growing pains in the hands as she gripped onto anything that would give her leverage.

 Pulling herself over the last ledge that separated her from her destination, Fae could have sworn she heard a shout out on the wind. Frozen she held herself still as she settled behind the ridge, thoughts of Wren forgotten for a moment as she strained to hear again trying desperately to figure out if she had been spotted. Her heart thundered in her ears and as she clutched her eyes shut she felt movement to her side. Knowing that even if she had been spotted there was no one that would be able to be here as fast as that, she slowly opened her eyes and turned her head to face into the clearing. A clearing that had now been blocked from view as a body took over her eyes, moving to lie down next to her. Shocked, it took a second for Fae to look to the face of the body next to her and when the amused face of Wren came into view she couldn't help but smile.

"Whatcha doing, Princess?" Wren enquired cheerfully, voice coloured in amusement.

The rest of the world rang silent as Wren took over all of her senses and she pushed herself into her arms, wanting — needing — her touch. Today it did not seem like enough. Tears reached and spilled over her eyelids as she held onto Wren, overcome with emotions she had not realised were lingering in her heart. The pulling in her chest that she had felt so many nights and days leading up to her first entrance to the forest that intensified every time she left and returned back to the castle, pulling her closer to Wren. Physically she could feel that intensity as she clutched to Wren's shirt, pulling her to her, the embrace not quite enough, wanting to meld their bodies together, feeling as if she ever let go she would lose her forever. The unknown force feeling as if it was coming to a climax as spluttered platitudes of longing and missing came from Faeryn's mouth, overwhelmed and overflowing with inexplicable emotion as uncontrollable tears poured from her tightly scrunched eyelids. The time they had been forced to bear apart, alongside the new revelations that she truly loved the woman she engulfed with her body accumulated into this overly stimulated mess of blubbered "I miss yous, and tears. Leaving her counterpart confused but coolly calm in the midst of her breakdown. Just another thing to add to the list of why she loved her.

Wren's coolness washed over her in a wave, subtle at first but increasing in vigour with each passing breath, like mint tea to the taste, cleansing her of her overwrought emotions and allowing her to see clearly through her tears, her heartbeat and breathing beginning to stutter back into a steady rhythm as she sniffed away her residual pain and leant back to look Wren in the face, eye to eye. It was like inhaling a cool summer's breeze on the top of a lonely mountain, taking your first real breath of fresh air after having been kept underground for so long.

"You're infuriating really," Faeryn breathed out, unable to say calmly what she really meant to say in that moment.

Chuckling and stepping back and away from her arms, Wren picked up a wooden sword from the forest floor, winking at Faeryn. "Let's train."

35

Faeryn

Training had been hard that day, with so much energy to expel and the determined pulling still itching at the back of her mind leaving her unable to abate the need to move, to wear herself so thoroughly that she was able to sit and rest a while without feeling the pull, the jitters and the anxiety that crept and overtook her sense, a sure side effect from the prolonged absence from Wren she had endured. As they fought with precise strikes, her eyes clouded over thinking of the way she felt, the pulling, wondering if Wren possibly felt the same way. Was she able to feel the pulling and make it lie dormant for periods of time? Unlike Faeryn, Wren had not seemed overcome with emotion upon their reunion the way that Faeryn herself had been and it left Faeryn questioning if Wren loved her the way that she herself and so recently discovered that she loved Wren.

Maybe she shouldn't share this revelation as hastily as she had thought she should on her journey down through the castle's hidden passageways. Had she been naïve in thinking that this was fated? With every grunt and thud of wood against wood her thoughts took over, seemingly egged on by the pulling in her heart that had in reality instigated this whole mind set. Should she leave it, or should she confront Wren with her feelings and end this game they had been playing? Or was this all in her head? Faeryn could not help but put all of these uncertain feelings into each hit against the practice sword, sweating with exertion, letting the noise of her thoughts build up into a deafening crescendo seeping through her pores.

Faeryn's body heaved as she began to falter, the exertion too much for her body to cope with; they had been going for what felt like hours and her stamina could no longer keep up with her mind's will to carry on working out the feelings running through her. Wren, she noted with slight annoyance, had seemingly not even broken a sweat despite having been here longer than her. Faeryn knew that she had not been training anywhere near as long as this beautiful woman but she had hoped that she would have been able to carry on and provoked at least a singular bead of sweat from her brow. Caught in her idle thoughts she had not noticed the slight flick of the wrist as Wren blocked her parry and as her wooden training sword clattered to the ground she too fell to her knees, panting as she looked up to her love with a half-amused smile.

"I feel like you've not been doing your strength exercises, Princess." Wren smirked down at her. Faeryn could never tell if it was love that twinkled in her eye when she did this, the slight hitch in her voice when she called her Princess was always noticeable and leant towards the idea that this could just be lust.

"Clearly you haven't," Faeryn drawled back at the woman now standing over her with her hand out in a motion to help her back to her feet. Gone was the simpering mess that had made itself known upon her arrival and now she got to her feet standing tall as she pulled Wren in with a jerk of her hand clasped tightly around the woman's forearm. Noses mere millimetres apart, Faeryn could feel the warmth of Wren's breath consume her as she locked her eyes onto the ocean waves that resided within Wren's irises. Once again the world slowed around them, all that there was was the beating of each other's hearts and the pulling urge in her chest, warmth rising up throughout her body and her unable to move a single muscle as she tried to keep her composure as she felt Wren moving in closer to her, lips skimming on her own. As she felt she was finally going to get release, a kiss so long to come to them after the weeks of being out of arms reach, a shout could be heard ringing throughout the forest.

Startled, Wren stepped away, broken out of the spell that had been binding them into their isolated moment. Faeryn stumbled forward, trying still to gravitate towards the warmth of Wren's skin.

"What... What... So-Sorry?" Faeryn asked, still confused as her mind struggled to bring itself back to present, acutely aware that Wren had said something, but not having the ability to process more than the fear on Wren's face. She had never seen her look scared before.

"Fae, snap out of it, that shout was surely from a guard. Did you not hear it?" Panic lacing her voice.

"We must go, they cannot find us here, not like this." Wren's state of panic bled through and hastened her movements as she frantically made to grab her bow and sword, eager to stash them away, notice pulled from Fae as her self-preservation instinct began to kick in. It was not until a harsh pull bruised through her upper arm that her heart faltered and began to slow.

"Wren, you need to calm your heart, breathe, and breathe." Fae looked into Wren's eyes, for once taking the stronger role between the two of them and urging her to take a moment and think rationally. That guard had with most likeliness not in fact seen them, but had been shouting to another guard on watch, either to alert him to change over or simply to reprimand him for falling asleep in the wee hours of the morning. It was not in all probability anything to do with them standing here in their peaceful opening of the forest. Holding Wren's hand to her own chest she took deep breaths allowing Wren to follow her own rhythm.

As Wren began to calm, Fae looked to the sky; the sun was slowly coming up and turning the blue hue that was their safety into first deep purples and then the beginnings of pale pink, red and oranges in the horizon. Their time in the forest was indeed up that night. Looking down at her strong warrior who was still taking in the long breaths keeping her heart beating at a steady rate and who from the slight crease in the skin between her eyebrows was clearly admonishing herself, Faeryn felt the love within her rise up with a calmness that she had never truly felt before. Without the ability to even think before the words came to her lips, Fae let out a secretive whisper.

"I love you, Wren." So simply and so calmly these words came out and danced along the wind that Wren had barely a moment to grasp them as they played in her ears.

Wren's eyes came up to meet with the Princess's in that moment and all fear left her and she felt as if she was floating on fine air. Fae heard a small laugh leave Wren's lips and a sharp wind that had previously felt so light hit her face. As her mind grasped for a reason for the sudden shift in the atmosphere around them, Wren opened her mouth to speak.

"Oh my dear, why now? How I've longed to hear those words from you and they come now as I am about to ask so much of you." Faeryn watched as Wren turned in on herself battling with her thoughts.

"What do you mean, Wren, what's going on? I thought you'd be happy," Faeryn asked, confusion filling her tone.

Walking away from her, Wren knelt down next to a tree close to the opening of the forest, seemingly rifling through the undergrowth. It wasn't long before Fae could see her bringing out a worn bulging satchel.

"Are you planning on going somewhere, Wren?" Faeryn asked, uncertain as Wren walked back across the clearing towards her.

"Fae, things are unsafe for me down at the village, I came here tonight with every intention of asking for you to run with me. Find somewhere new, somewhere they don't know you as the Princess and me as, well, no one." Wren's face looked pained as she said this. "We could find an island, where they don't know us, build a little cottage, be us, be happy... I love you too, Princess," Wren breathed out.

As happy as Fae felt when Wren declared her love for her, returning the feelings that Fae herself had let slip only a minute before, she couldn't understand why they needed to run. What was this trouble that Wren spoke of? She needed to know the truth.

"Wren, as happy as I am to hear that. I don't understand. Surely whatever has happened in the village you could fix. What could be so bad that you can't go back?" Faeryn rambled out, slightly haughtily.

"It's you! Don't you see! They know! That's why I was so afraid when I thought the guards were shouting for us. The villagers, they know about us; I'm sure of it. Your visit, you stood out as not being from there. Everyone knows everyone, I should have known it was too dangerous!" Wren's voice began to raise in volume.

"And, Fae, the messenger, the small boy, he was too clean, too well clothed to be from our area, even the scholars wouldn't have sent someone so well kept. The guards, that's when they took notice and Sergeant Rakoff has had it out for me since my father's death. Oh, Fae, there is no other option. I wish there was," Wren finished weakly, her face mourning the loss of the life she had previously had.

"I think you may have failed to factor one important piece of information into your thoughts here, Wren," Faeryn said with amusement.

"What?" Wren replied with little enthusiasm. "That I'm me of course," Faeryn said with a small smile.

"Come on, you, my love, are coming to the castle, my way."

36

Faeryn

Faeryn pulled a dumbfounded Wren behind her, far removed from her usually confident self, pushing her into a slide down the hill and through the undergrowth to her very own secret entrance into the forgotten passageways that mazed between the palace walls, glancing every minute up to the shadowy figures patrolling the wall's top, ensuring they had not indeed been spotted as Wren had feared. It was not until the curtain of vines that covered the entrance had swished back into place behind her that she could take a moment to pause and think about what she was doing and what Wren had told her. The implications of which she now realised had the potential to destroy them.

"Fae, I don't think this is a good idea," Wren said, knocking Faeryn out of her spirally doubts.

"Look, Wren, you said you needed to run away and I want you here with me. It's your turn to see how I live… plus if I am going to go with you I am going to need to get some of my stuff, aren't I?" Fae stated cockily, trying to hide the fear that had finally started to boil in the pit of her stomach.

She watched as Wren's face flitted through surprise, love, wonder and fear. Fae could see Wren battling with herself, wanting to give in to her heart but coming up with resistance from her head, clearly worried about the danger that this decision would surely lead to for Fae. It wasn't until Wren eventually met

Fae's eyes that she let out a small smile and she could see that her heart had won the internal struggle and she was assaulted by Wren pushing her up against the wall with a girlish giggle and lips met hers and all her overwhelmed emotions erupted from her in the form of uncontrollable giggles and kisses, elated as she pushed Wren back off of her and began again to drag her, this time through the passageways themselves, to go to where they met the palace.

As they approached the junction that Fae knew meant that they were now entering the palace itself, she slowed them to a halt, putting her fingers to her lips in a quieting gesture. Running through her head, the way back to her room, she knew this would be the safest way to show her love some of the palace without being seen. She could show her the window, the kitchens at least and then they could go on to her rooms.

"We are going to need to be really quiet from here on out. See that?" Faeryn whispered as she pointed at a break in the ceiling of the passageway which could only just be seen in the dark because of the slightly lighter colour of the stone ahead in comparison to the dull grey of the passage they had just emerged from. Wren nodded at her, unable to trust herself to be quiet with the excitement that still bubbled so close to the surface. She could not help but to lunge forward once again to scatter light pecks across Fae's face silently.

Shaking her head and swallowing down another giggle, Fae had to bring herself back to the seriousness of their situation.

"God, Wren," Faeryn breathed out. "We need to stay focused; I can't do that with you distracting me with your sweet kisses." She pulled away and smiled. "Do you want to see some of the palace before going back to my rooms? I'm sure we have time."

It was with this that they held each other's hands and walked on into the palace passageways, occasionally rubbing shoulders and letting out only the slightest whisper of giggles. Faeryn could feel herself getting more nervous the longer they walked. The first thing she wanted to show Wren they came upon while she was stuck in her own head, in fact it wasn't until Wren pulled on her hand and pointedly gestured towards some light coming from the wall ahead that she noticed. How had they gotten here already? Had she really been lost in her thoughts for the longest section of the passage? Breathing out slowly she collected herself and crept to the wall to look through the hole that she knew to be part of a door into the kitchens. Luckily, it all seemed to be quiet in there tonight, the dirty dishes from dinner were still by the sink, which was odd, but other than that everything seemed to be in order.

Waving Wren over to her she let her slide in front of her and pulled her midnight black curls to the side to whisper breathily into her ear.

"This is our kitchens, Cook and her two daughters work in here and once I was caught down here after hours having come through the passage. I made out I wanted some food but I'm sure…" Faeryn's story was then interrupted by a quiet clank in the room they were observing, making her jump in surprise and two shadows could be seen dancing in the candle light and hushed words unintelligible to Fae and Wren could be heard mumbled as Flora — or was it Dora? — came into sight followed soon after by a young man grabbing at her hips as he skipped into the room with a grin on his face. Faeryn watched as Flora whipped round and pressed her chest up against him and leant in for a kiss. Wren pulled her back just as their lips had been about to meet and looked at Fae with a face bright as beetroots whispering, "I think that's quite enough of that room. Where else did you want to show me?" Already making her way away from the peephole to the kitchen.

Faeryn's face began to colour as she realised that she had been watching the young couple unabashedly in front of Wren and she thought about what she would have seen if Wren hadn't been there and she had continued to watch. She could feel the heat rising in her as she looked back to Wren and realised that what she would have seen is exactly the sort of thing she wished to do with Wren right in this moment. Moving slowly and meaningfully towards Wren she brought her lips to Wren's in a passionate and heated kiss, the feeling of which was the furthest away from the sweet and innocent pecks they had shared with each other this day as they had been filled with the excitement of the admittance of their love for each other. The kiss built inside of her and she felt herself pushing forward into the kiss, jolting awake and becoming aware of their situation when the shock of their bodies hitting against the rough passageway wall knocked them back into the present. Quietly they looked at each other with curious eyes, and a resolution could be felt passing between them, the pull that had led them to the forest of Kasia, returning tenfold but now pulling them towards each other and onward towards their destination.

Continuing on forward, they curved with the passageway, bending right and left until they came upon the "window" to the guards' training grounds, the vision they saw there assaulted their eyes. Under a full moon two men could be seen leaning into one another and the far wall, under cover of the upper deck. Shirts cast aside and groping hands moved along torsos as they kissed.

Wren leaned into Fae at this point and muttered, "Is the palace always a hot bed of lust and love or have we brought the magic of the forest with us tonight?"

Shrugging, the Princess sighed, "I've never seen it quite this much in one night... but I can say I'm not against it, in fact, I would quite like to get back to my rooms and add to the festivities." Shocked, Fae could not believe that had come out of her mouth. Eyes wide, she looked up at Wren and brought one of her hands to her mouth. "I am so sorry, I can't quite believe I just said that."

Wren had a fiery look in her eyes and without a moment's hesitation she grabbed onto Faeryn's hand and started pulling her along the passageway, the time for sightseeing was over. Faeryn stumbled her way in front of Wren and began to move quickly down the passageways guiding her to her rooms, choosing to cut the tour short and skip out on the entry way into her mother's chambers, and discarding the idea of introducing Wren to her mother and potentially Tutor Tobin through the secretive gaze of the passageway peep hole.

As they neared the entrance to her room, Faeryn's heart picked up speed and her certainty started to waver, her palms became slick with sweat and her feet stumbled as the pull in her chest pushed her forward giving into the urges of her body as her mind frantically tried to catch up. She was nervous. Could she do this?

37

Faeryn

The dim light from the entrance hole into Faeryn's room came into sight as they rounded the final corner of the passageway. Bringing them to a slow walk, Fae squeezed Wren's hand and turned to face her.

"We're here," Fae let out in a rough whisper. "This comes through about a foot above my bed so be careful as you come through," Fae told Wren as she carefully drew back the tapestry hiding the entrance to her room.

Climbing down onto her bed with practiced ease, Fae quickly inspected her room to ensure they were safe before silently whipping around to hold the tapestry back for Wren to heave herself through.

Grabbing onto the sides of the hole, Wren was able to pull herself through with little fanfare, stumbling only when the drop became too long for her feet to meet the bed before letting go of her handholds. A small creak and rustle of the bed rang out in the room, muffled by the quilted covers of Faeryn's bed. They both held still, a moment of held breath and worry was soon let go as the silence remained from the door to Faeryn's quarters. Faeryn looked back to Wren with triumph and could not help but to let out a raspy giggle, setting Wren off into her own fit of giggles under her breath.

Wren was here, Fae could hardly believe it, her forest girl in her home at last. They both settled onto each side of the bed as Fae thought on the unimaginability of it all and the wondrous feeling of sheer love and magic that bubbled lowly in her chest. A peaceful drawn-out sigh left her chest, as she looked to Wren and then observed her surroundings, not able to think with a somewhat clear mind.

"How're you feeling, being in the castle after all this time?" Fae asked Wren, eyebrow arched in curiosity.

"It's beautiful, Princess. However, if I can give one note…" Wren said with a smirked lilt to her voice as she stood from the bed. "Perhaps we should make this, a little safer." Picking up the chair at Fae's desk, Wren crept towards the door. "This is an old trick I learnt from my mother as a child," Wren whispered placing the head of the chair under the door handle at an angle. "There we go, now if something were to happen, we have an extra minute or so for me to jump right on through that hole of yours."

Faeryn's face filled with blood as Wren said this, understanding that there was indeed some double meaning to what Wren was saying but too focused on the fact she had thought for a moment that they were truly safe. How had she not seen the possibility of danger here for Wren? Had she made a mistake bringing her here?

"Stop, come back to me, Fae, your mind's been taken by the Faeries again." Faeryn had not even seen Wren move back to the bed and settle herself crossed legged in front of her, too lost in her thoughts to see past her own eyes.

"I'm, here, I'm here, sorry, the reality of the danger I have created just hit me like a ton of horses. I'll understand if you want to leave," Faeryn mumbled out as Wren's eyes bored into her own and a steady hand came to brush the hair from her eyes and lay to rest on her cheek leaving tingles on her skin as Wren's fingers brushed against her.

"I'm not going anywhere," Wren breathed out so close to Fae's face that the hot whisper of wind came to nestle on the cheeks and the smell of nutmeg, fire and pine encased her senses. Fae could do nothing but lean in until her lips shadowed Wren's and the soft plumpness of her rose-tinted lips planted themselves against Wren's for but a moment. Drawing away, their eyes met with such focus on one another Fae felt as if the room had crumbled away from them and they were in the middle of a swirl of fire with nothing but the forest beyond as the pull in her chest burned bright once more. Wren's hand stayed caressing the side of Fae's face as they looked into each other's eyes, neither able to tear away. Fae could hardly breathe, the distance between them humming and coming to life as Fae could see the fire she had felt swirling around them, now not only just a feeling but something she felt her soul was bringing to life.

"Stay with me. Forever." It was the last thing Fae was able to whisper before Wren began to move closer and the time for words was over. Their lips were a breath apart as Fae swallowed down the last remnants of her fear and the castle finally fell away completely and Fae began to drown in the depths of Wren. Fae dared not move, heat coming from each and every pore of her being, and a tender aching began deep within her stomach as Wren started to move her lips against her own.

They both came to meet each other's bodies as they rose up to their knees on the plush bed, never breaking their lips apart, both afraid they would shatter the moment, their bodies clashed together in the gentlest of ways as they entwined their fingers and moved their lips together in sync. Their joined hands moving like a song inwards held effortlessly by their shoulders as fingers untwined and began to brush over shoulders, Faeryn was unable to do anything other than be in the moment and let the love they share wash over her, the pull in her chest finally fading after so many years.

Wren moved and framed her face within her hands and looked into Fae's eyes, asking for her to trust her without a drop of sound. Fae studied her face and found nothing but devotion and smirked as she once again moved forward in a passionate kiss, moving away from the tender fluttering of fingertips on skin she grabbed onto Wren's waist and with a movement of grace that Wren had not yet, despite their training, seen out of her flipped Wren round and onto the bed. Floating into place they hit the soft covers of the cover and Fae was able to feel a glimmer of satisfaction as she brought her lips to Wren's collar bone congratulating herself on her win. The moment did not last as Wren wrapped her legs around her waist and all in one swift movement was now sat atop her waist, mere inches above her most intimate area, even through her clothes, she knew Wren must feel the heat coming off of her but the worry soon evaporated as she saw the fire roar inside Wren's eyes. Fae watched as Wren's arms lifted above her body, shirt seam caught in both hands as they crossed and the olive skin of her taut stomach was exposed: so soft that Fae felt as if she needed to touch but her hands were trapped between Wren's thighs and her own sides. It felt like torture as slowly and carefully Wren continued her movement to take off her shirt and, as two perfectly rounded breasts bounced out from the underneath of her shirt, Faeryn could not help but to make a small choked out squeal, causing Wren to hesitate for only a second before pulling the shirt finally over the top of her mass of curly black shimmering hair and dropping it to the oak floor of the Princess's room.

As Wren leant down to her, her breasts a finger's width away from her own body, Fae strained her body up in an attempt to meet Wren's. Only for Wren to retreat and place an arm on Fae's chest and then move slowly across to her arms, so focused on her task Wren seemed to be, in Fae's eyes, that she barely noticed as Fae squirmed. It was not long before Fae's arms were free of their sleeves and her chest was also bare as Wren looked down at her from her perch on her waist. The warmth of the fire swirling them fizzled on her sweat-laden skin and a heat rose up giving her strength to pull her own body up jerking to meet Wren's own and feel the glorious tingle of pleasure as bare breast met her own skin. Faeryn scattered kisses along Wren's collar bone, ensuring she left a slight wetness with every kiss and delicately blew on each and every one to induce the goose bumps that were appearing on Wren's strong olive skin before making her way down to her lover's breast, the soft olive slowly coming to a peak at a warm brown nipple and, taking a moment to appreciate the goddess before her, Faeryn dived in and encased Wren's nipple with her mouth, not sure she was doing it right but encouraged by the small whimperings, that Wren had begun to let pass her sore and swollen lips. The pull on her own fiery red hair another sure sign of encouragement as she knew that if she moved away now she would be harshly pulled back in place.

Faeryn soon felt Wren's hand release from her hair and make its way down her back with feather light touches towards the dimples that lay at her lower back, pulling along with them the fabric of Fae's clothes. With each inch of cloth that left her skin, the Princess felt freer. Faeryn's heart pounded as both of their clothes were dismissed from their bodies as if they were walking off of them of their own free will, banished to a place outside of their own fiery forest and into the room beyond.

Wren kissed her neck and Faeryn was left without purchase, feeling as though she may combust as Wren began to move lower down her body, trailing those kisses in her wake, copying the technique she herself had used on Wren's collar bone only moments before. Her lips followed her finger tips as they journeyed down passed Faeryn's breasts and over the tight abs that she had helped build on her stomach, Fae's stomach tightened with every movement and every hot breath on her skin until Wren was there hovering above her most intimate part. Fae could hear each rustle of fabric, feel each whispering of skin on hers, her breath hiding behind her lips as she held herself in anticipation for what was to come, trying desperately to ensure she remembered to strain to hear the outside world, to warn them of any danger and yet Wren hovered there, looking up at Fae with nothing but resolute focus, love and fire in her eyes asking for nothing but permission.

Permission Faeryn willingly gave.

38

Wren

Wren saw the want in Fae's eyes, permission given, as she prayed to god she was going to get this right, nervously she looked down at her prize and began to move her fingers up towards her Princess's lips, she could do this. She let her fingertip brush across the supple lips in front of her and as she began to part them she could not believe how wet she was for her. Wren had never imagined she would be in this position, here in the castle, in love and loved in return by the Princess. For the first time since her mother's passing she felt whole and safe. The fire span around them and she wondered if Faeryn could feel it as heat whipped around the room with a subtle breeze when the heat became too stifling from the forest that seemed to have appeared through the fire's walls. As she pushed through and into Fae's heat the pull in her chest snapped, releasing and consuming her, she felt compelled. Her fingers curled of their own accord and she could hear the small moans of Fae pushing her onwards. Wren kept her movements short and powerful, having found a small soft patch within Fae that seemed to make her squirm more so than anything else she had done. It was when she felt Fae clutch to the covers that an idea crossed her mind, the smell of her love and the wetness was all consuming, drawing her in and she desired nothing more than to taste it. Slowing her fingers to a stop she began to withdraw as she looked up at her Princess, with a slight smirk to her face when she saw the glow of her eyes in the dark, reassuring her without words that what was to happen next would be worth the pause.

With the slightest of nods from Fae, Wren moved down the bed, adjusting her position to get the most leverage. Withdrawing her fingers completely from Faeryn, she glanced up through her hair one final time to see Fae's eyes closed again already before lowering her tongue to her and swiping it through her folds. She tasted like nectar, warm as if heated directly from the fire. It took but a moment for her to find the little bundle of nerves she knew to be there from her explorations of her own body, flicking her tongue over this in long languid motions, Faeryn began to buck her hips. Wren wrapped her arm firmly around Fae's thighs and set to work with a fever. Eliciting sounds from Fae that she had never heard before, as she felt her begin to shake, the fire around began to shimmer, as if cutting out to a fault, the breeze grew stronger and before Wren could realise what was happening two strong and rough hands had gripped onto her shoulders and ripped her away from her place between Faeryn's legs.

She could hear the shouts of guards, the outraged cries of a woman, a voice that terrified her to recognise as the Queen's. Wren stumbled back as she was pulled away, falling from the bed and with hunched shoulders looked up from the floor to see the Queen grimacing at her with such disgust she could have been a rodent in her supper. Looking back to Wren she whimpered as she saw the fire leaving her body, her eyes blinking to wake herself up from this mess. A cry ripped out from nowhere and from her mouth and Fae's all the same. "I lo…" Before her mouth was gripped roughly to a close by the guard on her right.

Her heart hurt, the pulling back like a crescendo within her chest, the pain drowning out the pinches and grazes she was getting from being restrained by the guards. It was like a dazed dream, or nightmare should I say, that went as she was pulled roughly from behind and out of the door of Faeryn's room. Her heels ripped open and her skin was as cold as the cold stone of the castle that banged against it as the guards dragged her further into the depths of the castle.

Through hallways, lined with the finery of the richest of people, tapestries hung to the hallway walls, pristine without the slightest hint of dust, the maids and other servants that they passed in their journey, each gasped with dismay and migrated to the sides of the hallway, whispering as they got far enough away to not be heard distinctly. Soon the entire city of Ekoni would know that there had been an intruder in the castle, but they would not know the true extent of what had happened here. They would not know of the love torn asunder, of the cries of pain from the Princess or of her.

It felt like an age of humiliation that she was dragged through the castle, before they made a sharp turn and came into the opening of a staircase. Without hesitation they pulled her through and down the steps of the winding staircase, narrow enough that only one of the guards could grasp her while the other trailed behind cutting off any escape route she may have had, if it were not for the strong muscled grip of the guard left holding her. The staircase was rough, dust covered the corners of each step and Wren could feel the cobwebs cling to her feet as her still-naked body scraped down each step. As they came to the end of the staircase it opened into a large bare room with nothing but a door at the far end, this room, she noted, was far less like the rest of the castle and more akin to what she imagined her own home may look like If it did not have the furniture in it or was subject to the vigorous cleaning she had done over the years.

Wren knew then that they must be nearing the dungeons. Wren's mind ran away with her as the realisation of what had transpired began to truly sink in, they were going to throw her in the dungeon, and she would never see the light of day again. Or would they sentence her to death, would she even get a trial? They surely would not want this getting out. What would Faeryn do? Would she save her?

A tear slipped from Wren's eyes as they pulled her through the room and opened the looming solid oak door at the end of the room, a peep window lined with metal bars at its top and a large deadbolt across its width, she shuddered as it made a low creaking noise. The guard that had a hold of her let go of her arm for a brief second as he used both hands to push her back straight through the door and slam it shut as she stumbled through. Wren felt a sharp cut to her knees as she fell to the floor, putting both hands in front of her to catch her as she fell further forward, scraping her palms as they came into contact with the rough, gravel-covered stone floor. As she gathered herself she shifted to a seated position and inspected first the cuts on her heels, then knees and hands. If she had been at home she would have had Letta and her girls look them over and apply ointments to ensure they did not get infected. But she was not at home; she had allowed her love for Faeryn to cloud her judgement and now she was here, the bowels of the castle, a prisoner and probably not long for this world.

Shaking these thoughts from her head, she knew that Faeryn was not to blame, she was just as enamoured and just as in love as she was and neither of them would have guessed that this would happen, how could they? The passageways were supposed to be a secret. She would have to figure a way out of here, she had been going to run tonight anyway. Wren knew she would just need to think of this as a delay. She would escape, find Fae and run.

That's what would have to happen. Wren nodded resolutely to herself and began to look at her surroundings, the room was bare, there was no window so the only light came from the dimly lit room she had passed through to get here coming through the barred window and from the seams of the door. She could hear the clanging and heaving breath of the guards standing watch outside the door to her prison. Her cell had nothing but a small pile of straw against one wall, she supposed was meant to be a bed, and a bucket in the back left corner. That was something she did not want to think about just yet, she was sure the room would end up a stinking mess if the guard didn't come to change the bucket if she were to be here that long.

Shuffling herself slowly so as to not damage her body any further, she moved herself to the straw laid out and tried to warm up, covering herself with some of the straw. Wren was unsure how she would last if they left her like this, her body was shivering with the cold and it felt as if ice had made its home in her bones and soul.

39

Wren

Hours passed as Wren lay huddled in straw within the dungeon, the tips of her fingers and toes turning blue. She could not be sure of the time of day any longer because there seemed to always be a candle lit in the room beyond. The only way to guess at it had been from the changing of the guard, which had happened two times as far as she could tell from her spot on the floor. This she assumed meant that it had been a considerable amount of time since she had been chucked in here with nothing on and no food or water.

It was as she thought of food that her stomach began to rumble and her mouth began to feel like cotton when a scraping from the door took her attention away from herself and a young man came in with a cup of water and a nub of bread on an iron plate. The young man was the same one that had delivered her the note Faeryn had written to the market all those weeks ago. A picture began to form inside Wren's head as to how the Queen must have found out about them as the young man backed away from the room and the door was once again slammed shut and the room descended into more darkness. Wren felt her way around the floor, joints creaking from the ice inside of them, looking for the precious water and food that he had brought her. As he shakily reached out to take the cup in her hand, what looked like rags fell from the barred window of her cell and thudded onto the floor, knocking over the water that was so nearly within her grasp. IN panic she let out a crackled squeak, floundering to pick the cup back up, hoping against all hopes that there was still a dribble of water left in it. Managing to take hold of the cup she brought it to her lips slowly and a small trickle of water washed over her lips into her dry mouth, enough to wet the dried-out muscle but not enough to quench her thirst. Spluttering in hatred for her situation and the inhuman cruelty she was being subjected to in the dungeon of her love's castle she reached out to grab at the rags that had taken her resource away from her. As she picked the rag up, more cloth unfolded away from the rest; in her hands she held rags, yes, but made in the form of clothes.

Someone was helping her, even if it was just giving her something to stave off a miniscule part of the cold. Hurriedly she pulled on the shirt and pants that were in the bundle, slightly small and ripped badly. Wren knew she must look a sight, but this one small act had given her back some of the warmth she desperately craved to carry on.

What must have been days passed by as Wren lay, paced and thought to herself in the dungeon. Why weren't they coming for her? Had they forgotten, was she supposed to be dead? Did Fae know that she was a mere few floors below her, still within reach? Ultimately her thoughts always returned there, to Faeryn, her Princess. Wren tried to sleep as much as she could, her dreams were full of the forest and the pull in her chest didn't feel quite so bad in her sleep, her dreams allowed her to remove herself from the harsh reality of the days in the cell and she had become accustomed to the scratching straw on the floor of the cell. The only people that she came into any contact with in her waking hours were the young men and woman sent to bring her food, always the same cup of water and stale nub of bread for her to pick on, a routine she had become used to as the door would scrape open and shut and she would spare them nothing but a look as they silently worked to replace the bucket and leave the food.

She tried to sleep through it so she did not have to bear witness to the looks of pure disgust on their faces, she often wondered why they thought she was in there.

Trapped in her own thoughts, just like any other day, the cell door scraped open and Wren ignored it, laying on her side, blocking out the world. However, this was not the usual visit, a sharp jab in the back told her as much as she was kicked out of her own mind. Turning over in fear and a little bit of indignation, Wren's eyes widened and she scrambled as close to the wall to her back as possible as her eyes took in the sight of the Queen standing in front of her.

"What is your name?" the Queen barked out.

Wren stayed silent, still in shock, as she sucked in as much air as she could.

"You will answer your Queen," screamed a guard stepping forward only to be blocked by the Queen herself holding out a jewel encrusted arm in front of him.

"Wren, Your Majesty," Wren managed to splutter out as the Queen took a menacing step towards her.

"Leave us," the Queen commanded in a shrill voice, focus clearly attached to Wren's face.

"Ar-are you sure Your Majesty?" the guard said worriedly.

"You dare question me? Leave at once!" the Queen shouted, sparing the man a withering look as the guard stepped away and the door swung shut in his place.

Wren shook as she was stared down by the Queen; what could she possibly want with her, now, after everything? Wren's fighting spirit chose this moment to rise up from a forgotten place within her and she imagined the forest around her and the heat she had felt from the fire as she said her next words quietly but forcefully. "What do you want?"

The Queen seemed taken aback that she had spoken to her that way and Wren took a little satisfaction from the fleeting look of surprise before the Queen's face scrunched into anger.

"You have no right to question me; I am your Queen, you disgusting girl!" The Queen's face reddened as her anger came out in her words, lip shaking with venom.

"You are nothing do you hear me? Nothing but dirt beneath my shoes! You and your devilish, seductive ways!"

Wren's face settled into an amused look as she surveyed the Queen. "I think you'll find, Your Maajjeessttyy, that your daughter is the one who seduced me. Now if that is all." Wren spoke with a swagger of false confidence, flicking her wrist towards the door as if to show the Queen the door. Her amusement was quickly replied to with a sharp slap to the face as the Queen's anger grew.

"You filthy degenerate, not my daughter! She is nothing like you. She is to marry, she is to have a husband and have children. You will be nary a blip in her life, she will never remember you!" the Queen spat out.

Wren let out a snigger at this, knowing Faeryn would never do as the Queen suggested willingly, earning another closed handed punch to the head. This time she felt it as the Queen's rings ripped into the skin of her head and could smell the fresh blood from the wound as it trickled down her hair.

"Faeryn will soon see that this love you have is nothing but fake, a bewitched lie that lustful daemons such as yourself spew onto their victims," the Queen said, punctuating every point with another forceful punch to a weakened Wren's head.

"We love each other," Wren managed to croak out between punches, too weak to stop them, too strong of heart to let go of what she knew to be the truth. "How do you expect to stop us?" she let out in a garbled whisper as blood ran into her mouth from a busted lip. She had always been too stubborn for her own good.

Finally the punches let up and a ruffled Queen stepped away from her and looked down at the beaten Wren on the floor.

"You're an abomination, Wren and you are banished from MY lands," was the last thing Wren heard the Queen say to her as two guards came into the room grabbing onto her as she lost consciousness.

40

Faeryn

Faeryn felt Wren shift her fingers into place; she could feel the warmth as they drew closer to her and could feel Wren's eyes still watching her as fire began to crawl up her as Wren parted her lips. Fae moaned as Wren's fingers gently entered her, wincing slightly as the pain of pleasure took its hold, quashed ever so slightly by the wetness that had built up since they had ventured onto the bed that night. Faeryn felt as though she could not breathe, only able to moan out as Wren's fingers curled inside her with the precision akin to her sword exercises. Shivers grew up her spine and shot to all corners of her body as Wren continued her ministrations. Fae clutched her fingers into the covers as she felt the fire within her turn up to heights unknown. Just as she felt as though ready to explode, the movements of Wren's fingers stopped. Fae was barely able to open her eyes to look down at Wren in consternation but all that greeted her was a mass of black curls as Wren slowly repositioned her body, moving lower still before settling at the arc of her legs and looking up with a glow in her eyes, once again asking for permission. Fae made the slightest movement to nod, not wanting this moment to end, and Wren without further delay looked back down to her heat. Fae's mind went blank as Wren lowered herself to her, finding a new feeling altogether. Fae felt her body all at once but very slowly burn brighter than she had ever felt before, her body vibrating with her want and love for Wren, never having known the tenderness that this expression of love could give. The heat within her intensified as she arched her back off the bed, Wren's mouth moving at an unprecedented pace, wet and warm, heat coming off her tongue and into her that reached to every tip of her body. Shaking, Fae could not help but to buck as Wren wrapped her hands around her thighs. Sweat breaking out on her chest as she could feel the explosion ready to wrack through her body.

And then nothing. It all came to a crashing halt as the fire inside her was smothered with a cold aloneness that she had not felt in many years. Wren was ripped from her, muffled shouting was the only thing Faeryn could hear as her senses came back to her and she fought to open her bleary eyes, Wren's voice ringing out to her a terrified, "I lo…" before her voice was muffled by what Fae could now make out was a hand.

A guided hand of chainmail muffling out the voice of her love. Looking around, now able to make out the room around her, the swirling fire and forest of their privacy gone away with the distance between them.

Guards, guards filled the room, her mother standing next to the door with a quietened Wren at her side held back and struggling with two guards holding her still and silent.

And with a raised brow of her mother she was gone, dragged through the door of her chambers as guards filed out behind her and her mother stepping around them.

"This is for your own good, you selfish child," the Queen menacingly whispered at her, practically spitting the words as Faeryn began to move forward, finally out of her haze, moving in slow progression towards her mother and the door before it was slammed in her face and the thunk of the lock twisting into place shattered her heart.

A blood curdling scream left Faeryn's throat as she found her feet and scrambled to the door of the quarters, pulling on the handle and crying out for Wren, her mother, anyone to open the door to let her out and to her love.

Her wails of pain and protest did no use and she began to claw at the door, trying to find a way through. For hours she clawed at the door wailing, her nails chipped to pieces and blood smearing on the door from the cuts she had made trying to make a dent in the door until she finally came to a stop and turned in on herself, curling into a small ball at the foot of the door. How could she have done this? Why was her mother so selfish, so cruel, to have done this? Just when they were making headway in their relationship. What of Wren, surely she was already dead?

Her mother, she knew, was not a gentle being, she knew that Wren's punishment may very well be her life. How could she have been so stupid as to bring Wren here, she knew it wasn't definitely safe, but they came anyway? Wren must hate her now. The cold she had felt as Wren was ripped away had spread over the hours feeling like frost seeping into her skin and muscles, the fire in her room blazing in the fireplace did nothing to stave off the cold. The pull in her chest hurt deeply. Sitting all the way up, the pit of her throat pulled her voice away from her as the tear tracks on her cheeks froze as her silence wore on.

Faeryn moved herself to her bed, snuggling her face into the covers that had held her and Wren as they made love, Wren's smell lingering ever so slightly warming the edge of her nose. As she lay there, days went by, maids came and went, leaving food and juices for her to eat; she could not bring herself to go near them and at the end of every day the maids took away the still food-laden plates. None had tried to speak to her, none had tried to dress her but all had shot her stricken looks from under their bowed heads. Fae knew she must look half dead. As time passed Fae did not realise that the blood had been wiped away from the door, leaving only small gouges where her grief had clawed into the door looking for a way out. The only thing left in the room in fact that was dirty, was her.

41

Faeryn

Daylight came in through Faeryn's window as her eyes fluttered open, red and swollen still from her silent tears, she sniffled as she lay unmoving, now awake yet again in her misery, the smell of Wren had disappeared from her covers the night before and she had cried herself to sleep as she mourned once again for her loss. Body sore, she shuffled and turned her body to face the door to her room. Startling, she came upon the figure of her mother watching her leaning against the stone wall next to the door of the room. Faeryn wondered how long she had stood there, had she noticed the marks on the door she had made? Faeryn said nothing, only watched as her mother stepped forward towards her, eerily calm, a stark contrast to how she had last seen her. Unable to stay quiet any longer, Faeryn rasped out:

"What have you done?"

The Queen smiled, her eyes wide with a crazy calm look to her eyes. "I have fixed your situation, my dear daughter," she said in a sickly-sweet tone, sitting at the end of Faeryn's bed.

"What do you mean you fixed my situation?" Faeryn sat up, the anger of a thousand fires suddenly bursting from her chest. "I had no situation to fix, only a woman I loved, that you tore away from me!" Fae's fire drew back to embers as she mentioned Wren, the loss still too great to warm herself from the ice inside her veins.

"Insolent girl, she would have ruined you, ruined this family and killed our lands! I did what needed to be done! And now so will you," the Queen retorted, the last part coming out in a calm whisper.

Faeryn looked at her mother as if she had never seen her before, never known the woman she truly was.

"Now so will I?" Fae whispered to herself. "What do you mean so will I? I will do nothing for you, Your Maajjeessttyy," she said in a mocking tone.

Faeryn had sounded exactly like Wren when she said this, and the Queen flinched for a split second, seeing for the first time how close the two girls had really gotten. Righting herself, the Queen pushed forward, still feeling as if she had surely saved her daughter from a world of disaster and pain. "You are going to marry, Faeryn." The Queen stood. "You are going to marry a man of my choosing, of good standing, I gave you a chance to do this a different way and you threw it back in my face. You have shown me how gullible and idiotic you can truly be and now you must marry. For the good of the Queendom."

Faeryn could not help but to shrink back and disappear as her mother said this, sounding so unwavering; she knew she would not be able to argue herself out of this. She would have to run or figure out some sort of plan before it was too late. She watched dumbstruck as her mother walked towards the door, leaving her to her thoughts.

As the door began to close, her mother poked her head around one last time and said, "Oh and by the way, that abomination, has been banished. You won't be seeing her again." And with a smile, left.

42

Wren

The sound of crashing waves and the clipped call of a seagull were the first things Wren heard as she came to, she felt her body, beaten and bruised, roughly grate against a wooden floor, splinters digging into her fingertips as her stomach ached and nausea overtook her as she felt herself rocking. The air smelt of salt, vomit and stale wine and as she blinked open her eyes she could see a knocked over barrel, red stained wood and a pile of vomit were the culprit of the smell invading her nostrils. Quickly moving to sit, she held her head in agony as it thumped loudly in her ears and the pain split into her head. Waiting for it to calm again from her movement she held herself still to once again open her eyes and survey her surroundings.

Everything was wooden, apart from yet more bars across a criss-crossed gate into her room that she could see through plainly. Looking to the floor around, her hands moved across wet straw that, as she brought it to her lips, she could smell the salt for what it really was, sea water.

A ship, Wren was in a ship. Pushing down her panic, she tried to remember what had happened. The last thing she remembered clearly was the Queen herself dealing punches to her head with ring-laden hands, shouting at her as she smartly replied with sass. Oh god why had she done that? Letta always said her mouth would get her in trouble someday. Neither of them would have thought that it would have caused something like this. As she fought to remember, a voice slowly crept into her mind. "Banished," it said. The Queen had banished her.

Tears slipped from her eyes as she finally understood why she was on a ship, but she knew that she and Faeryn both had said I love you at the end, when she was being dragged away from her and to the dungeon. It had kept her strong, and it would keep her strong now. She would get through this, she would get back to her Princess.

"Faeryn," she whispered out.

Looking down at herself she saw that her rags had been replaced with red britches and a royal blue shirt, no shoes though. Curious, Wren thought to herself, what are they to do with me? At this thought, Wren looked up and scrambled to her feet. Thumping footsteps approached and, as big black boots came into view, Wren raised her eyes to see a Queen's Ship Captain in his naval uniform.

"So you're awake then?" he gruffed out informally.

Wren did not reply, only lowered her eyes again and closed them ready to turn away, sluggish from her previously unconscious state and unwilling to cooperate as her grief made her go in on herself.

The Captain did not relent, however, throwing a mop and bucket into the brig as he opened the door.

"Wake up, girl, this is the first day of the rest of your life. Come on," he shouted as he turned away, leaving the door swinging on its hinges.

Wren looked after him, her face setting into a determined grimace. If she was to be a Swabbie, so be it, but one day she would go back, when she was strong enough, she would go back.

"I will find you, Faeryn, I promise," she swore to herself, picking up the mop and bucket and making her way to follow her captain.

END